Salty

Also by Kate Myers

Excavations

SALTY

A NOVEL

Kate Myers

HarperVia

An Imprint of HarperCollinsPublishers

SALTY. Copyright © 2025 by Kate Myers. All rights reserved. Printed in the United States of America. No part of this book may be used or reproduced in any manner whatsoever without written permission except in the case of brief quotations embodied in critical articles and reviews. For information, address HarperCollins Publishers, 195 Broadway, New York, NY 10007.

HarperCollins books may be purchased for educational, business, or sales promotional use. For information, please email the Special Markets Department at SPsales@harpercollins.com.

FIRST EDITION

Designed by Yvonne Chan
Image of boat on page iii © GN.Studio/Shutterstock
Image of women on page 1 © Lana_Samcorp/Shutterstock
Photograph of boat on page 81 © wmaster890/iStock/Getty Images
Photograph of yacht on page 81 © alexandr6868/iStock/Getty Images
Photograph of water on page 81 © Westend61/Getty Images
Image of palm trees on page 185 © Kusumaillustration/Shutterstock
Photograph of bed on page 185 © Dmytro Duda/iStock/Getty Images
Photograph of sea and sky on page 185 © Carolina Santos Torre/iStock/Getty Images
Photograph of lionfish on page 253 © Dorling Kindersley/UIG/Bridgeman Images

Library of Congress Cataloging-in-Publication Data has been applied for.

ISBN 978-0-06-338548-1

25 26 27 28 29 LBC 5 4 3 2 1

For Zoe

Across all the passing lives and deaths,
the endless waves of swimming joy
and quiet losses of exquisite creatures . . .
there is nothing the ocean has not seen.

SALLY ANDREW

Part
One

Chapter

1

You wouldn't know it was happening until the water reached your bed.

Something this big doesn't go down fast, like a beer can to the bottom of a pool. Density, buoyancy, mass, and fiberglass—I'm not getting into that with you.

Trust me. It takes a very long time. Overnight, for example. And I'm telling you, if you're asleep, after you've had a few, you're not going to notice.

You might hear the water before you feel it. But that's the thing, you know, the sound of water is extremely pleasant. Come on, that's what you're paying for in the first place, to hear the water all the time. Middle of the night, in a sleepy state like that, it wouldn't necessarily be crystal clear that the water was inside rather than out, lapping up against the boat like usual. You're probably enjoying it.

Granted, alright, you might also hear things floating around, that decorative stuff they've got in there, potpourri bowls or bird statues or whatever, you know what I'm talking about. Water's going to lift those items off the floor or off a low table and bang them around a bit, sure. But hey, again, water's a very effective muffler.

And like I said, in this particular case, alarm's a no-go if the system line's snipped. Not like you're going to notice the lights are out—you hit the switch yourself when you went to bed. Problem is the deck lights go out, too, so the boat goes dark on the surface. How often have you been swimming in the ocean at night, friend?

No way, you just wouldn't notice, the average person. You'd be in the middle of a dream. What do people like him even dream about? Or does a guy like that just have nightmares about guys like me? If he's dreaming about some beach or a pool, the water's going to feel just right. A little REM-state smell-o-vision. But the soaked bedding would get anybody—not a pleasant sensation. So that's it, you won't know something's going on until it hits the mattress line, soaks your sheets. And guess what? That means you're in two, three feet of water.

And anyway, soon as that happens, the second you bolt up and shake your wife awake, all hell breaks loose. Of course, first thing you do, you spin around and put your feet on the floor, and whoa—it's up to your knees, your waist even, if you've got one of those fancy high-up beds. Good luck to you.

Even that's misleading, though. Most of the boat is completely under-water at that point—only the downstairs suites haven't caught up yet, thanks to the valves. My handiwork, funny enough. You wouldn't know yet that the entire boat is most of the way gone. If you saw it from shore or from another boat, you'd only be able to see the top deck, the cockpit up there waving a Hail Mary.

You can make it out of your suite, maybe, if the big door that goes from the main deck down to the living rooms is sealed. But as soon as you open that, like I'm saying, the rest of the boat's below the waterline. You're in your underwear staring down a wall of water, and the last thing you ever hear is your wife saying the dust ruffle's ruined.

So no, for the tenth time, I'm telling you, there wouldn't be any survivors.

Chapter

2

Never question the owners.

The owners made choices about the boats and it was her job to accept those choices, no comment. To wonder aloud, for example, about that silver tubed fountain in the bow was to insult them. Denise knew this; she'd learned it a million times.

They were ten minutes into a tour of a boat she'd already spent weeks at sea with. But there was a redesign that triggered the safety walk-through protocol, like throw pillows were keeping the Coast Guard helicopters at bay. The owner paused in the bow to emphasize a word that was meaningless to Denise—*herringbone*—and gesture at the banquette seating that wrapped around the plunge pool. Denise squinted at the uncanny silver spout arcing a stream of water from the pool into the sea, chlorinating the ocean.

Her phone buzzed in her pocket. Exactly seven people had Denise's number, all of whom knew to call her if and only if they were sucking in their last breath.

It was her sister, Helen.

Decline.

She shook her head clear and turned back to the pool. "Is that like a . . ." she started, then clamped her mouth shut.

Goddammit, Helen. Kicking Denise in the shin from six thousand miles away. Denise should have known. Better yet, she should have blocked Helen's number.

The fountain was a sea cucumber, she was brusquely informed.

Two hours later everyone else was on board—her crew, the guests—
and the boat pulled out from the marina. Seventy feet long, three stories
high, the boat had been redesigned to look like an embalmed aquarium:
eel railings, conch shell doorknobs, squid chandelier, wall-to-wall oil
paintings of fish from the Rio Grande to the Yangtze.

As they cruised toward the inlet that led out to the ocean, the low
sun reached the perfect angle in the sky to taunt her, beaming insult
to injury. There was a silver matrix of scaffolding going up two lots
over from the marina, and it streamed a blinding white light across
her dashboard. Just today, after weeks of rods and ladders at all angles, the scaffolding had locked into a shape that finally looked like a
real building. The sight of it made Denise want to throttle this forty-
thousand-pound machine into overdrive, creating a giant rooster
tail of white froth behind her, and ram it into the shore.

The party below her on the main deck already clinked and
clanged, glasses and laughs and forks and farts, rich white noise.
The wide deck in the bow was packed with twenty people in tuxe-
dos and slippery looking gowns, all of whom were barefoot at the
owner's request. All toes had been stubbed.

The owner had been ice-cold, hadn't spoken a word to Denise,
which was fine by her. He sat far behind her at the stern edge of the
top deck, facing the boat's wake, which frothed along the water in a
silvery line; he didn't want to know where the wake ended and the
moonlight began. Next to him, in a twin teak lounge chair, was another man his age, and from behind she could not tell them apart.

For an hour she'd let their banter of birthrights wash over her as
she focused on the tide reports instead, but then a few words rose to
her ears over the rumble of the engine.

"Falcons sold out the new place."

"You're kidding. It was just scaffolded."

"Wait list from the other lagoon properties."

One of them let out a whistle. "How the hell'd they even get those permits? I mean, come on."

"Gotta break a few endangered bird eggs . . ."

Denise's left hand tightened around the silver wheel so hard her fingernails dug into her thumb. With her right, she pressed the throttle a quarter inch forward and the engine responded to drown them out.

Boats were for business. Vacations were business, grandchildren time was business, and parties were serious business. Owners never used the boats for pleasure, as far as Denise had seen in her twenty-plus years with Ahoy. They were floating offices, unmoored boardrooms.

They were the perfect place to talk about disemboweling the pristine peninsula where Denise had grown up and turning it into a hideous—no, dangerous—monstrosity.

The DJ tooted an air horn and she flinched.

"You two good?" Rod, a deckhand in his fifties, shirt untucked, sweating in sixty degrees and a breeze, popped up from the stairs to ask the men. They waved him off.

Embroidered on the breast pocket of Denise's polo shirt was a jaunty shrimp at an old-fashioned wooden steering wheel. It made her furious that the shirts were all the same. The shrimps of her crew should be carrying trays or tying knots. Only the head shrimp was at the helm.

All her requests to reembroider had gone unanswered.

All her phone calls and letters to elected zoning officials had also gone unanswered.

Champagne corks parabolaed into the sea. Hands flung over the boat's edge in animated conversation, often losing their grip on glasses with *oopsies*! At one point, though no one else had bothered looking, Denise had seen dolphins swimming on both sides of the boat, now concussed.

Her crew of shrimps floated among the crowd. Her first mate, Stew, an uptight meatball of a man who refused to acknowledge he was no longer size-medium material, took a pile of crumpled mono-grammed napkins into his hand, slipped his pinkie through the handle of a used espresso cup, and slid half a dozen used canapé skewers—mini plastic swords—into his pocket. If anyone would be stabbed in the thigh tonight, it would be him. He was the father of three terrible small children and it showed.

Her second mate, Kaylee, a white-haired human harp sound, could've been fifty or sixty-five. Her paperwork revealed the doodle of a shooting star on the birth year line. She pinned a guest's hairdo with one hand, squeezed a lime into a glass with another, and slid a chair over for a guest with her foot. Her voice was feathery soft; in her presence guests often found themselves closing their eyes and *mmm*-ing along in agreement that certain cults did have a point. The constant gentle motion of her body gave the impression that she had tentacles.

Why the hell had Helen called?

At the half hour mark, Denise did her pat-down self-check. Air horn on the belt, electromagnetic anklet ready to emit a high-pitched shark deterrent field when it contacted salt water, waterproof taser clipped onto the side of the open-water-certified bathing suit she wore in lieu of underpants, jellyfish-proof petroleum jelly, and a neon-orange inflatable Croakies strap to hold her head above water if she passed out in the drink.

She'd seen how other captains dressed, and if they wanted to face off in nature's coliseum armed with a friendship bracelet, they could knock themselves out.

Stew and Kaylee wove through the crowd to hand out sparklers while the DJ, chronicling the night with bursts of one-word poetry, leaned into his microphone, made Y's with both sets of fingers, and shouted, "Pyromania!"

Denise picked up the black radio.

"Ahoy," she grumbled. Her resentment of the marina name and

the necessity to say it out loud was bottomless. "We're coming in ahead of schedule." Normally she'd cut a wide sea donut for another half an hour of cruise time, but she didn't feel like it anymore.

"Denise, no sirree. The schedule says ETA one thirty." The onshore dispatchers were overly attached to pieces of paper. "My Zodiac is still in the slip. I was going to whiz around to catch some snook after my shift. You're saying you want me to move it now?"

"Now or after I crush it with this boat, your call."

"Denise! Not again, last time you—"

She clipped the radio back onto its dock and wiped a smear of petroleum jelly off the console.

The owners of these yachts were not titans of industry. They were at the bottom of the top of the food chain, middling millionaires, regional bigwigs at best. The titans had full-time staff and private marinas, and this rung had Ahoy: a yacht management company that provided a captain and crew on a certain schedule, brokered rentals if you needed the cash flow, and kept your boat clean and properly paperworked. Catering to the low end of the very rich was the bedrock of the nautical gig economy. Ahoy employed a wide swath of humanity, from aromatherapists to armed security, all seaworthy.

Captain Denise, adjusting the crotch of her shorts around the bathing suit groin, was the jewel of their offerings.

The boat cruised to within sight of land again, drawing confused looks from those passengers who hadn't clocked leaving it. Stew began his preliminary line check under a chorus of advice from people who attended a week of sailing camp twenty years ago. Below a preposterous spray of stars that arced over the charcoal horizon ahead, the dolphins were back astride the hull, asking for it.

She hadn't spoken to Helen in six months and nine days. Not that she was keeping track.

The yacht slipped from the ocean back into the narrow inlet, then cruised down the palm-lined waterway. It was a wide river that ran parallel to the sea and was dotted on both sides with interchangeable mansions, looking into a mirror and absolutely loving it. A few minutes in, the peninsula extended its long green finger out into the water and at the very tip was Ahoy, the boats like white petals reaching out from the stem. A large empty slip waited for Denise with open arms.

She kept her eyes down at the controls. If she looked at the new scaffolding from up here, where she could see every single piece of that thing, she didn't trust herself not to shotput the anchor into it.

"He's back!" Rod stood again in front of the owner and aimed two thumbs-up at his own chest, revealing crescents of sweat beneath his arms.

Denise spun and glared at him. "Down." She eyed the stairs.

Rod held up a finger. "Real quick. Heard you two gentlemen talking about the new Falcon place, and it's big and juicy alright." He rubbed his palms together, then clapped once. "I'm thinking I've got to shoot my shot here, carpe damn, to go in on one with you two."

"Now." Denise raised her voice.

"Maybe you're thinking one condo's small potatoes, but you need to feel the market, and I live in a condo, alright? You're the money guys, we get our feet wet, split it two ways—you two, I mean—I'm the intel guy, and we go from there. I overheard you and had to come—"

Denise took a single step forward and tased him.

The two old men shot back into their chairs. Rod opened his mouth, and it was beyond satisfying to see his lips move and hear nothing. He crumpled to the floor.

"You're fired," she said, into the abrupt silence afterward.

From downstairs, Stew released an unsanctioned "Woo-hoo!"

The owner stood up and handed her an empty crystal champagne flute. "Home. Now."

In Denise's pocket, her phone buzzed again.

Chapter

3

Three oceans, six time zones, and one equator away, Helen was returning to shore and feeling great about it. She bobbed up and down on the balls of her feet at the stern of the boat, ready to help dock and assist the passengers onto the pier, her freckled shoulders soaking up the remains of the day's heat. The sleeves of her blue staff polo shirt were rolled all the way up the way she liked them, and the bottom was untucked because she hadn't put her pants back on after taking a thirty minute swim on her ten minute lunch break.

The fancy little yellow boat swiveled and nuzzled its way up to the pier, churning the turquoise waters off these Marshall Islands into an astonishing swirl of orange and green. Helen had just wrapped up a tour of the islands' turtles, seals, and little neon fish populations that was very impressive, if she did say so herself. People loved to hear about danger in the water; it gave them an excuse to stay out of it.

The engine was cut, throwing the crew and passengers into silence.

"Woo-hoo!" Helen shouted, raising her arms and waggling her hips. Silence was no way to remind people they'd just had a ton of fun. The guests flinched and reached for their wallets, filing off with startled goodbyes, and palms full of bills, a conga line of gratitude. Nothing like a safe return from sea to make people appreciative. Helen tied off the stern of the boat to the nearest cleat, pinched away the curls that always stuck to her sunscreened forehead, then climbed off the boat herself.

The boat's crew was already elbow deep in their cleanup operation.

"Domo arigato, amigos! Maximo fun, as always. Ciao!"

None of them waved. They were grizzled yachtsmen who'd seen a dozen freelance nature tour guides come and go, and they'd see a dozen more before the sun set on their time in the Pacific.

At the end of the pier, Helen took her time with a few squats and stretches to keep the blood flowing and joints limber. Tour guiding was crazy physical work—people had no idea. The guests needed a minute to get on shore before Helen was allowed to follow, as she'd been instructed to keep a very specific distance between herself and clients on hotel property.

That's where the boat suites came in handy.

She had another gig that afternoon leading a snorkel excursion. Was she driving the bus there? She couldn't remember. Sometimes they gave her a driver, sometimes they didn't. Her life's work was knowing stick shift and enough fun facts to skate by working at fancy resorts as a "nature expert" these days. A journeyman of hospitality, she had traced a zigzag of gigs and demotions across time zones and remote island nations. Moving around a lot and never getting promoted was the key to not having to fill out the paperwork required to legally work abroad.

Someday she'd open up her own hotel. Or a restaurant. Or a boat where people could mix tiki drinks and pick up trash out of the ocean. Something. She wasn't sure specifically how she wanted to cash in on everything she'd learned, but it would come to her someday. Six countries in, two countries kicked out of—she was a woman of the world.

"Helen?"

She froze mid-squat. A woman in a ballerina bun holding a clipboard had appeared next to her.

"May I have a word?"

"Yowza, you scared me. Sure thing. Are you doing a clip or scrunchie for that thing, let me see," Helen craned her neck to look at the back of the woman's head. "Bobby pins, damn. Now that's a bankable skill." She flipped back her sizable hair with both hands.

The woman did not move her lips. She was not wearing a name tag, which was alarming. The low-level staff all wore name tags. "We will be letting you go. Thank you."

"Now? But, wait, why?"—even though Helen already knew. She murmured a half-hearted "oh no."

"I believe you do know why, from our last conversation."

"That was with you?"

The woman nodded. *Shit.* Helen vaguely remembered a stiff conversation about *staff comportment*, which she could only say in a deep phony accent, but she could've sworn that was with a different blazer-lady. Those chats all blurred together.

"I wore my hair down," the woman conceded.

"Right, but I thought it was five strikes," Helen raised one eyebrow, hopeful, skipping over the fact that she knew the number perfectly well, and *five* was not it.

"On today's tour"—the woman looked down at her clipboard— "Sylvia made a phone call after your . . . meeting."

"She called you? From the boat? After—" Helen stopped herself.

The woman read off her notes. "As per her own company's HR policy to self-report, out of an abundance of caution, and to avoid any future conflicts."

Helen huffed out a laugh. "Conflicts with who? We're never going to see each other again!" She put her hands on her hips.

This was a first. She'd been ratted out by two other crew members, caught in the act once, needed medical attention that other time, but self-reporting? These people were supposed to be on vacation.

"Okay, you got me. I'm sorry. How did she even get phone service out there? But listen, there was consent out the wazoo, okay? No complaints from Cecelia—"

"Sylvia."

"Or any of the other . . . s." Helen looked across the pier at the crew still on board, and they all looked away. She lowered her voice. "Is there a way to, like, give me an extension? Just one, this one time. Self-reporting, I mean, come on, that came out of nowhere."

The woman furrowed her brow and spoke in halted chunks of words. "You'd like . . . an extension . . . of how many . . . incidents . . . you can have . . . like this?"

"Seven? Or six, compromise."

A moment later Helen was signing a piece of paper that ended what she called her career. Normally she would've wasted no time and booked it right over to the next island to learn the magic number of incidents she'd be allowed there. But then a long-dreaded set of words sealed her fate.

"We've had some calls regarding the status of your work visa. It seems several other organizations, ours included, have been unable to verify your legal employment status."

Helen slowly walked down the pier and across the sand without looking up. She trudged to the little alley, canopied by enormous palm fronds, between the staff entrance and the parking lot, and straddled her yellow bicycle.

The black plastic ends of the helmet straps gently tapped against her cheeks. It wasn't her style to brag, but her bank account always had enough money in it for a one-way international flight. It seemed that time of year had now come when she'd need to spend the account all the way down.

The phone was already in her hand; momentum was on her

side. Her life was the sum of all the first ideas that had ever popped into her head. And this idea, the idea she had right now, was hardly a retreat. It was an adventure into the heart of the darkest mystery of her life; a wild unknown awaited at the other end of that ringing line.

But, of course, Denise didn't answer the call.

Chapter

4

The little waterway peninsula was perfect, and everyone talked about it that way. They said *the peninsula* the way you'd say *the neighborhood*, with all the same kinds of groups, gossip, and gardens.

The water flowed from dark, brackish brown in the muddy shallows to a blue that brightened to turquoise as the water reached out toward the ocean. Round white birds with scrawny orange legs stepped gingerly along the scraggly shore, darting their beaks in between the leaves at silver flashes of herring skimming the sand.

Ahoy Marina took up the entire rounded end of the peninsula. Its campus layout included the glass-walled welcome center, a small pink building of administrative offices, and behind a set of hedges away from the water, a village unto itself with blue-and-white striped bungalows for crew members who spent the night. The welcome center was the crown jewel, prisming all over the place into the eyes of anyone who approached under the direct sun. Reaching out along the piers around the tip of the land were the modest white yachts, about ten in all.

Next down the peninsula, after a row of hedges, was Heracanes, the sixty-five-plus all-women community next door. Forty residents lived in a sweet set of large pastel cottages, like a cluster of bed-and-breakfasts, with a bean-shaped pool, a kayak rack, bocce courts, wide decks with cozy lounge chairs, cupholders galore, and a dozen extremely well-attended garden beds. The emphasis at Heracanes was on active living, and its residents were mostly former athletes, mothers of three or more, or both.

The lot at the very end—or the beginning, where the peninsula connected to the mainland—was Conch Cab. It was barely a lot but rather a pinkie finger of a business made up of a single pier with six boats, three on each side. It provided water taxi service to the restaurants and hotels all along the waterway, picking up and dropping off between noon and midnight every day. Where the pier met the shore, a battered palapa—a thatched-roof cabana—shaded two picnic tables. The owner, Randy, a handlebar-mustached forty-something fond of the leather-vest-and-bathing-suit combo, parked his motorcycle at the end of the narrow bike path that led out to the road and let his dog, Styx, run wild around Heracanes all day. The residents didn't mind. Each of the taxi boats had a different-colored awning on top, a rainbow of nautical livery, and Randy employed a rotating cast of captains who wouldn't pass the background check at Ahoy.

The whole peninsula appeared to undulate in constant motion. Shielded by nothing, it was incredibly windy, and its people seemed to be in solidarity with the ever-flapping leaves. The Ahoy crews were in a perpetual state of cleaning, their little maintenance rafts circling the yachts like those tiny fish that lick the scum off bigger fish, and they marched up and down the piers all day, carting supplies and fetching orders. The Heracanes residents were in competition with one another over perceived longevity, with limbs zigging and zagging in lawn games and leisure sports, not to mention the chasing of grandchildren. And of course Randy's water taxis buzzed in and out of their slips at all hours of the day, circling the peninsula and tooting their horns every time the captains thought they saw someone wave, which was every time a Heracanes resident stretched.

Until recently, there had been a small empty lot in between Heracanes and Conch Cab. It had been Denise's home, her mother's place really, where Denise and her sister, Helen, had grown up in a rancher fighting for its life against the weeds. Ten years ago, when their mom moved to the Bahamas, she'd sold it to a single retired woman like herself, who'd spent her whole life in an office and now wanted to do nothing but sit in the sun all day. In due time, the new owner was dead of melanoma. The lot was then sold to the Falcon Development Company—and with a snap of their fingers, the Falcons had the zoning laws "updated." It used to be that you couldn't so much as install a hot tub on this land, a delicate shoreline, surrounded by water on both sides. But the dam of the zoning ordinance gave way under the pressure of a rushing river of money, and last year the Falcons began the work of obliterating any trace of what Denise remembered of home.

The house was one thing; frankly, it was overdue for a bulldozing. Her heart could've withstood a new house—even a big, embarrassing one. But the dense, wild jungle of a yard had looked the way it probably used to look two hundred years ago, and it gave her the feeling of being comfortably, proudly in the middle, squished in between two certainties with her tan arms outstretched to hold those two times together. Wildness long before and wildness long after. That was what she couldn't stand, the anger she was bathed in, that she'd had one tiny little piece of planet to protect and had utterly failed it.

From sunup to sundown, they'd practically lived outside, always a trio. First, her mother, her father, and Denise. And then, after her dad died, her mother, Denise, and Helen. They lost him when Denise was ten to a car accident while he was on his way home from a job. Helen, who had just been born, had the morbid privilege of not remembering him at all. But Denise did. The lot, their land, their yard, their home—that was the last place she'd had him; they'd known the place together—its skinny trees, low tides, salt smells, and bird songs, all two acres of it—and now it was gone.

Six months ago, the developers started to dig a giant neon-blue hellhole whose edges reached both sides of the lot. It was a lagoon, and it was big enough that neighbors could reach out and dunk their hands into the water. At the rim nearest the shoreline, the surrounding sand curled down toward the waterway; it seemed possible fish could just jump from one body to another. Pools were too small, too denatured; lagoons were apparently part of a new, loathsome trend to pave paradise and dig a bigger, plastic paradise with an in-ground liner that lasted twenty-five to thirty years.

The lagoon made Denise feel like she might be dying—like she was upside down and all the blood was pooling in her head and eventually would have to go somewhere, and so her head would probably explode. Month after month, she watched the hole grow larger and deeper and morph into shades of ever-brighter blue, as if a light were being turned up at the bottom so the whole thing could be seen from space, and every single week it became more and more clear that there was absolutely, positively nothing she could do to stop it.

The scaffolding for the planned building looked like the skeleton of a robot. It was a towering pile of chrome rectangles with huge metallic balconies that caught the sun at all the wrong angles and lasered blinding beams onto the neighbors like an enemy from the future.

There was a reason laws had existed to prevent people like the Falcons from constructing something like this on such a narrow strip of land. Water hugged the peninsula on both sides, eroding the shore a little bit every year. The Falcons had ripped out the roots that kept the land stitched together, injected an extra two hundred thousand gallons of water right into the middle, and planned for people to live right on top of that.

It was as if they were trying to kill someone.

Chapter

5

It was a special occasion, their first lunch together since the lagoon construction was finished. Poppy followed the host through the gold vaunted-ceiling atrium, past the ten-foot-high floral arrangements on thick marble tables, the purple wingback chairs facing the windows that overlooked the pool and beach, the plush Oriental rugs that went on and on beneath their feet. Versailles with aquariums.

She turned left toward the beach club dining room, but the host half-turned with a raised hand to indicate they would not be sitting at their usual table. Instead, Poppy and the surviving Falcon family stepped into the cavernous ballroom that faced the golf course. Sunlight flooded through the towering arched windows, and aside from a grand piano, their table was alone in the room, an island set for four on an acre of black-and-white checkered floor.

As he held out her chair, Tim Falcon pursed his lips and widened his eyes at her. She completely understood what he meant: This lunch was big.

The menu at the beach club dining room held a special place in Poppy's heart that she'd never told anyone else about. The first time her fiancé, Tim, ever took her here, she read the words *Coastal Sophistication* embossed in gold at the top of the specials list. She lifted her head and thought, *That is how I'm going to describe my life*. It was as if she'd been searching for words like these to guide her, and here she was now with this incredible man who'd chosen her out of everyone. He was giving her this gift, a North Star, a proverb to orient her at every fork in the road of life. In the years since—it had been a long engagement; the Falcons were understandably particular about the wedding details and hadn't yet decided on a date for the couple—Poppy had used the phrase in countless circumstances. When the contractor asked her to describe what she had in mind for the new bathroom: *coastal sophistication*. When her mother asked her again last month what she was doing marrying into a family like this: *coastal sophistication*.

Tim's older brother, Alden, waved over the waiter and said they'd all do the prix fixe lunch.

"Nope," Tim said before the server could walk away. "Club sando for me. Not so fast, bro grande."

Poppy loved being ordered for. All the more exciting this time, because she hadn't even had a chance to look at the prix fixe list, and she loved surprises. Left to make her own decision, she always chose the wrong thing, always too elaborate for the occasion or that drew attention, like something called a flambé or what turned out to be a baby animal that someone across the table commented on. She usually tried to ask Tim what a few of the italicized words on the menu meant, but he never quite told her the right thing, just that a dish was a "rad call" or "super yum."

The waiter returned with their drinks, and Poppy raised her glass.

"Cheers to being in the Cinderella ballroom!"

Linnie and Alden shared a glance then slowly lifted their iced teas toward the center of the table.

"Have you heard from Raul this week?" Linnie asked. "I'm seeing him for dinner tomorrow, of course, but it'd be best if his people were looped in with yours. That way everyone's got the same set of information, directly."

"Who?" Poppy asked. She was still smiling from the cheers.

Alden nodded his head while swallowing a large sip of his drink. "Agreed. I'll follow up."

"Old-school Raul, love that guy," Tim said. "Family friend, babe, you met him. Mom knows what's up, top-tier talent time only. He does all the land and dirt stuff for us, makes sure we can build wherever we want. He gave us the huge green light on this one so all the tree huggers would back off. We owe him a serious solid. You remember, he's got that pad in Pinecrest with the waterslide I dominated."

Poppy nodded. Raul sounded sort of familiar. Now that she split her time between a few different houses, she sympathized with how hard it could be to keep up with the different people associated with each place.

"You want me to reach out? I could DM," Tim suggested. He was really good at that kind of thing; it was one of the departments he oversaw at the company.

"No, thank you, sweetheart," Linnie said and shook her head firmly. Her white hair was pulled back in a low ponytail, and she wore a vintage white sundress. Poppy wondered when a dress was just a dress you'd had for a while and when it became vintage. She'd ask when there was a break in the conversation.

"We've got something else for you, actually, if you're up for a bit more responsibility." Alden gave a single nod when the waiter placed the crab avocado stack in front of him.

"Shoot," Tim said with a smile, jutting out his chin. He was wearing one of his new Hawaiian shirts, the one with panthers on it. Poppy smiled, too, so that Alden would understand how supportive she was of the family.

"We're very nearly over the hump here, dear." Linnie hadn't touched her food yet. "All that kerfuffle with the group concerned about the peninsula lagoon, saying we shouldn't build, that's all wrapping up. Quieting down finally. And Alden and I can't thank you enough for all your . . . fundraisers."

At this, Poppy beamed and gave her own ponytail a little shimmy. She'd helped Tim plan a series of parties to benefit a local sea bird charity; they'd even rented out the pool here one night and raised nine thousand dollars. That hadn't covered the cost of the rental, but so many people said it was an interesting cause.

"Anytime, Mom." Tim winked at his mother across the table. Any woman would melt at that, and Linnie was no exception.

"You are sweet." She separated out each word. Poppy looked over at her but did not receive a look back.

"So this is a little more under the radar, a little stealth mode." Alden put his fork down. He always used these kinds of terms, company jargon that made him seem like a bit of a blowhard, in Poppy's unspoken opinion. "Obviously we're planning to take a look at the branding after all this, possibly even a name change, though I'm hoping it doesn't go that far. But certainly some new messaging, a bit of a marketing massage."

"Absofruitly." Tim speared a chunk of crab off Poppy's plate and popped it in his mouth. This was why he was the CMO of Falcon Development: He had a way with words.

"And if I know you," Linnie said in the same kind, teasing voice she had used after Tim spoke to that investigative real estate reporter about paddleboarding, "I know you're my outdoorsman, and your head is always so clear, and you do your best thinking when you're on the boat."

"That is true," Poppy agreed.

Linnie winked at her, and Poppy felt her chest flood with warmth.

"So here's what I'm asking, brother man." Alden put both elbows on the table. "You go on the boat for a few weeks, get out of Dodge while we've still got these green freaks, those reporters, all those distractions you don't need, and just do what you do best: Get your arms around the big picture. Come up with a big, juicy rebrand, a whole new look for the company. I've heard you've had some really thought-worthy ideas in the past, so now's the moment. Your moment. And we'll go over everything when you're back and get the team on it like you wouldn't believe."

"Your moment." Poppy was nearly brought to tears as she placed her hand on Tim's thigh. She kept her chin raised, eyes softened, and head slightly tilted at whoever was speaking, prepared to be included again.

Without looking her way, Linnie and Alden continued describing to Tim exactly what he'd be working on: messaging, reinvention, image; new, sturdy, structurally sound, green, clean, fun-filled lagoons. Poppy took this opportunity to eat her next course, a lobster club salad. The chunks were too large and unwieldy to put into her mouth in one forkful, and usually she would've left them on the plate and glanced down at them longingly, wanting them very badly but not willing to get caught mid-conversation with a mouthful and mayonnaise smear. But now she had an open runway while the family went back and forth. The salad really was delicious.

Tim nodded vigorously along and finally replied. "Razzle dazzle—I get it. But clean. And very juicy. I'll have to hand over some serious reins to Janine, I guess," Tim said, then fanned his hand forward. "Ah, she'll get it." Janine was the SVP of marketing, Tim's number two, and every time Poppy saw her, she looked upset and very cold.

"Oh, and one last thing." Linnie turned sideways in her seat and rested a heavily jeweled hand on Poppy's shoulder. "It seems like just a bit of paperwork, but it means so much more than that to me. I hope you both have a sense of how eager we are to welcome this young lady into the family. So, I'm delighted to announce we have decided to put the boat in Poppy's name."

"Me?" Poppy's eyes bulged. As she lunged to hug Linnie, she looked through the centerpiece at Alden, who didn't smile but nodded. When she pulled back from her future mother-in-law, she grabbed the collar of her own dress in excitement.

"Like a wedding gift, alright?" Alden said through a mouthful.

"That's exactly right," Linnie agreed, smoothing her skirt and bestowing upon Poppy a tight smile and little scrunch of her nose.

Tim's eyes shone. He took his fiancée's hand and looked back and forth between his brother and mom. If only his father were here, Poppy thought, and hadn't had that second stroke when Tim burned down the lacrosse locker rooms at Bucknell.

"It's settled then," Alden said in his deep voice, which Poppy used to find intimidating and kind of mean but now realized was just extra warm—paternal, even. "And Mom, Raul tomorrow? You want me there?"

Linnie nodded, swallowing a tiny corner of that stiff lettuce that looked like a green Frito. She was a lady who knew exactly how and when to take the perfect-size bite. Poppy had so much to learn from her. "And I'll call Geoff this afternoon," Linnie said.

Poppy looked all around the table and beamed, feeling herself at this moment to have reached the very height of coastal sophistication.

Chapter

6

The valets hadn't remembered to roll down the windows as she'd in-structed, and because they'd insisted on parking her car out front in the full sun rather than in the garage, the saddle-leather interior was so hot that the first breath Linnie drew inside seared her lungs. She turned the key, and warm air wheezed through the vents. The Mer-cedes was a vintage beauty, made in 1956 and exorbitantly restored and maintained—not unlike herself.

The lagoons had been an absolutely fabulous idea. She had to remind herself of that now that things had veered this way. The idea was dynamo. Pools were done, so passé. If anyone could have a pool, why would anyone want one? Concrete and chlorine, done and done. Nature was in right now, and that was exactly what she, Linnie Falcon, had brought to the market: Super Nature.

She pulled out from the semicircle of like-minded cars around the gargantuan stone dolphin fountain and gave a generous wave to the staff, then cruised slowly down the wide brick drive toward the gate. The flowers lining the way were spectacular, bird beaks of orange-pink, vertical ribbons of purple petals, feathered red fists.

The paperwork remained on the passenger seat. At the last min-ute, she'd decided not to bring it in with her and instead let the girl and Tim marinate in the excitement of it all before they signed any-thing. *Don't make it about paperwork right away*, Linnie thought. Let them really think of it as a gift—let a signature be an afterthought. Better yet, let that needlepoint belt of a man, Geoff over at the marina office, handle the details. God knows he'd made smarter people sign off on worse things.

If she was being honest, that was why she'd pursued the fabulous idea with so much unbridled gusto in the first place: because of her late husband. Not *for* him—not in some lasting tribute, "he would've wanted it this way" way—but in spite of him. Not once in thirty-four years had he taken one of her proposals seriously; even if he had, later he would have claimed to her face that he'd come up with the idea himself. To her, their whole marriage had been decades beat to the gentle drum of pats on the head: *Don't worry about that, Lins— now why aren't the kids using the new bikes?* When the man finally passed, he'd handed it all to her. Over the course of years, delicately, she'd convinced him that she'd be the ideal steward, mediating between the two sons so that each one would feel he'd received a fair deal. If she was the chairman, both of them would have equal say, she assured her husband. It didn't even occur to him that Linnie would more or less cut both boys out and take total control herself.

The idea had been so fun, honestly. And flashy. Lagoons! Truly, they were beautiful. As if God had pressed down a finger at each one of their condos and left a glowing, cerulean print. Tanzanite jewels along the shore, a shade of blue that chlorine could only dream of— and the fish! This very week they had just now installed brand-new, gorgeous fish, and they were magnificent looking.

Someone at some luncheon was complaining about this fish with red-and-white silky fins, about how there were too many of them, "invasive," but when Linnie saw the pictures, she thought, *Bingo.* They photographed beautifully. Swimming alongside exotic creatures seemed absolutely wild, unheard-of—even so out-there as to feel slightly dangerous. It was just that thrilling of an idea. And the condos were selling accordingly.

Of course there were hiccups. At the first lagoon property, they went through construction workers like water: They kept slipping on the plastic lining and breaking parts of legs she'd never even heard of. At the second, two cranes demolished two heron habitats, which sank a fortune in Audubon donations. And then at the third location, some out-to-lunch parents complained their children nearly drowned because the Falcons had built right next to a playground—as if the view hadn't been vastly improved. Then the whole fourth location bungle when a cement mixer dumped into the wrong river . . .

A lesser woman would've stopped to take stock.

Changing the zoning for the new peninsula property, the fifth location, was so easy, she'd laughed out loud when she was told what it would take. Over the years, they'd laid the groundwork, of course—gigantic checks folded up and paper-airplaned into every single little conservation cause in the area to pave the way. Nonetheless, she'd been prepared to go to war, considering the way the wind blew on these things these days. Instead, all she had had to do was to cut half a dozen checks for twenty-five-thousand-dollar campaign donations and to invite three wives and one husband to her annual hydrangea gala at the club. Done.

She arrived at her own gate now and leaned out the window to buzz herself in. On the manila folder on the seat beside her, *Poppy* was written in Linnie's beautiful cursive. The girl would be charmed by that touch, perhaps more by the personal penmanship than by the gift of a sixty-five-foot yacht.

After all the trouble the company had caused for her these past years, Linnie did sometimes wonder whether her late husband knew exactly what he was doing by giving it to her. She would've loved to blame him. But the truth was the trouble mostly started once she'd embarked on this lagoon business. People were just relentless with their criticism, their opinions about how she should do *her* job.

It was as if they thought she was trying to kill someone.

Chapter

7

Helen: Pick up!

Denise: Are you dead? Is this Helen or her captor?

Helen: How would I be dead? Aloha from the Marshall Islands!

Denise: Shark, bus crash, rogue STD strain.

Helen: I'm at the Fijian deli getting these new nuts they invented. Yummmm.

Denise: They don't invent new nuts. And they don't say *deli* there.

Helen: How would you know? The Marshall Islands are in Oceania. Doesn't that sound like a mermaid's middle name? Maybe I'll change mine.

Denise: Goodnight.

Helen: I'm getting these new nuts on my layover, by the way. Next stop—home sweet home, Denny! I called you!

Denise: Don't call me that. No. Christmas was two weeks ago, Mom tie-dyed you a sarong.

Helen: WTF, no spoilers! I like to do my presents when I'm back! Ughhh. I hate knowing that. Can she make me something else? Tell her you ruined it.

Denise: Are you seriously coming here?

Helen: Ahoy! Yeah, to come work for you. You said I could come work there if I ever needed to, so ahoy, sissy! Wintertime funtime, dynamic duo back together.

Denise: Never said that. No openings. Not a duo.

Helen: I heard you tell Mom I could always come work for you.

Denise: Stop eavesdropping. I said that so she'd stop stressing out about you and talking to me about it all the time.

Helen: Too late, mate, on my way to the airport.

Denise: Take the nuts somewhere else. Spin the globe and close your eyes, like we used to.

Helen: I hid beer in that globe, it got gross, threw it out. Equator leaked.

Helen: Hello? Did you fall asleep?

Denise: We might have an opening.

Helen: Hell yeah you do! I have sooooo much hospitality experience now. And a Filipino bus license.

Denise: What happened? No, never mind. Don't put it in writing. Why don't you just go stay with Mom for a while?

Helen: Janet.

Denise: Janet.

Helen: Are they ever getting married?

Denise: Don't ask.

Helen: No bc then they couldn't torture us and say every five minutes they're roommates with benefits.

Denise: Last week she told me call me Bamama.

Helen: So after ten years she's our common-law Bahama mom.

Denise: Congrats to us.

Helen: Bamommy dearest. Plane's about to take off. I'm staying with you. Four months tops.

Denise: No. Can u pass a background check?

Helen: In many countries, yes.

Helen: Ooo, I also want to see the lagoon thing too, Mom says you told her it's really crazy, wacko.

Helen: You still there? Okay, yeah, I'll try calling again. Pick up!

Helen: Hello???

Chapter

8

They were ten years apart.

No one was expected to be close with a sibling who was ten years older or younger. When people asked, "Are you close with your sister?," all Denise or Helen had to do in response was to shrug and say for the millionth time, "We're ten years apart."

The distance between them was Helen's fault, because she'd moved so far away. Multiday differences in time zones were a barrier to both regular communication and coming home for holidays. Now that the girls were grown and the ten-years gap actually didn't feel as gaping as it used to, Helen was on the opposite side of the planet.

It was Denise's fault, because she'd never gone anywhere at all. She'd happily spent her entire life on one little peninsula, working her way up her first and only ladder. After a while the struggle to keep up with each other's day-to-day stopped feeling worth it. Denise's emotional thermostat was set low to begin with, and appeals to any vague sentiment of sisterly attachment never landed. What was the point, exactly, if they'd never be in the same place? She brandished the self-inflicted responsibility of remaining here and felt like everyone was always leaving, and leaving her with the bag, and it left a film of anger on the inside of her skin that she couldn't wash off.

It was their mother's fault. Babs was underwater from the minute the sisters' relationship began—widowed, broke, mother of a screaming newborn and a ten-year-old gone silent, the new owner of a marine plumbing business she'd just inherited. There was always work, there was always a child to bring to the worksite, there was always someone who needed something from her, and she always had to say yes and she was always exhausted.

The moment Helen moved out, Babs cashed out whatever she had; bought a tiny, hilly farm in the Bahamas; quickly met Janet, her partner of almost ten years now; and stopped communicating with the outside world all that much herself, finally having stepped into a life of her own choosing.

It was their father's fault because he was dead. His passing pulled loose one of the strings that could've tied the sisters together for good. Denise missed him, and Helen couldn't. They had essentially both been only children, and for some reason, each resented the other for that fact, as if they'd had any cosmic control.

Their relationship had frozen at the ages of eighteen and eight, the last time they'd lived at home together, until now.

Chapter

9

On the back of a motorcycle with her legs wrapped around a suspiciously handsome, mustached man named Randy, Helen tried hard to imagine what it would be like to see Denise again.

Was she excited? Yes, and that was all wrong. She should've been nervous, or irritated at least, that Denise had sent someone to pick her up. But Helen couldn't help it: She was excited. Excitement was her default feeling, something she liked about herself; she was aggressively forward-facing. Case in point, home looked and smelled the same as ever, and the big-leaved, salted air of tropicalia was remarkably like that of the islands she'd just left, but this was a connection that hadn't occurred to her until right then.

She let out a whoop.

For the first time in a long time, she didn't have to arrive somewhere new and immediately start thinking about the next place. This was not borrowed time. In fact, on this prominent peninsula, the nautical flags lining the road to Ahoy spelled out *ISLAND TIME*.

Denise had memorably described Randy in an email once as "a man." Meeting him, however, completely warped Helen's entire view of her makeup-free-zone, self-hair-cutting sister. The fact that this guy was objectively extremely good-looking was something Helen hadn't been prepared for at all. It made her think of her sister in a new, basic light, as someone who would be interested in something so obviously hot as an anchor tattoo under a cloud of chest hair.

Helen's own appetites mirrored her travels: omnivorous and fast-paced. Working at Ahoy would mean boats holding men and women captive—in other words, buffet tables. In her wide experience, furthermore, people tended to be significantly gayer at sea.

It shocked her how giddy she felt. To both her right and left she had a view of the water, slice by slice through the ten thousand palm trees on either side of the road. They cruised past the new construction, which her mother had told her Denise was flipping out about, and now they were passing Heracanes, and then on to the marina. Every time the bike slowed or stopped for a traffic light, the humidity caught up with them all at once and drowned both their bodies.

They stopped now behind a backhoe grinding its way over to the construction site, and Randy's pleasant baritone explained the water taxi business to her.

"They're out here barfing off the side of the pier and, boom, I'm swooping in. You get on the restaurant pickup route, after hours, they don't know what the fare is, man. They're at sea so we're talking no laws. *Is this guy taking me out into the ocean? Is this guy going to drown me?* No, man, I'm taking you home, and I'll get you there safe, but I'm charging you twenty big ones for it. And they leave fifties, no change! The old owners, they did the whole sunset cruise thing, early bird special, little toot down to dinner and dessert. Hell, no! I'm grabbing this business by the ping-pongs. Flag me down when you leave Marge's Margs. We use those big plastic cheese ball tubs, you know, for tip jars, and I'm telling you, I'm eating cheese balls all damn day this week because I need to put two on every boat. That's how it's going."

He lifted his right arm into the air and held up only his pointer and pinkie fingers to emphasize exactly how rock and roll the situation was.

"I'm in the wrong business," Helen shouted.

"Damn right you are. Well, you're getting closer at least now. Denise'll tip you out alright."

"How long does it take to get a captain's license these days?" she wondered out loud.

"*Pssh*, they're real uptight. About five years?"

Helen winced.

Randy twisted to look back at her. "Man, you look like her, you know. It's a trip. Like I'm meeting Denise ten years ago—wham! And I'm telling you, I wish I had."

She liked Randy a lot so far.

"So why'd she send you to come get me?" Helen asked. She knew the answer, that Denise was avoiding her the same way Helen was avoiding Denise, buying herself a little buffer between the concept of reuniting and the reality. But Randy was a talker, and Helen wanted to take advantage before Denise elbowed him to shut up.

"Girl can't sleep at all right now with that condo going up—she's losing it. You know about the lagoon thing. She spent the whole night on my computer looking up how to get away with draining it or setting the whole thing on fire and making it look like lightning. Problem is, you want lightning, you get a thunderstorm, some rain, no more fire. Uphill battle."

Helen rolled her eyes, not that Randy could see. "It's not our house anymore. They can do whatever they want. She's not the president of the peninsula." This was borrowed directly from her eight-year-old self.

"Just wait until you see it, might change your tune big-time. Plus, come on, for you two, it's the last place you had your dad. I do get that. Every time I drive past a Wendy's, I think of my mom. Her name was Wendy."

Helen's muscles froze. She was not in any way prepared to talk about her dad with Randy. It was shocking to learn that Denise did, or that she talked about anything with anyone honestly. It was not a topic Helen ever brought up herself.

She swallowed. "Maybe Denise will change her tune," she said with more force than she felt.

Randy barked out a laugh. "Not much of a tune changer. Here we go."

Helen tried to relax her shoulders.

Randy took a sharp right, and soon they reached a tall metal gate emblazoned with an anchor logo and cursive *A*. He leaned over and told the small black box he was here for Denise.

"You're meant to use the secondary entrance," a British voice piped through the speaker.

"Screw you, Geoff," Randy replied.

A huff came through the box. The gate opened, and they pulled inside.

Chapter

10

You guys are thinking about it like some guy lifts up the hood of a car and cuts the brake line. Like one snip breaks all hell loose. This is not that.

The original engine design for that boat came from the Norwegian military. And guess where they got all their ideas? The Vikings. So yeah, there's a reason why those guys are some premier yacht people, every Bjorne and Leif I've ever met has a primo consulting gig. You should get one of them over here talking to you. Beautiful, beautiful boats, gorgeous, right down to the bolts.

You know some of these dopey owners want every little piece engraved like that? I'm serious. Think about the type of human being who wants every one of those ten thousand nuts on his boat engraved with his own two initials. That's the kind of person you insurance guys are working for, just saying.

These are serious, sophisticated machines with the kinds of design elements that people like you and me would never even think to care about. No offense. But the mechanics are fundamental, for all boats—they're all the same at the end of the day. It's about being able to tinker with the engine and then with the tech layer on top of that. The boats are outfitted like spaceships these days.

Really would be a two-man job, pulling off something like that.

Chapter

11

Helen pulled off her helmet, and her hair exploded skyward. From her backpack she pulled out an angular straw hat she'd bought at a market in Palau. Now that she was back in a first-world nation, it was her responsibility to use these small fashion choices to teach others about native cultures around the world, and she took this responsibility very seriously. She pulled the strings of the hat around her chin so it would not blow off.

Her shoulders were hot to the touch at the edges of her linen crop top and crochet skirt, the thinking woman's mesh. The backs of her legs were slick with sweat.

From around the side of the glass building, Denise marched toward them holding a clipboard and a life jacket. The clipboard elicited in Helen a Pavlovian sense of dread. Denise thrust out a stiff arm toward the man standing behind the front desk of the building, as if to stop him from following her.

To Helen, her sister looked exactly the same; she was born forty. Her sunglasses tan wrapped a wide white band around her upper face like war paint. Short black-and-gray hair that defied both description and wind blew straight up and back as if she was being electrocuted. What could generously be described as bangs flopped over the sides of a red visor with a shrimp on it. She wore basketball shorts beneath a white captain's polo embroidered with *Ahor* in green. One of her flip-flops was duct-taped together.

"Misprint," Denise said, pointing to the breast pocket when she arrived in front of them. Her voice was as rough and raspy as ever from years of yelling at crews over the wind. "Got a box of fifty in the truck for dirt work. If you don't keep up with Zodiac maintenance, it'll bite you in the ass. What are you wearing?" She was the one to ask.

Helen opened her mouth but found she couldn't say a word. She pressed her lips together and forced a weak smile that couldn't possibly hold back the water she felt suddenly rising behind her eyes. What had she been expecting?

"Hey, this is a big old moment." Randy leaned back, made a large V with his arms, and pointed fingers at both women. "Denise has told me a helluva lot about you. You've seen Guam?"

This was the drip. Helen was a cumulative crier, holding it in for a hundred little drips, filling up all along, and she never had any idea when the last little drop would fall, the one that overflowed the whole thing. Apparently, this was it. She started nodding uncontrollably, faster and faster, as if that could stop anything, until tears started to roll down her cheeks. All at once, the time change, jet lag, hunger, exhaustion, and the sad realization of where she was, *really* was, and the very beautiful places she'd left behind and the nothing she had to show for it and the grease-stained, worst babysitter of all time who was standing in front of her with no plans to even ask her how her flight was all crashed down on her.

"Whoa." Randy raised both hands in surrender. "She was all good on the ride over, I swear." He whipped off his do-rag and extended it to her. Helen blew her nose into it. Randy kept a hand on Helen's shoulder and gently elbowed Denise. "You know your sister did a camper van in Japan?"

"Yeah, I know." Denise sighed. She pulled a white rag from her back belt loop, put it over her shoulder like a burp cloth, then extended her arms.

Helen stepped forward and hugged her sister, smushing her streaked face into Denise's shoulder. Denise wrapped her arms around Helen, and they held the stilted embrace for a long moment. The blue-and-white marina flags flapped out on the pier, and the waves crashed over the big gray stones of the breakwater. Helen's breathing slowed. It was the most they'd touched in years.

"Why are you even wearing eye mascara?" Denise asked, her chin pushing into Helen's neck with every word.

"Are there other kinds?" Helen blubbered. "Wait, is it getting on my linen? It's made out of bamboo."

Denise sniffed her hair. "Gross. Don't tell me you dye your hair, do you know how toxic—"

Helen pulled back and wiped her nose on her bare arm. As if she'd thrown up after too many drinks, she felt better already, empty and clean. She took one big step backward and clapped once.

Randy flinched and his head swiveled between the two of them as he witnessed the speed at which they completed a full cycle of sisterhood.

"So, here I am!" Helen sniffled and power-smiled, forcing her mood up and out, a trick she'd learned from meeting a lot of CEOs on vacation. "Put me in, coach." She swayed side to side and bent her arms at the elbows to indicate physical readiness.

With one finger, Denise slid her sunglasses down from atop her visor and over her eyes. "Mom knows you're here, right?" She crossed her arms. "What is your plan exactly? With details."

"Relax. I'm going to call Mom later—she knows I'm here. If I call her right now, she'll ask me to hurry up and go visit, and I want to get settled in first." She yanked her suitcase off the bike, and it smacked the ground and fell over. "Do they have outdoor showers here? I haven't showered indoors in a really long time. I don't know if I could handle that kind of culture shock right now."

"Call Mom."

"Why? I will! Lay off already, it's been two seconds. You know, people who work in places that look like this are supposed to be way less uptight. Ask me, I know. Proximity to water lowers your heart rate."

"Now tell that to cats," Randy said.

"You cannot park there, Randy! We've discussed this!" The man from behind the front desk called out from inside the glass building through cupped hands. He wore shorts with a jacket and tie on top.

Randy leaned over to kiss Denise. "I'll see you tonight," he said, then turned to Helen. "And I want to hear your Japanese. We're doing sushi and getting the weird stuff." He revved the engine then drove through the gate, and they both took cover under their arms from the silvery cloud of dust that rose from the oyster-shell parking lot.

The mood became palpably tense once no third party was there to perform for. The only way through the familiar awkwardness was to arrange themselves into the existing grooves of the roles they knew how to act out. Denise played angry, Helen played peppy, and eye rolls greased the wheels.

Helen usually stuck with the safe topics of things they both hated: fancy restaurants, sports and their fans, and the whole raisin-craisin family. But wasn't she too mature for that now? She wasn't a kid anymore. Now she would say whatever popped into her head.

"Can I ask, I mean, I'm asking—a boyfriend? I love that guy, he's, like, actually a good guy, I think. And yikes, holy mustache. Hubba-hubba. How long has that been going on? When's the wedding? Double wedding for you and Mom?" Helen cocked her head toward the gate but kept looking at Denise.

"Stop."

A boat horn blared in the distance and both women turned their heads toward the water. Helen felt a familiar weight pushing onto her shoulders, as if the wind was blowing down rather than sideways. Denise fanned herself with the clipboard and grumbled something Helen couldn't make out in her raging voice—their mother's voice. Every conversation a battlefield. Neither Denise nor their mom suffered fools and considered every single person on earth a fool, Helen included. But for some reason Denise's grumbling felt weirdly comforting now, like the warm but itchy blanket the family had kept around for years.

Denise crossed her arms. "Okay. Are you for real about working here? For longer than a week? Because I'm warning you, there are people here you are not going to like working for. It's not fun-time-family-vacation people, it's serious—people like the Falcons, alright? You can't quit every time your feelings get hurt."

Helen stared at her. "Millenium? Peregrine? Atlanta?"

Denise moved her hands to her hips, leaned forward, and squinted at Helen like she couldn't believe her eyes. "The lagoon people. The people who own our land now?"

"Oh." Helen stood up straighter. "Wait, you work for them? Here?" She looked around as if one of them might pop out and introduce themselves. "I love that. So there's still a connection there: us, them. We're all still a part of the whole thing. That's sweet to, like, keep it in the family some."

Denise huffed and lifted up her arms, then let them slap down to her thighs. "Are you kidding me?"

"No! It's nice. Sometimes things are nice, Denise. Hate to break it to you."

"People who are about to obliterate this peninsula? I hate them, Helen, and you should, too. It is not nice. I sent you like a hundred petitions about this. They are killing the shoreline, our shoreline, in case you forgot. I don't even like seeing their name on here." She thrust the clipboard out as though she wanted to smack Helen over the head with it.

Now Helen huffed. It had taken all of five minutes for Denise to go fully berserk. "Well, which one is it? Am I supposed to hate these people, or am I supposed to work for them?"

"Both!" Denise pointed at her face.

Now Helen threw up her hands.

"I'm telling you we don't bring all that personal stuff here. You're invisible. Even if it feels wrong, even if it feels like absolute shit, no one cares how you feel. It's a job. The boat is a relationship-free zone. I'm saying you need to put every single thing away, none of that, and just work."

"Invisible is in the eye of the beholder. If people see me and they like what they see, there's nothing I can do about that," Helen explained. "Hold on. Does Mom know you work for them?"

"I do not work for them; they're just a client of Ahoy's. Geoff knows I'm not getting that close. Are you even listening? Yes, she knows their boat's here—she's done bilge repair jobs for them before."

"Wow. So I guess you both have zero maritime ethics."

"Helen, oh my God. We both have mortgages, how about that? And please. Your moral compass went overboard when you lost your virginity on my kayak."

"Yours? You didn't even live at home anymore, that was mine. And whatever. It's fine with me. If I see them, I won't say anything. I'm invisible. Pretend I'm not even here, like when you made me sleep in the tree house alone all summer, when I was seven."

Denise brought her fingers to her temples.

Helen crossed her arms and craned her neck toward the row of shrubs at the property line. "So I need to go look at that lagoon thing, huh?"

"Yes, you do." Denise turned around and started walking past the glass building toward the piers, and Helen fell in step with her. "I'll figure out one of the cottages for you and just . . . stay in there."

Denise took the suitcase from Helen's hand and pulled it for her.

Then Denise stopped on the deck in front of the piers and faced her sister directly. "Just level with me. If I need to find someone else, I need to find them right now. I have charters coming up. How permanent is this?"

Over Denise's shoulder, Helen could see the stretch of lawn where the cute crew cottages were. Half a dozen great-looking young people in shorts and shrimp visors were performing calisthenics. Yum.

"Very," Helen said.

Chapter

12

"That is what's so amazing about it, Mom, I didn't have to pay for it." Poppy paced back and forth along the wraparound second-floor balcony of her and Tim's house with her yellow tasseled caftan billowing behind her. From up here, outside the French doors of their master bedroom, they had a quadruple water view: hot tub, pool, waterway, then ocean. Down below, people in cargo shorts trimmed the purple jacaranda trees, power-washed the pool house, and scrubbed the sides of Tim's sailboat at the end of the pier.

Poppy waved to them every time they looked up at her, which was a lot over the past hour. She was loudly telling her mother the news.

"Well, how'd that work out exactly? Who just gives somebody a giant boat?" her mom asked.

"It's a wedding gift!"

"For the wedding they can't find a way to fit on the calendar."

"*Mom.*" She drew out the word. "Don't go there. This is a sign. You have to see it. If you saw it, you would totally understand how big a deal it is—it's a very big boat. We could live on it. And Tim says he's renaming it, but he wants it to be a surprise. He's going to show me the paint job tomorrow. I think he's going to name it after me."

"That's one way to lay claim."

Poppy draped her arms over the ledge and beamed.

Inside the bedroom Elena was putting together their suitcases. Poppy had been told to pack, which she learned last year meant just telling Elena they were going on a trip.

"You know," her mother said, "I see the ads for those buildings with the lagoons sometimes on TV. Your father and I thought maybe we might see some of you on there or something. You're so pretty, they ought to have you be the one on-screen. And at one point you said Tim was talking to some reporter. It should be you."

"Oh no, he's not doing that anymore. His mom said he's all done with that. You know how it is—the more you talk about how great something is, the more other people talk about erosion. They're just worried about the shoreline and it being too much water moving around there and all. It's so hard to get everyone to agree, but I think what could bring people together is that lagoons are very nice to look at."

"Water moves on its own. It's called *waves*."

"Exactly. Hold on, mama, I'm getting another call." Poppy stretched each side of her neck. "Hello?"

"Hi! Is this Miss Poppy Wojcikski?"

A smile bloomed across her face. She pressed her shoulders back, lifted her chin to the sun, and adjusted the sides of her caftan. "It is!"

"Ahoy," said a charming voice with a British accent. "This is Geoff with Ahoy Marina."

Her mouth opened. "Oh! Yes, right. Fine, thank you. Am I supposed to say ahoy now?"

"No need, thank you. Excellent. Well, I'm sorry to bother you, but I'm calling of course to introduce myself and also to extend an invitation." His accent made her chest flutter. She'd never actually spoken to someone from another country.

In the past, whenever she'd heard Tim and his family mention Geoff, always next to the word *arrangements*, she imagined some kind of white-bearded captain, a sea Santa who took care of everything boat related. But this man sounded younger, crisp and polished. She pictured his clothes having gold buttons.

"Do you need me to help on the boat?" Her stomach wobbled. It hadn't occurred to her that she'd have to know anything about boats.

Geoff laughed, and she felt her cheeks flush. "Quite right, Miss Wojcikski. So, would you like to do a run-through? I know neither nut nor bolt of it has changed since you were last aboard, but all the same, it's all a bit new to you in this light. This could be a good moment to see how it all works, from an owner's perspective. There's nothing you necessarily need to know, of course, but in case you're interested, we'd like to offer a walk-through with myself and one of the captains."

"Oh!"

A set of doors blew open in Poppy's mind. This could be her hobby. Tim was always trying to get her to have hobbies. He had so many: windsurfing, collecting drum sets, a small mine in Peru.

"I'm a boat person now." She said it out loud and immediately felt more important.

"Indeed you are. Is there anything you'd like me to take care of in the meantime?"

Not only could she funnel her time into this, she could do all the nice things she always thought about doing but never seemed to be able to find the right outlet for. She wanted to do good. The Falcons did so much charity work, and right here, right now, this was her opportunity.

"I'd like to make the boat carbon-neutral."

"I—"

"And gay-friendly."

"Of course we can't stop any particular person from getting on the boat, so—"

"And no guns allowed."

"Well—"

"And definitely a woman captain."

"Yes! There we go. Certainly, that we can arrange."

Poppy nodded once, firmly. She'd tried to get involved with several of Linnie's charity groups, but none had taken up any of her ideas yet. And now look at all the good she'd done in just one conversation—changing the world.

"Outstanding decisions," Geoff said. "So, the walk-through then, Wednesday afternoon? Two o'clock?"

"You'll do the walk-through with me?" She knew he would, he'd already said so, but she loved the way his voice sounded.

"Right by your side."

A little swirl of something she'd rather not think about frothed inside her stomach. Her eyes darted to the door as if Tim would walk in at that moment and see her smiling like this.

"Two o'clock," she agreed. How silly to think that being An Owner didn't come with any kind of responsibility—of course it did. She had to *attend the walk-through* and *make arrangements* with *Geoff.*

A little shimmy overtook her upper half, then she turned back to head inside the bedroom. "Elena?" she called. "I'm sorry, I can't help you pack anymore." She threw her arms open wide. "I'm going to have a meeting!"

Chapter

13

Twice today, Geoff had been asked where the bathroom was—
and not by clients, mind you, but by contractors wearing snorkels.
What his bosses didn't understand, and what Geoff had tried to
explain to them in at least a dozen formally formatted emails, was
that stationing him at the front desk diluted his brand. He was a
concierge, a *senior* concierge, as he bolded in his signature.

Those who snorkeled professionally did not need concierges.
The snorkelers of the world having the same level of access to Geoff
as the yacht owners was hardly the exclusivity of customer service
Ahoy claimed to provide.

But his presence at the front desk was deemed a "temporary re-
assignment" to "pitch in" during "staffing transitions," and so far all
of Geoff's questions had gone unanswered.

He hung up the phone with Poppy Wojcikski, evidently the new
Falcon owner—an imminent in-law, which was not for him to wonder about—and made a note of her upcoming walk-through.

On top, he wore a sky-blue linen jacket with the coral Ahoy anchor
insignia tie; on the bottom, pleated khaki shorts and rubber, perforated Top-Siders that could withstand a hosing.

He'd gracefully handled the most delicate of conversations, from
helicopter pilot snafus, to monogramming catastrophes when initials added up to a word you'd rather they not, to tense exchanges
with an owner over his wife's inexplicable, repeated, violent assaults

on the horseshoe crabs in Grace Bay. Any day now, surely, he would be returned to an office.

The two Ahoy locations, here and at the Bahamas port, were identical down to the interior plant choices—mirror images across the Caribbean, purposefully designed to standardize guests' experiences as they boarded and disembarked. No matter what had gone on at sea, and Geoff was delighted not to know, one came home to the familiar bleached hug that was Ahoy.

Geoff looked out to the docks. Between the office and the piers was a thin band of grass along a wide wooden deck that spanned the marina with a spacious array of lounge chairs, should guests wish to wait there for any reason. No one ever did—guests, of course, preferred to wait on their yachts, and Ahoy staff were not permitted to touch the lounge chairs—and thus no one had ever once lounged there. Their yellow-and-white striped cushions were laundered every other day.

The bottom half of the blue Dutch door at the landside entrance swung open. Denise marched in, trailing dual exhaust clouds of humidity and dissatisfaction.

She whipped off her sunglasses and pounded both elbows onto Geoff's desk, her weathered hands dangling among the dongles behind his computer. Geoff stopped himself from mentioning yet again the array of well-intended grooming products he'd laid out in the crew locker rooms.

"I'm going first," she said. She spoke in an emotionless, clipped style that frightened him, though he would never admit it.

Geoff pulled his head back for a moment before lowering his shoulders and squaring his jaw. "Denise. Would you prefer to speak outside?" Dealing with this woman directly was demotion personified.

"You'd like that, wouldn't you?" A glob of neon-green gum smacked from within the horrid depths of her mouth.

Geoff had a remarkable gift for holding the muscles in his face completely still.

She hoisted herself further over the desk and picked up a napkin Geoff had saved from his lunch. She spit her gum into it and placed the wad into her pocket. "Crew hole. I'm bringing on my sister, and I want to go light on the background check."

The hulking blue landline at Geoff's desk rang. He flinched, and Denise grinned with half her face, her prey on edge. He pursed his lips as if looking at something unsavory. He did not care at all for this component of the job. So far today, he'd received calls from a lost lobster distributor en route, a billionaire's business manager, then the business manager's ex-husband's divorce lawyer, and finally an employee requiring a larger uniform after a chest procedure. All unsettling.

He had no choice but to pick up the cursed object.

"Ahoy?" Not a word usually subject to question marks, but a more effusive greeting had frightened elderly callers.

Without taking her eyes off his face, Denise took the phone from Geoff's hand and placed it back down onto the receiver.

"You—"

"Alright? So we're done with that. Now what did you want?" Around Denise's neck was an unsanctioned accessory, a camouflage-patterned sun buff that he'd seen her wear up to her chin like some kind of ocean warlord. Without looking down he knew about the shoes, an HR battle lost long ago: amphibious footwear of the woman's own construction that was, as she pointed out to everyone, bite-proof. Last summer she'd left some poor creature's triangular tooth in the toe for weeks.

Geoff pressed his palms onto the desk. "The Falcons," he said. She straightened her spine, and now it was his turn to grin. "There is a new ownership structure in place, and they've requested a female captain."

"Nope." She shook her head. "Part of my deal. Not working that. You know that, Fern knows that."

"What would you have us do, then? We are utmost at the service of our—"

"Hire more female captains."

He emphasized his accent in hopes that it conveyed a sense of hierarchy. "I believe we can avoid Fern altogether for this arrangement, as that seems to be your preference regarding your sister, was it?"

An hour earlier, Geoff had entered the HR office himself to document the new Falcon ownership and had been nearly knocked backward from across the desk by the sheer force of Fern's frosted teal eyeshadow. As usual, she'd been mid-craft, and the nozzle of an active glue gun dripped its contents onto her notes beside a pile of mini shells and a canvas of collage-by-number. Her neon fingernails clacked along the ancient keyboard like radioactive crab claws, and she skipped the top-left row of letters completely as one sleeve was glued to her desk at the wrist.

Denise stared at him, and Geoff hoped it wasn't apparent that the back of his neck had begun to sweat. Suddenly she placed both palms onto his desk and leaned forward. Her rough elbows spanned sideways like wings.

"You've seen way too many pieces of paper around here, so they can't fire you," she said. "The suits stashed you here until you hate it so much you quit."

Geoff felt a sinking sensation behind his ribs but lifted his chin. "And?" He could see the muscles working in her jaw.

"Fine," she growled.

The phone rang again; Denise picked it up and slammed the receiver down.

She jammed her hand into her pocket, retrieved the wadded-up piece of gum, and threw it at his desk.

He had to find a way out of here.

Chapter

14

Behind the main Ahoy building were the striped crew cottages, each with a window flower box and an Adirondack chair out front with a seahorse-shaped lumbar pillow. No one lived here full-time, though many crew members came close. Owner schedules were fickle. In the winter during high season, the bungalows were full nearly every night, and often enough there was more than one occupant inside.

Like all modern communities, this one was segregated on the basis of exercise: those who did it and those who hated them. The majority was known, by the minority at least, as the grunts. They made noises like tennis players no matter what they were doing. Lifting a laundry basket: *Ughn!* Opening a door: *Yugh!* Stretching a post-run thigh in the most visible part of the courtyard for everyone to feast their eyes on: *Guh!*

This group spent every waking minute on shore working out and wore a self-imposed uniform of tank tops tucked into shorts with tiny crotch pockets for sweat-drenched keycards. Every one of the grunts had a single-syllable name—Tim, Tom, Kim, Kat—as if their parents' greatest dream was maximum efficiency. They were all twenty-seven.

Denise believed that if she ever had to pick up something heavy and accidentally released one of their mating calls, she would be strangled in spandex until she accepted their idol, the electrolyte water bottle.

She shoved past them out toward the piers. Thank God Helen's first charter today was with Raul, so Denise could at least make sure her sister kept everything in her pants before the goddamned Falcons got involved. A manatee swam slowly under the pier in front of her, about to head-butt the boat on the other side. A concussion sounded incredible right now.

It was just after 9:00 a.m. and already outrageously hot. Stew and Kaylee helped the delivery team unload packaged snack foods; soaps; linens; bath and beach towels; a pile of magazines tied with an ivory grosgrain ribbon; cases of wine, liquor, champagne, and beer; individually wrapped dark chocolate truffles; dog food; and the one-two punch of evening plans: fireworks and a defibrillator. The chef would arrive shortly with the fish, steaks, vegetables, fruits, spices, and a portable herb garden. The farm-fresh florist clomped down the pier in clogs with fieldfuls of peonies in long boxes, all an identical shade of neon pink.

They would be gone one night.

Helen was off to a promising start, stealing one of the peonies and sticking it in her ponytail. The shrimp polo shirt looked great on exactly no one except Helen apparently, which irritated Denise to no end. The whole situation irritated her—that Helen was right, Denise *would* give her a job the moment she needed one, and that Helen had no idea what her sister had sacrificed to do so.

Helen wore a chunky Polynesian bracelet of wooden beads and a belt patterned with alternating Greek and Korean flags. Her entire wardrobe consisted of conversation prompts designed to bore people to death. She was not better than everybody else just because she'd taken a lot of planes in her life. *Sophisticated.* Once Denise had heard their mom use that word to describe her other daughter's world travels. So sophisticated, she had an HR-violation punch card. Denise rejected the word as the marker of a life correctly lived.

A caravan of feelings rolled through her, one after another, too fast for Denise to get a good look at each one, then crashed into a pileup inside her chest when Helen winked at her and waved from the base of the silver ramp. Denise felt sorry for that little girl whose big sister had not wanted to spend any time with her growing up, felt sorry for herself for being saddled with babysitting her whole teenage life and never getting any credit. And she was angry at Helen now for forcing them back here like this, in exactly the same formation.

She wanted to want to *roll with it*, a concept people had tried to explain her entire life. Letting things come, letting go of things, being carefree. But why would anyone want to feel like that—a walking target? If you didn't care, if your guard was down, if you were simply building a stick fort in the backyard, letting your mind wander to what might be for dinner, then you might look up one minute and see your mom walking through the knee-high grass, carrying a newborn baby in her arms, and falling to her knees, almost dropping the baby, before she could reach you with the news that your dad was gone. That was called being surprised, and it was what you got for being carefree. You had to care, to stay vigilant and ready for bad news at all times, or better yet, you had to be so far out ahead that you were the one delivering bad news, always. It was infuriating to be told to *roll with it*, and every time she tried, and failed, she was mad at herself and everyone else in circles like a dog chasing its tail, except the tail was on fire and her nose was always getting burned, but she could not stop herself.

She stopped in front of the ramp and her crew stood before her.

"Did we get the old cot bedding back? If we get those Patagonian tundra, snow-proof sleeping bags again, I'm doing nights in the kayak up top, and you know what I don't sleep in." Stew's sweaty, blond crew cut glistened in the sun.

Answering just encouraged them.

Kaylee raised her hand as slowly as joints could possibly extend. "We've talked about gut health, Denise, so many times. Was there something you had for breakfast that disturbed or confused your microbiome? Because I'm getting a rawness from you, a kind of very dark halo orbiting—" Kaylee waved circles at her own belly. "So I need to ask, from the bottom of my heart, how much yogurt is on board?"

"And who is she?" Stew jabbed a thumb toward Helen.

Helen waved both hands in front of her. "Aloha, team! I'm an ice-breaker girl, so." She leaned against the piling to take a rest from watching others work. "Helen, recently turned twenty-eight, just moved here from, well, all over, as you can see—" She hoisted up her hand and thrust out her hips. "Technically I'm new to yacht life but definitely not to boating. Favorite food, okay, that is a tough one, but I'd have to say either pork adobo pancit or mushroom pizza. And yes, I'm Denise's sister."

Stew glared at Denise. "You never said anything about a sister. This will not change the tip outs."

Kaylee turned and wrapped Helen in a long hug. "I believed Denise had someone like you in her heart, a twin spirit."

"We're ten years apart," they both said at the same time.

Kaylee bowed. "Welcome. I can also sense your digestive halo, and I'm so impressed and just want to say thank you for honoring your inner flora with the peace and respect it deserves. Here." She reached in her pocket then handed Helen a white feather.

Stew looked Helen up and down as though she'd just crawled out from under the pier. "She's a junior deckhand, right?"

Denise nodded once.

Stew dropped a shoulder bag at Helen's feet. "Bring this on board. Put it below the cot closest to the biggest fan. I'm a sweater, remember that. Can you do calf massages?"

"Besties," Helen said to Denise once they were alone. "Right? That was so good, they love me. Amazing."

"Do not assume that everybody likes you. They were going easy because I'm here. Wait till we're out there doing the work. And chill out. You cannot put on the Helen show around the guests, do you understand? You work for Stew and Kay—do not talk to anybody else."

"No, I'm pretty sure everybody likes me." Helen bobbed her shoulders.

A car door slammed on shore, and Denise saw Raul Williams's driver walk around to open the door for him. "Just listen to me. Do less, be less, fade into the background, don't drop anything. And you're welcome, by the way—you know you haven't actually said thank you yet."

Helen heaved Stew's duffel onto her shoulder. "I'll thank you when you honor your inner flora."

Chapter

15

Raul Williams was Denise's favorite owner, a low bar.

He walked on board with a silver cane tapping out his arrival at every step—Dialysis Iglesias himself. He was a foot shorter than Denise, and she'd never seen him wear anything but a uniform of beige short-sleeved linen suits and tan loafers. He seemed impervious to the weather, appearing cool even on the most suffocating, humid days, and the little remaining hair he had was shaved into a frost of white across his head. He'd been an engineer by training long before he'd made a fortune partnering with real estate developers on groundwater solutions, and he still had the clinical aura of a scientist about him. It didn't seem as though he touched anything or even came close; it was as if there was always a cane-length distance between himself and the world. He was pristine and self-possessed, and every room he stepped into became a controlled environment.

Four defeated-looking people in business casual with briefcases, two of whom had seriously miscalculated and carried tennis rackets, trailed behind him. This group was what Raul called his exoskeleton, a layer of lawyers, accountants, and assistants that went everywhere.

Denise checked her watch, then ducked down below deck.

The living room suite was larger than Denise's home. Two curved couches made a pair of thick blue parentheses. Between them was a giant glass coffee table that acted as a magnifying lens for the frog-patterned rug beneath it, enlarging the already bulging eyes.

Bookshelves were built into the curved walls, filled with framed photographs of Raul and his late wife. There was a chrome wet bar with four stools along the back and a dining table for twelve.

Where most people had a large TV screen, Raul had something else: a floor-to-ceiling terrarium.

It was a grid of four glass rectangles, each filled with a perfect brown gradient of soil, a pool of water, some neat little plants, and a lizard. They were gorgeous. Raul and Denise were both enthusiasts, it was what they'd bonded over, in Denise's first and only experience bonding with an owner. She knew she was looking at over half a million dollars' worth of Reptilia here.

Her eyes scanned across the glass from one set of little eyes to the next, fellow travelers on the paths of most resistance. Tiny dinosaurs, survivors. She had neither the budget nor the schedule for pets like this, so with her resentment in check, it was a pleasure to work for someone who did.

She took one last look, then jogged upstairs to the cockpit.

It took roughly four hours for them to cruise to Musha Cay, a private island owned by a successful magician, and they arrived in time for cocktail hour. The crew commenced a perfect waltz to anchor the yacht off the white-sand shore. The lush vegetation of the island's interior swayed back and forth in the strong breeze, exposing the purple-flowered shrubs and pink bougainvillea behind the enormous green leaves.

An orange crescent of sun clung to the tops of the palms.

As the guests descended onto the small chase boat that would deliver them to the island for dinner, Denise observed Helen hand out last-minute snacks, fix hairdos, laugh at jokes, and hold four empty glasses in one hand.

Stew and Kaylee were the closest thing Denise had to family here, and she felt protective of them now that her actual family member threatened to barge in. Kaylee had come from the world of luxury spas, kept a moon rock in her cargo shorts, and once told Denise she was born on one of the Keys that didn't "usually" appear on maps. Stew was a short man of astounding musculature who came from the world of Disney cruises, where he'd handled pizza night logistics for five hundred; he was the father of multiples and had just had his husband's parents move into the second floor of his house.

Kaylee and Stew could handle anything, and it seemed, Denise had to admit, that Helen could, too. Denise was embarrassed by the childishness of both sets of her feelings about Helen's evident competence. Part of her, of course, wanted Helen to be terrible at the job, as Denise had suspected she'd be. But the other part was afraid, in a childlike way, that Denise had finally captured something she didn't even know she would be allowed to capture and that it might escape again.

That night Helen was too exhausted to even try to hang out with her sister after the guests went to bed. Denise sat up on the third deck with her feet on the console, leafing through the dossiers that Geoff prepared on every single guest. The source of his power was professional-grade gossip and bolding the word *highly* in emails.

The navy blue sky glowed silver at the horizon and held an astonishing number of stars. Waves lapped the hull. Behind her, she heard the faint clang of a ring tapping against the metal railing, rising toward her one step at a time.

"Why am I not surprised you are a nocturnal animal," Raul said.

He was winded from the climb and breathing heavily, leaning over in his robe. Oxygen tanks were placed throughout the boat, despite her insistence that these increased the chances of an explosion dramatically, and he pulled on one now. Denise helped him with the nozzle but said nothing.

"You want one?" He opened the mini fridge and pulled out two bottles of beer.

Denise took one and opened it with a *twist-hiss*. "The dirt down there looks really good," she said, and they tapped the tops of their bottles together.

"I know. I knew you would like them. And I like your little sister, by the way," Raul helped himself to a lounge chair. "A bit chatty, but she knows her lizards, too. *Cortada de la misma tela.*"

Denise shook her head. Their closeness did not extend to discussing their own species. "What's up, Raul?"

He took a long swig and sank down farther into the seat. Denise hated seeing him here—if she was being honest, she always bristled when owners got anywhere near the controls—but there wasn't a thing she could do about it. "I never would've gotten so rich if someone had told me how much time I'd have to spend with those guys," he said.

"So you came to my office instead." She couldn't help herself.

"Other people's work is so easy."

A gust of wind rushed over the boat and with it the smell of salt, earth, and chlorine from the pools on the island. Raul closed his eyes and leaned his head back. Denise crossed her arms. They stayed like this for a long moment. If he wanted relaxation, she didn't understand why he'd come up here to subject her to it. The man could not be alone, from what she could tell. Ever since his wife died last year, he was never by himself for more than a few minutes before he pulled someone to his side. The exoskeleton kept expanding yet pushing in closer, and she'd seen him chatting with Helen earlier today at lunch, unable to stomach dining solo.

"Raul?" A voice rose from the stairs.

He lifted his head.

A woman in a buttoned-up set of full-length blue gingham pajamas stepped onto Denise's deck. Her thick-framed glasses slid down her nose. "I'm sorry to interrupt," she said. Her hand was cupped around the bottom of a phone. "Melinda Falcon again."

Denise looked at him. Raul curled his lips down and shook his head. "Too late," he whispered with a flap of his hand.

The woman slid her glasses up and nodded. "So sorry." She disappeared, and Denise could just make out her voice delivering the news into the phone.

She narrowed her eyes. "What do you need from the Falcons?"

Raul leaned back again. "Please. Nothing."

"Then why the hell are they calling you at ten o'clock at night?"

He sighed. "I would never work with people like that. They believe they invented real estate because they dug a bigger swimming hole. And I know Linnie's husband, used to know him, and he would have hated that whole thing. Not as much as you hate it, but a lot. He was more about working with what was there." Raul waved his hand in the direction of the island, the sea, the stars.

She scoffed. "Falcon founder, environmental hero."

Raul swept his eyes around the yacht and very slowly extended his pointer finger and arced it over toward the console in front of him, landing at the fuel gauge. "As the lizards say, Captain Denise, glass houses."

Chapter

16

The next morning, the minute Stew told her she could leave, Helen hopped the fence to Heracanes. Her headband was made out of sea-shells from a beach in Vietnam, yet not one of the grunts had asked her about it; she hoped these women were more worldly.

The sun was at full blaze without a single cloud in the sky, and the wind whipped in all directions. The palm fronds flipped and flapped as if they were giving the day a round of applause for being so beautiful.

The Heracanes pool splashed with lap swimmers, and card game players tittered on the terrace. Also underway were cornhole and bocce matches and a yoga class where half the participants were asleep. A flock of white-haired kayakers circled offshore.

None of this crop would recognize her, but as a kid, Helen had spent plenty of time here. Her mom had tossed her over the fence for babysitting weekly; she'd used the pool, let the old ladies fawn all over her, and helped herself to a dozen grandmothers. She loved it here.

Her eyes were trained on the lemonade and cookies spread on the patio when she saw someone her own age standing beside the table.

"Want some?" The young woman wore short overalls and a tank top, and her pixie cut had streaks of neon pink in it. She pointed at Helen's headband. "Olive shells."

Helen slowly reached out her hand and forced herself to blink. "I love shells, too. I'm Helen."

"Those are olive shells, right? I always wanted a belt like that. But also, it's like wearing a bunch of dead mollusks' houses, you know? Feels kind of disrespectful? I'm Jules." She took a sip from a Dixie cup and wiped a drip of lemonade from her chin.

For the millionth time in her life, Helen was in love. "Do you work here?"

"Yeah, and finishing up grad school. I've been here for five years, God. Why, you want to work here? You like paddleboarding and getting your hair French braided?"

Helen was pretty sure this woman was reading her mind. "The hair does look good," she said and took a small step closer.

Jules shook her head so her hair mussed itself up.

"I have a job," Helen said. "At Ahoy. You might've met my sister, Denise?"

Jules squinted. "I don't really think of Denise as having relatives of any kind. More like the US Navy and the ghost of Steve Irwin came up with her in a lab, minus any of Steve's personality."

Well, now Helen had to marry this woman.

"You're hoofing it. Where are you going?" Jules asked.

Helen cocked her head toward the construction site next door. For a second, she thought about telling Jules she used to live there and used to come here and everything else there was to know about herself. But she thought better of it—plenty of time for that if they were neighbors. "Just scoping things out, keeping tabs, getting the scoop. What do you think of all that?"

"Not my speed, not even a little." Jules handed her a cup of lemonade. "Roadie. After you're done over there, you might want to come back for a spiked one."

Straining every ounce of coolness she'd ever had, Helen did not turn around to look at Jules as she walked away. Damn. If someone like Jules had been working at this place when Helen was in high school, she never would've left.

Along the next fence, bordering her old place, there was a wide, meticulously kept garden bed. Helen took one giant step across it, then hoisted herself up and over toward home.

Her feet landed on sand. Sand. The peninsula, and her yard, were made of dirt and grass. Landing on this felt to her like landing on the surface of the moon. She looked up from her crouched position.

The blue shocked her. Her mouth opened as though she had something to say to someone, but no one else was there, and there was nothing to say.

Her yard was now the color of a melted popsicle, glistening slime blue. The flat surface rippled beneath the breeze, and it was hard to tell whether the water was two or twenty feet deep. Instinctively, her head turned to the left where her house had been, the yellow rancher with the sloping front porch. There instead was the metal skeleton of a small building, silver and cement, three stories high, with jutting metallic rectangles of future balconies. She swallowed hard, and the lemonade on her tongue went sour.

The lagoon was eerily mesmerizing. Her face turned back toward the water, and for a moment she almost forgot where she was entirely. It seemed that rather than a new place landing here, the piece of earth she'd once lived on had dislodged, floated upward, and transported itself onto another planet. This didn't feel like the same place at all, in any way.

She had a horrible thought, maybe the worst thought she'd ever had in her life: Denise was right.

A hollow freeze seeped into her chest. It was just gone. The house, the yard, the grass, the pebbles, the roots. All her chances. It was all supposed to stay in place, right here, for her to think about in a vague, fuzzy way, and to rest assured that someday, whenever she had the time, she could visit. One day, she was sure of it, she would be standing here and the way the light fell over the grass would finally make her remember the warmth of a big arm cradling her tiny head; the creak of the porch step would remind her of a nose touching her nose and whispering, "Hello, little one"; the bird flapping its wings in the shade of the mahoe tree would be the heartbeat inside the chest she'd fallen asleep on.

But that would never happen now. All the chances she ever had to try to stitch together a single memory, anything at all, about her dad were gone.

Only now did it sink in how much she'd taken for granted, assumed home would always be here, waiting around for her to come rake her fingers over the ground to uncover some kind of artifact. Not just that, she had rolled her eyes at how this place never changed at all, resented it even, and it made her sick with shame now.

Here she was, finally standing still here, and there wasn't even any dirt left to run her hands over. It was sand now. Someone else had done the digging, and whatever they'd found, they'd tossed and left in its place a giant hole.

A hole that was frighteningly too big and too deep. That the shoreline might crumble and cave in, that the water might claw and drag away this place completely made her legs feel weak. How could they do this?

Something moved inside the lagoon.

Helen dropped to her knees and stretched her head out over the water. Her fingers dipped in. It was so warm. A ribbon of red-and-white stripes rippled by. It looked like a swimming flower, bright scarlet with fins waving outward from all sides. There were dozens in there, and she recognized the fish immediately.

"Bonjour." She wiped her eyes.

The tour guide in her sparked to life. They were lionfish, native to French Polynesia, slow-moving, fins akimbo to tangle their prey. They preferred living in dynamic marine environments like coral reefs or shipwrecks, so they'd be disappointed here alright, plopped into a roid-raged pool. It was all wrong. Deep in her chest she felt a surge of sympathy for them that made her tear up all over again.

She stood abruptly, brushed the sand off her legs, and turned her back on the lagoon. Maybe she'd find Jules again, or maybe she'd go cannonball into the Heracanes pool for old times' sake; she just didn't want to be alone, and she wasn't ready yet to see Denise. She wasn't ready for the *I told you*. Not yet.

She hopped the fence again, careful to avoid crushing the flowers on the other side, and tried to remember any other fun facts about those pretty fish. Oh, look, the kayaks were back, maybe she'd take one out. Or snatch another lemonade. She never was very good at her job and had either never known or completely forgotten that lionfish were also extremely poisonous.

Chapter
17

"Dude, nailed it. You knocked it out of the park. I've got to know, how'd you get that swirl on the *G*?" Tim Falcon pressed his palms together and bowed to Geoff.

From behind the desk, Geoff tried to keep his eyes within their sockets. He had not, of course, painted the side of this man's boat with its new name. It was beyond disturbing that he'd been mistaken for a tradesman.

"Hey now! There she is, our new big-time, Superbowl prime-time owner." Tim drumrolled on the desk then rushed to the door with his arms wide. "You two had your little phone date already, right?"

And there, my God, framed in a white rectangular halo of winter sunshine, was the most beautiful woman Geoff had ever laid eyes on in his entire life.

"I'm here! I can't believe it's real!" Poppy beamed, bunched up her hands into fists, and did a little hop. Her reddish hair bobbed at her shoulders. "Wow. I am just dead."

Geoff thought he legitimately might be. He scrambled out to greet her.

The woman extended her perfect specimen of an arm toward him. "Poppy," she said. Their faces were just inches apart. "And I'm really not the owner. I mean, obviously. Well, I am, actually, but not, like, officially. *Pshhh!*"

"You so are, babe. Geoff Boyardee here's going to show you the ropes." Tim finger-gunned him.

Geoff took her hand in both of his and stared into her magnificent face. "Geoff," he breathed, trying to make the word last as long as possible. She didn't look away from him. An unmistakable electric current slithered up both of their arms. Geoff felt sublime gratitude that his omniscient, brilliant superiors had placed him at this desk.

She looked out the window to where a grunt carried an unmistakably nonowner laundry basket. "Do you live here?" Her profile revealed the length of her delicate, pale neck. "Jeez, that seems like so much fun. So cozy, you know? I love having a lot of people around. That's the nicest thing, to always have someone to talk to. We have people at the house all the time, but they're always working, you know?"

"Woof. Dorm life? No thanks. Back at the frat no one wanted to be my roommate, and I said, 'Bros, that's a good thing.'" Tim pecked at his phone.

"Sure is better than the view I had at my old job," she said. "Tim remembers how dark it was in those cubicles at the office."

"I don't, actually." He didn't look up from his screen.

Poppy turned back to Geoff. Her fingers rose to cover her bottom lip. "I can't believe they did this."

Neither could Geoff, actually. Apart from cases of death or forced sale, not once had an owner transferred the title of their boat to someone else—let alone someone outside the family. Something was strange, but now that he'd met this creature, it made absolute, perfect sense to him that she would be given anything she ever wanted.

"Shall we?" Geoff tore his eyes from Poppy's face and escorted them outside.

There were always extraneous crew members around at loose ends between charters, and for this occasion, Geoff had wrangled ten of them to stand in front of the renamed boat. A grunt had been given a fog machine tutorial, as was requested for the unveiling. Fog hovered around the hull now, obscuring the new name. The ten grunts looked at one another, shrugged, and started applauding as Tim and Poppy walked over.

"Nice! I told you we'd get a crowd. Party people! Everyone's here for you, babe. Pop-Tart's time to shine!" He air-guitared.

"Thank you!" Poppy waved with both hands. Her tasseled, sequined, gold-buttoned sundress lifted, fell, and swayed, hypnotizing Geoff.

A silver champagne bucket stood at attention. Tim plucked out the bottle and blasted the cork straight into the water. The fog dissipated, and the five-foot-high name *Lagoonatic*, in cursive, came into view.

Tim's phone rang, and without a word he slammed the bottle back into the ice and walked back to shore.

Geoff looked up at Poppy, winked, and poured her a glass. "Congratulations, Miss Wojcikski. Your captain is on her way. Now, just a few quick items to go over." He opened a glossy Ahoy folder.

At the sight of the documents, Poppy emitted a porcine squeal. Geoff was utterly enchanted.

He opened his lips, and for the briefest of moments he did wonder again: Why had the Falcon family skipped over their son Tim with this boat? And, more important, did that mean that someone—like Geoff perhaps—could look past him as well?

Chapter

18

On the morning they were set to meet the Falcons, Helen pulled Denise into her new cottage and closed the door, looping the dangling metal hook into the flimsy eye to lock it.

"Okay, I'm with you. I am all in," Helen said. There were four snow globes on her nightstand, each with a different, culturally inexcusable Santa inside.

Denise bent her knees to peer out the small window. "God, you can see right into Geoff's cottage. Disgusting. You're in what?"

"We need to get that lagoon fixed or taken out. Talk about disgusting. I hate it. Hate it, hate it, hate it, I've decided—so much. And I know," she said, holding up both hands, "it took me way too long to get on board. Fine. Totally on me, I had no idea. But I saw it and, whoa, yikes, nope, that thing's got to go. It's a hazard, environmentally and also emotionally. Have those people ever heard of erosion? Because it's also eroding right here." She patted her chest.

Denise stood up to her full height and squinted at Helen for a drawn-out moment before she spoke. "Alright. Yeah, no shit. Okay. Welcome, finally."

Helen relaxed her shoulders then rubbed her hands together. "Okay, so what are we doing? What's the plan? You're never not midplan, so just tell me and I'll do it."

Denise let out a long exhale, releasing about one-tenth of the frustration she felt about just how well any of her plans had worked so far. "Well, yes, I sent those petitions around. I called. I called about two hundred times. Filed formal complaints. I reached out to the county, state, everyone-who-might-fucking-care-dot-gov, all of them. Nothing! Nothing. That's the plan. Plan's over. Now the plan is to just take it and watch that building go up. The whole thing is legal."

Helen looked around as if to make sure they were alone, then pulled the gauzy curtain over the window. "Denise. Why are you messing with petitions? You have access to their boat. The mother lode. You can get on there, figure out how the hell this whole thing happened, how they got that done because, nope, I will not believe that it was legal, no way. Then you can light them up! You're always saying all they do is work on that thing—it's like a giant cubicle on there, I saw Raul's whole setup—so there's totally some smoking gun, paper trail thing on board. Right? It's at least worth looking around, bare minimum. People would kill to have boat access."

"Do you hear yourself? Slow down, Erin Brockovich."

"Um, yes. Exactly!"

Denise lowered her voice to an angry whisper. "Helen. You've hated them for five minutes, I've hated them for years now. You have a lot of feeling like shit to catch up on. I'm not jeopardizing my entire job so I can go snooping around inside some file cabinets. Looking for what exactly? And what am I supposed to say when I find something?"

"When, not if. See?"

Denise held up a hand. "'Hey, Dickhead Falcon the Third, who doesn't even remember my name, let's get into a fun chat about corrupt local zoning officials and toothless construction regulations?' What do you think they're going to say? You want them to fill in the lagoon and plant a bunch of native grasses and designate it a nature park and name it after Dad?"

Helen blinked, and her lips parted. "That would be so amazing."

The muscles in Denise's face went slack, and she shook her head. It was too much to ask that Helen would even begin to understand this set of feelings, the back-to-back waves of rage and futility that just kept coming every time Denise saw that place. Her sister had never expressed one ounce of concern for the land until she could make it all about herself like this and stir up as much drama as possible. Denise tucked in her shirt as tight as it would go. She pressed a finger into Helen's chest before stepping outside. "Be out on the dock in half an hour, invisible. Do not get us fired."

Chapter

19

Denise forced herself not to think about anything, to go blank, to shut it out, to put blinders on and focus on the job. The key was to picture it: Her ears were wide open for the wind to rush right on through—nothing in there. Clean as a whistle. *You are a professional,* she told herself. *You are a vessel. You are a captain, dammit. You face down hurricanes. You are doing your job. You are not thinking about killing anyone.*

As he usually did before delivering horrible news, Geoff stood on the pier looking giddy. "Denise, darling. There you are." His voice bounced; he had never been this friendly to her in his life. "This is Poppy Wojcikski. Now, what is Poppy short for? I have to know." He turned to face her.

The tall woman grinned from ear to ear and extended her hand to Denise. "Penelope. I'm so honored that you're a woman."

Denise shook the proffered hand, keeping her eyes on the patch of sky above this woman's head.

Poppy let go and looked up at the clouds, shielding her eyes with a purple manicure. "Is it windier during the day?"

"Quite right," Geoff said. He adjusted his lapels and shifted his weight, making his rubber shoes squeak. He looked like the Monopoly Man had been spit out on the other side of a Buffett concert. "It has everything to do with the moon. See, you're getting the hang of sea life already."

"Tim's my fiancé." Poppy shimmied her hair. "In case you're all like, *What the heck is she doing here?*"

Geoff's face fell into a grimace. "Well."

"Can I go on? I'm dying to go on. I mean, I've been on before, duh, with Tim, but not like this. Can I go up? Am I allowed?"

Denise and Geoff looked at each other. "By all means!" Geoff motioned to the silver ramp that led up from the dock. Poppy handed Geoff her half-empty glass.

"You will have to speak to her," Geoff said once she was on deck. "Technically, as you are aware, she is not a member of the Falcon family. They're barely engaged."

"Keep it in your pants."

Helen, Stew, and Kaylee walked up behind them. "Is that her?" Helen asked. She elbowed Denise, who hadn't thought it was possible to clench her jaw shut any tighter.

"Indeed it is," Geoff said, and drank the rest of Poppy's champagne.

Chapter

20

Raul walked into the waterfront dining room and immediately pointed to the bare window with the missing curtains, just as Linnie had known he would.

"What happened here?"

"Cheers," she said first, and they clinked glasses.

When she was last in Scotland, she'd seen a summer tartan that she adored; she had it ordered for curtains, but somewhere along the way, the measurements had been lost in translation. Feet to meters to one enormous empty window. She happily explained this all to Raul now. It gave the evening a charming crutch, a simple refrain they could come back to conversationally, one that made Linnie look exactly as she wanted to appear: forgetful, shallow, distracted.

They sat down to dinner just as the sun was setting, casting a golden-orange glow that bounced a thousand tiny rainbows around the room from the chandelier. When it was time to eat, her chef carried in two piled-high take-out containers from what she knew to be Raul's favorite hole-in-the-wall in Little Havana.

"You could've just sent me a card, Melinda," Raul said, wiping his mouth. "This is a little above and beyond. You know it was nothing—it was just the truth."

"Your truth," she pointed a fork at his chest, "is very valuable. I would sooner say it was a lifeline."

Raul Williams was the Falcons' partner. When building on waterfront lots, they needed a lot of groundwater work done, and Raul was the best of the best. The work had been standard on every other location, extensive soil testing to make sure the land was solid enough, but the peninsula property was a bear. Those nasally voices that always chirped at the Falcons' heels were louder than usual because of the laws that Linnie had had changed: *It's an environmental abomination. It'll cause erosion. The damage to the shoreline! Oh no, not the endangered cormorants! What happens after thirty years? Linnie Falcon, it's all your fault the planet's burning to a crisp!*

But Raul had stood by the Falcons, never wavered. His testing of the soil there was bulletproof. The land was good, so what was the worry? His reputation as someone who cared, apparently earnestly, about conservation and animals and whatnot had been the cherry on top.

The partnership had made him a great deal of money. They'd make even more together with more lagoon locations in the years to come. There was no reason whatsoever for a few green nuts to put a damper on all their good work. Raul had greased the wheels, naysayers be damned, and Linnie was grateful.

"People love those things. It's been a tremendous deal," he admitted. "I am only human."

"Superhuman," she winked. "We really can't thank you enough. Phew!" She mimed wiping her brow.

"Where are the next lots you're looking at? *We're* looking at." Now it was his turn to wink. This dinner was going beautifully.

She nodded and covered her mouth with a napkin for a moment. The plantains really were absolutely delicious. "Here and there. And I have to say, the lagoon-first idea, having it put in before the building is finished like we did on the peninsula—divine. The sales," she snapped her fingers.

He nodded. "People see the water, the sand—"

"They have to have it."

"Who could resist?" He smiled tightly.

"Well," she said. "To us." She raised a glass.

"To the bumps in the road," he said. "Behind us."

Truth be told, the bumps had spooked her more than she'd let on.

Unbelievable, the very idea that these environmental lunatics or some low-level civil servants could take away what was rightfully hers. And who knew when they might pipe up again, and how loudly? What if it was all snatched away?

Linnie had taken precautions.

As the complaints against the company mounted, it occurred to her that the wise thing to do would be to shield at least some of their family assets. Just in case. If the worst happened and any one of these minor problems escalated to the point that assets were potentially seized, they would not be able to touch the yacht.

She was a mother, after all, and needed to provide her family a safety net. That was why she'd given a boat key worth sixty million dollars to a woman named Poppy Wojcikski, who was not, critically, married into the family just yet. Give the girl the boat, keep it separate from the family for the time being, then bring it back in when the time was right, when the storms had passed. In addition to having an enviable natural hair color, Poppy was also a perfect vessel for some light asset maneuvering.

Raul took a slurp of wine. "Ahh, mmm, it doesn't get any better," he said through another mouthful. "How did you know this is the exact meal I was in need of this week?" He put his napkin to his lips for a moment, then plunged his fork into his takeout container for another bite. "You thought I looked too skinny?"

"Raul." Linnie playfully swatted at him with her napkin. "Now, didn't your mother teach you to eat quietly?" But she recognized him doing the same thing she was, presenting himself as he wanted her to think of him—sloppy, unsophisticated, cavalier.

He wiped his mouth again. "She taught me to appreciate the difference between bad *ropa vieja* and good. And when it's good, it's so good, and you'd better enjoy it like this, savor it—you never know when you'll have the good stuff again."

And wasn't that the truth. One week later, the Falcons' peninsula building collapsed.

Part Two

Chapter

21

Now you have to look at the benefits of registering your boat in the Bahamas. What's the whole point of that? All I know is two things: One, you can sail around there and nobody has to know when or where you're coming or going; and two, if something does happen, you're dealing with Bahamian cops, not US ones.

But I'm guessing there's more to it, sure. You're the paperwork people, you tell me.

Is one of you a lawyer? No? So you don't know anything. All you insurance people know is how to hang on to the money. Doing everything you can here to make sure you don't pay out on this thing—if it was an accident. You still think this whole thing was an accident?

Alright, alright. Yeah, yeah, back to me. Star of the show here. Like you didn't already know everything there is to know about me the second you picked up that phone. Ahoy told you there's exactly one person they trust to handle all the boat maintenance.

Navy, eight years, specializing in exactly what we keep talking about. I did mechanic jobs on aircraft carriers—marine engineer. Little bit larger piece of work than your average pleasure cruiser. Engine room the size of your rich buddy's suburban house, and let me tell you, that's all I saw. Travel around the world, alright, tell that to me staring at a wall of pistons every day and night, with some fun little breaks down on my stomach with a flashlight looking under the pumps. I hear I was in some very beautiful countries.

Then, you know, on one of my leaves, I was sitting solo at a picnic table in a bar in Islamorada, and next thing I know, the right guy plops down next to me at the right time and boom: I'm being offered more money than God to fix the guy up before he leaves on his fishing trip. Took me an hour, and he gave me a beer, too. Ridiculously thankful, fawning all over himself like I built the thing from scratch. He had no idea my last gig was being shot at right before going down to fix a compressor in Somalia. This was a breeze. Forget I said that.

All from this one guy, popular guy I guess, one gig like that comes after another. You never know who's on the next seat over, right? And I work my way around and up the Keys until I get a gig doing serious yacht repair and upkeep, no more fishing trips. These are the boats you're interested in.

I do bounce around a lot, that's probably what you're getting at. Wait till you hear this list: Oceans Club, Vista Voyages, Moorings, Charter Corp, Sail-ebrations, Ahoy. Sounds like a kid's birthday party on a pirate ship, but you're looking at it on that paper you've got, those are the top yacht management operations in the country. I've done work for all of them, plus the side jobs. Not every repair job's on the books—hate to tell you paper people that.

So I'm technically not an employee of Ahoy, just a freelancer. They've asked me to go steady there about a million times, but it's just not my thing. But they keep me on. They love doing their fancy voice to go out there and say, "We have a world-class Navy engineer maintaining our fleet."

I know you're recording this whole thing—you want me to start saying the name? It's not like we don't know whose boat it is.

Chapter

22

It seemed complicated at first, but by now Poppy really did understand. They'd talked it out a lot, and Linnie had been so nice to include her in the big family meeting.

They sat in the Falcons' living room, the one with the horse paintings in the heavy-looking frames, and it felt extra cozy having all the blinds down and curtains drawn. Only every now and then, when someone peeked to check, could you maybe see one of the reporters on the lawn. It was a nice orangey light inside, and they were all sitting on the big, squishy couches that faced the pool room—it had a pool table and you could walk out to the pool from there.

They all leaned closer toward the big screen and watched it together.

There was just one grainy video from a security camera. One minute it was so peaceful. The peninsula property really was nice; it had little yellow umbrellas and chairs all around it, and the water was so gentle, you never had to worry about waves. That's what was so funny about it, in the video it just looked super calm and gentle, that hammock with the little tassels swinging back and forth between the two palm trees. They planted those to stop all the erosion, and look what happened anyway.

Around one minute and thirty seconds, the whole scaffolding leaned over to the left. Then, slowly at first, the bottom just started to flake out to the right, over the lagoon, like cards flying out of a deck. And then floor by floor, boom, boom, boom, they all just pancaked one after another. The camera shook with each one. Three floors was the height limit, and they'd stuck to that. Then the whole screen just became a big, gray cloud of smoke.

It was very lucky no one was inside. No one was taking a tour or anything; it happened around ten o'clock at night. The sales lady was actually scheduled to give her first tour of the new units in the morning, so they really were fortunate. Alden already got that lady a new car even though she hadn't even been there yet and her old car didn't even get damaged or anything.

There'd been a big thunderstorm overnight. And, of course, the ground was unpredictable; that's what everyone always said. That's why they'd planted those palm trees in the sand, because they always took every precaution when it came to *land integrity*, a term Linnie and Alden used a lot. Builders had to be the ones to think about things like that. Because that lagoon was their biggest property yet, they'd been super careful. They built the building *in good faith*, another term Alden liked and Poppy loved the sound of. It reminded her of Sunday school.

Watching the video made her feel a little queasy. One time, Tim had told her those condos would be a perfect place for Poppy's mom to live—"Fauxceanfront for somebody who can't tell the difference," he'd said—and she kept thinking about that. What if her mom had finally agreed to move out and had been living in one of those units? What if she had been asleep when it happened?

But no one died. That's what Linnie kept saying over and over, and she was right. But it still made Poppy sad.

Chapter

23

It happened. It actually happened. Denise's breathing was out of control.

Gone. It was gone. It collapsed. She had said it would. She knew it. Had she made this happen? Was it her fault? Were the sirens coming for her? Did believing that this exact thing was going to happen every single day for over a year make this actually happen? When she had pictured it happening, there was fire, but there was no fire now; she couldn't smell anything, her nose was full of dust. Was she happy? Was anyone dead? She could not be happy if anyone was dead. But probably no one had died. Right? What about a security guard? Someone from Heracanes? What if someone had walked over there to look at the lagoon? Wait, Helen had just done that yesterday. God. But Helen was right there. She was fine. They were safe. *Don't smile. Don't let anyone see you smile. Breathe. Get your breathing under control. Slow down. Helen is right here.*

Her sister was pacing in figure eights at the front of the Zodiac, making it bob up and down and lurch from side to side. They were floating just outside the cloud of gray smoke that hovered in front of the Falcon shoreline.

Ten minutes ago, they'd all been sitting around the crew cottages playing cards in their pajamas, listening to Stew perform the list of his husband's ex-wives when they heard the boom of a lifetime. Denise and Helen had sprinted out to the pier and leaped onto the nearest boat.

"Hold still," Denise barked. She held up the walkie-talkie and listened to its frantic crackle about who was coming to do what, where, and why—an angry stream of men's voices shouting about ranks and departments.

The boat moved closer toward the shore. Helen came aft to stand next to Denise, their shoulders touching, and they both stared straight ahead. The smoke was barely starting to clear, tiny visible particles falling gently into the water, creating a rippling, silver film.

The entire lot was covered in towering dunes of charcoal-colored soot, and where the building once stood was a jagged mound of rubble, with scaffolding piled like a huge plate of french fries dumped into the lagoon. The water there was a slick of gray sludge. An eerie handful of bright purple hibiscus flowers glided toward the shoreline, like survivors reaching to be pulled out of the rubble.

Helen's hands disappeared into her mass of hair. She turned to face Denise and yelled in a whisper, "Did you do this? Was this you somehow?"

Denise spun on her and whisper-yelled right back. "Shut the hell up! Don't even say that out loud."

A siren whooped behind them, and they both jumped.

Denise holstered the radio she'd been gripping in her hand and throttled the boat into reverse. Emergency responders were starting to arrive in their neon-yellow boats. "Are you trying to get us arrested?"

"No! And there's no way it's 'us.' You're the one who said you'd do basically anything to get rid of that. That it 'had to go.'" Helen extended her arm and jerked it toward the shore.

"That was you! You said that! You said you were all in!"

"Shh!" They stared at each other for a long second with identical V's in their foreheads, then turned back to face the ruined heap. A small white emergency Coast Guard boat pulled up with blue lights ablaze, blasting its horn with no regard for the sleepy seniors next door. It rammed its nose onto the shore, and three men in baseball caps clambered out.

"I was just there," Helen shivered all the way down to her fingers. "What do you think even happened?"

"I don't know."

But of course Denise knew.

The ground had had it, that's what. Just as Denise had said it would, a hundred thousand times, loudly and vehemently, to anyone who would listen and to many people who would not. The peninsula could not sustain the injection of a gigantic lagoon; it was too much water—it was that simple. And so the peninsula did what it had to do. She felt a surge of perverse pride, like a mother whose child had shoved off a bully.

"It's spectacular," she muttered. She hadn't exactly meant to say that out loud, but she felt an irrepressible giddiness rising in her chest.

"What is wrong with you? Stop smiling, they're going to arrest you." Helen turned to the boat cops and gave a huge smile, waving as if they were about to raft up and share a cooler. "Look nice for once. Look sad. Don't show teeth."

A monotone voice piped in over a bullhorn. "This section of the waterway is closed to all recreational boat traffic." They looked around; Denise's boat was the only one out. She resented *recreational* but gave a tight wave back and turned the boat around. As they pulled away, she craned her neck to drink in every last glimpse.

"Pull over," Helen elbowed her. A crowd had formed at the end of the pier at Heracanes. A dozen seniors, some in appropriate nightwear, stood gaping at the smoke and rubble. Denise sidled up the boat beside them.

"What happened?" a woman wearing bird pajamas with feather-trimmed sleeves asked. She had two long white French braids, and she stepped out in front of the group, their surrogate, to address Denise and Helen.

"Oh, Donna, you can't believe it. It is completely gone. Pancaked." Helen made a slicing motion in the air. The women gasped and tightened the belts of their robes. "Is Jules here? Is she okay?"

Donna took Helen's hand. "She's fine, dear. You know I've seen her watching the boats go out every day now, maybe looking for a little someone on board." Donna patted Helen's hand and winked.

Amid everything, Denise couldn't help but clock that, in one week's time, Helen had become close confidants with whoever Donna was and had developed a crush on someone named Jules.

"Now, sweetheart, how are you holding up?" As Donna turned to her, Denise noticed that her pink lipstick matched her slippers.

"Donna's the chair of the landscaping committee," Helen explained. She lowered her voice and whispered. "But she's term-limited."

"Okay. I'm Denise, by the way. Nice to meet you." She had never, ever said that phrase before in her life. It was never that nice to meet anyone, but right now absolutely everything seemed very nice. Denise was trying to tamp down her delighted lips, which couldn't help trying to smile. She needed to be peer-pressured into the correct emotions; she looked at the lines on the foreheads and cheeks in front of her and tried to arrange the skin of her own face in a similar way.

But you know what's a lot easier than calling all the county officials to complain, creating and circulating a dozen petitions, mailing endless complaints to environmental watchdog offices, and spending hours researching how to impeach a lower-level city council member for not responding to constituents?

For the building to fall down.

"Don't be silly. We know who you are, dear," Donna answered Denise. "You've been going steady with that lovely young man, Randy. He gives us vouchers for all the taxi rides we want before

5:00 p.m. And the two of you," she pointed between the sisters, "are the spitting image. Aren't they?" The group nodded and murmured affirmatively.

"Team Randy," Helen held up a fist.

"Oh my, I hope there aren't teams. Are there teams already? The two of you are such a good fit, personality-wise. What has it been now, two years? Terrific chemistry," said Donna, a person Denise had never met.

"Disaster zone," Denise said, jutting her chin next door. "No way they'll build again. Not now."

"Oh, they probably will," Donna chuckled, giving her shoulders a little bounce. "They always do. Speak of the handsome devil—"

A water taxi emerged through the smoke in the air and sped toward Heracanes way too fast. Randy was at the helm. "Denise!" he shouted with his hands cupped around his mouth and then waved frantically with both arms as the boat veered toward the pier.

Her stomach flickered. An entire building had been swallowed by the earth mere feet from Randy's business, and it hadn't even occurred to her yet to call him. A wave of, what exactly—fear? regret? shame?—rolled across her. She cleared her throat. "Randy! Babe! Are you okay?" she shouted back through cupped hands, hoping the volume sounded like sufficient worry and counted for something.

Helen leaned over. "*Babe*."

"Shut up."

Randy threw a dock line to Helen. In a romantic V, he jumped up onto the pier then down onto Denise's boat and wrapped his arms around her. He wore red plaid pajama pants and a Doobie Brothers T-shirt with the sleeves cut off, and he smelled like the sensitive-skin shaving cream she'd put in his stocking at Christmas. Her shoulders and neck instantly relaxed; she realized she'd been clenching them this whole time.

The Heracanes women applauded.

"Hell's bells. Are you alright? Why didn't you call me? You weren't over there, were you?" He kissed her then put his palms on her cheeks. "Hold on, maybe don't tell me if you were. But I've got to know, were you there for this? You?" he whispered.

Denise tightened her jaw. She was equal parts pissed and proud at the insinuation.

"My sister, Denise, was with me all night," Helen said very loudly to the group.

"Damn right she was." Randy nodded and kept an arm around Denise's shoulder. "How are you doing, Donna? You all might not want to be out here breathing this in. Nasty stuff, I can feel it on my nose hairs."

It was a crowd that didn't need to be told twice to go back to bed. Donna winked at Randy more suggestively than Denise liked and led the group back to the building.

The three of them stood shoulder to shoulder at the end of the Heracanes pier looking into the smoke.

"I'm serious," Randy said. He took Denise by the shoulders, squatted a bit to get at eye level with her, and brushed a thumb across her cheek. "Are you alright? This is some scary stuff. A whole-ass building just up and out of here. Boom. When I heard it, I thought, I just . . . I don't even want to say what I thought." He looked at Helen. "And you were just over there, you know? Anyone know what the medical situation is? We need to find out. Man, this is getting to me." His eyes watered.

Helen and Denise stared at Randy, then looked at each other and visibly cringed before gazing away. Randy was an emoter.

With a flat palm, Helen patted him on the shoulder, as if softness might be contagious. A few years ago Denise would've probably done the same, but she'd learned. She'd evolved, and she was proud of her progress—something she and Randy had talked about a good amount. For three full seconds, she put her head on his shoulder and allowed him to kiss her hair.

The excitement in her chest was receding. She was exhausted suddenly, and the sight of red and blue lights splashing across the water as more boats pulled up to police next door was dampening her spirits.

"We're doing their charter tomorrow," Helen said. "Aren't we? How?"

No normal person on earth would hop onto their yacht the day after a disaster—so the Falcons just might. A boat is an escape valve; a boat is a getaway car; a boat is a good excuse to get the dumber end of your relatives out of here for a while. "Maybe," Denise admitted. She could still hear the boom-scream of the collapse, as if remnants of the noise were floating in the air on the dust.

Blame the rain. Blame the earth's crust. Blame the regulators and the protesters for not regulating or protesting enough, for letting the Falcons let this happen. She was too antsy to be mad, circling to find the next landing strip for her anger. Surely, they would still get away with this, even now. She wasn't able to imagine a world in which she wasn't still furious at them.

Helen put her hands on her hips. "So what now? What're we supposed to do?"

They all answered at once.

"I want to say investigate," Helen said.

"Celebrate," Denise muttered.

"Help them clean up," Randy sniffled.

Chapter

24

There were swarms of reporters in the area and Geoff was not op-posed to making a statement. Finally, a crisis befitting his talents.

Thanks to his effusive outreach and reassurances, the Falcons ended up back at the marina sooner than he would've thought pos-sible. Two days later, Tim and Poppy stepped into the Ahoy office.

Geoff stood at the door with his hands clasped at his waist. "I am so sorry," he greeted them with a pronounced frown. "On behalf of all of us at Ahoy, we offer our most sincere thoughts and prayers, if you'd like them—but if not, we understand, and ours can be re-directed."

Tim clapped a hand onto his shoulder. "Thanks, muchacho. Big week. It was a serious downer."

Geoff nodded. "Indeed."

"Technical term for when a building goes down."

"Of course." Geoff stole a glance at angelic Poppy, who was nod-ding solemnly.

Tim held up his phone. "I've got to take this. Crisis mode." He blew air out from his cheeks and stepped away, facing the wall. "I told you, bid eight hundred on the limited edition."

Geoff turned to Poppy. "And what about you? How are you hold-ing up?"

She lunged forward and hugged him. Slowly he placed his hands on her back and accepted her closeness, his body bubbling over. Over her shoulder, he watched Tim, who was pacing outside now, not paying them any attention. Geoff pulled her in closer for a moment and took an indulgent sniff of her hair (a magnificent coconut) before she pulled away.

"You're the first person who's even asked me. Can you believe that?" For a fleeting moment, her eyebrows rippled the slightest wrinkle into her flawless forehead.

"You've been through something terrible."

Her eyes widened. "There were reporters at our house. And we're not allowed to say anything to them. Tim's not even allowed to say hi and get a good word in for his new line of windsurfing shorts. And you know the scariest part about the whole thing? It could happen to anyone. I mean, there was that thunderstorm—it didn't even last that long—and *boom*. Linnie said it was all about rain, and there are only so many buildings that can handle that much rain. Any building could just . . ." She shook her head, and the genuine fear in her eyes made Geoff's heart seize.

He pressed his lips together and nodded, their eyes locked. "Land be damned," he said. "You're almost safer on a boat, out on the water."

She touched his arm. "Oh my God, I thought the exact same thing."

Her hand was still on his wrist.

Tim walked back. "Never ends. It's all about management, top to bottom. Geoff gets it. I'm trying to manage down, but the problem is I am being managed by my mom, and so I need to make sure I'm not just copying her management style, you know? Need my own spin cycle on it, the secret Timmy sauce drizzled all over. Because that's what makes my team click."

Geoff coughed. "Should we make our way to the boat?"

He wedged himself in between Tim and Poppy and escorted them down the freshly power-washed dock, gleaming white in the full sun, the polished cleats like diamonds lining the walk. It was jarring how pristine Ahoy looked considering the abject ruin just a hundred yards away, and for a moment Geoff felt a tinge of guilt before he quickly grabbed the wheel and U-turned that feeling into pride. Here, under his watch, the world was made perfect for the people who deserved it most, like the woman beside him.

The silver passerelle that led up to their boat shone like a divine stairway. Waiting there in a tight semicircle were Denise, Helen, Kaylee, and Stew, dressed in identical red polo shirts and roomy shorts, all with their hands clasped behind their backs.

"Poppy, you've met our top team here," Geoff said. Stew used this moment to extract a wedgie.

"Poppy! Hello, hello!" Helen said and waved.

Geoff and Denise stared daggers at her.

Helen stood up straighter. "I mean, ahoy, ahoy!"

"Denise, of course, is your captain." Geoff widened his eyes in her direction and modeled a smile. Her face did not budge, but she lifted her arms and pulled apart the two ends at the back of her visor. The sound of Velcro ripped through the air, and Poppy flinched. Denise strapped the visor onto her head more tightly, turned, and strode up the ramp to the boat.

"She is very good with boats, however," Geoff gestured after her with his clipboard.

"As long as one of you is very good with a little old mixology." Tim pointed to the crew one by one then skipped up the ramp himself. "It's noon somewhere."

As the crew boarded, Poppy lingered in front of Geoff. "Well," she said. "Off we go. I really hope I can sleep. You know, I keep having nightmares about the house just being sucked down into the earth's core, and Tim doesn't sleep in the same room, he says I snore, so I can never fall back asleep. I think I need to be around a lot of people, all close together, you know? And to get away from the ground for a little bit."

"And your registration, of course," he reminded her. The entire point of this charter was for Poppy to complete a round of paperwork certifying her ownership.

She palmed her forehead. "Oh jeez. See? I really do need a good night's sleep. It's the biggest day of my life, getting this boat officially, and I'm all—" She jostled her hands in the air. "Thanks for reminding me. I wish you were coming with us. I mean, you could help keep us organized and all."

Geoff swallowed audibly. "I very much wish so, too."

As Poppy reached the top of the passerelle, she turned to wave to him. He bit his lip and waved back.

Usually, it was his greatest joy to watch guests leave. But now, as he stood there under the baking sun, he felt a physical urge to hurl himself into the water headfirst and windmill his arms and kick his legs through the wake until he reached the boat, which was now pulling away. How was it possible that he wouldn't see her for several whole days? What was happening to him? And how did he know, just know, deep down in his awakened heart, that she was wondering exactly the same thing at this very minute?

He jogged back to the office.

Geoff looked down at his enemy, the phone. The blue abomination had a pink starfish affixed to its handle that made it impossible to hold comfortably.

He picked it up and dialed.

"Hello, Mr. Falcon Jr.?" Geoff coiled the phone line around his fingers and watched out the window as another crew ferried cases of champagne down the dock on their backs like French ants.

"Speaking."

"It's Geoff, sir."

"Boat Geoff?"

". . . Yes."

"Did something happen with Tim?" Alden Falcon barked. "I do not have time for Tim shit right now."

"Of course not. All is completely fine, sir, and I apologize for disturbing you. I will be in Nassau this week, and so I'd like to offer my services as a concierge, if you will. Several times now, I've assisted clients throughout the re-registration process. To make sure they're in the right places, at the right times, with all the correct documents in hand. It can be quite onerous to attempt to complete, and since this registrant, Poppy, is a new entity, I thought—"

"Stop. Got it. Yeah, alright. I can't have that getting messed up right now. Fine, sure, better off with Tim staying on the boat. Go with her and get it done."

"Excellent. Then I'll report back."

"Don't call me again."

"Right. Bye, now."

Superior service, he knew, meant addressing the desires of your clients before they were even aware of those desires themselves.

Chapter

25

Helen stood across the fence from Jules. She was wearing a different pair of overalls this time, and a black camera dangled from her neck on a thick gray strap.

"Are you hanging in there?" Helen asked. Her hands rested on the cool, curved metal top of the fence, and she tightened her fingers to keep them from reaching over and adjusting any number of Jules's straps, as she was desperate to do.

"Totally. It's the most exciting thing that's ever happened here. They love it. Look, Donna's been gardening nonstop just so she has an excuse to kneel down at the fence line and look over there all day." Jules cocked her head, and Helen looked over her shoulder.

Helen cupped her hands around her mouth. "Donna!" The woman looked behind her, waved, and blew Helen a kiss with dirt-covered hands.

"Do you ever get bored working here?" Helen asked. She reached over and touched the camera—surely that didn't count. "Trying some new hobbies?"

Jules scoffed. "No. Somebody just moved in. It's her first week, and I just saw she finally got out and started Pilates, so I had to get a picture. It's really important that they invest in permanence here— like, whatever their permanence looks like, you know? Everyone has all these framed pictures of their families, kids, dead husbands, whatever, so I try to get one of them doing their thing here, as soon as I can, and I frame it for them so they can have that up there, too. I don't know. The first week is important. I think so, anyway. And this is a freaky first week for that lady."

Helen had never liked someone more in her entire life. "You know, it's basically my first week here, too."

Jules took Helen by the shoulders, turned her around, then lifted up her camera to get a picture of both of them, side by side. Helen's chin rested against Jules's forehead; her hair smelled like lemonade and the chemical, charcoal scent that had been wafting through the air ever since the collapse. Helen placed her hand around Jules's shoulders and squeezed.

"There." Jules pulled away and placed the camera back onto her chest. "One of the gals now. Ideally, and hey, call me a perfectionist, there wouldn't be a post-environmental-disaster hellscape in the background. Or Donna. But what can you do?"

Chapter

26

No one died. No one was hurt. No one died. No one was hurt.
No one died.

Linnie repeated these words to everyone she spoke to, put one heel in front of the other, and did not stop moving for a minute to let any of this sink in one bit. You had to match people's emotions; that was what they'd done with the protesters and the regulators, and it's what they'd do now. People were upset, they were frightened, and so she would be upset, she would be frightened. She was responding appropriately.

It was on the front page of the local newspaper and led the regional TV station's news that first night. Beyond this concentrated hullabaloo, a blip of media sensationalism, the coverage hadn't gone further. Thank God. Because no one had died and no one had gotten hurt. It was a private property issue.

This was the regulators' fault. If there truly was a dire matter of safety involved, then the laws should be utterly impenetrable. It was ludicrous that these people had just rolled over and said yes to everything she wanted. The blame lay squarely at the feet of those who claimed to know better and were yet susceptible to the slightest temptations.

This was the lawyers' fault. They should've seen the entire lagoon opportunity for what it was: a fool's errand. It hadn't been a door to march through; it was just a window—an opening to peek out and say, "Now that's an idea, but there's probably a good reason why no one's done it before." But no, they were too eager to please; they'd been the ones to push this, like show dogs jumping through loopholes.

This was Alden's fault. He was the one who knew the business. He'd worked at the company since college, for Christ's sake, and never had a single other job, and he was the one who crunched the numbers for the whole project. He'd cut corners on the lagoon's lining—which was, to be fair, an outrageous expense, but something they clearly should've sprung for. Not to mention a million other little cuts he said would be fine. *Fine, fine, fine.* He was also the one who said not to spring for the extra trees. Thanks to her brilliant son, a storm rolled through, and it was like filling up a water balloon with a fire hose.

This was the weather's fault.

This was Raul's fault. Soil science snake oil. He told them the ground would hold, and now she was going to bury him in it.

Chapter

27

If the Falcons had allowed a forensic investigation into the collapse, which they never would, this is what they would have learned.

It was the sand's fault, in many ways. Despite the idea that a lagoon was better than a pool, a reasonably sized pool would've been fine here surrounded by concrete, not sand.

The lagoon's excessive size brought it too close to the building itself, leaving only about ten feet between the water's edge and the load-bearing beams of the lower balconies. Ten feet of concrete is very different from ten feet of sand and dirt.

The building materials were middling quality, nothing to write home about, and that certainly didn't help. Corners had been cut, but corners were cut every day in every way all over the world, and the earth didn't swallow up a chunk of a peninsula as a result.

The rain filled the lagoon to the brim, and when it overflowed, it pushed the sand perimeter outward. A wet, muddy, sandy outskirt oozed up to the edge of the building. Mud worked its wonders, and the ground beneath the outermost scaffolding began to slide.

Under the ground, there just wasn't enough room. It was a narrow wedge of solid, dry earth, not nearly enough to support a large structure. You could've had a lovely building or a lovely lagoon there, but not both. The wedge wobbled, pressed in, and cratered, and the building collapsed.

And that is what happened to the part you could see: the frame of a three-story condo building cascading, piling onto the ground.

As for what happened below the surface, the plastic lining of the lagoon itself held up surprisingly well. It was cheap, there was no doubt about that, but of course many pool linings are. Even a thicker, stronger, more expensive lining was no match for a steel beam that javelined into it from twenty feet in the air. It skewered the lining like a toothpick through a slice of ham.

And that created a hole. Not an enormous one but an eight-inch-wide crack that allowed the water in the lagoon to drain into the ground below. The crack was on the far side, where the lagoon abutted the Heracanes property; that was the beam's fault for aiming in that direction.

It wasn't a gaping black hole below there or a sinkhole sucking the whole building down into the ground—nothing nearly so dramatic. The debris that fell—slabs of concrete, drywall, planks and rods, construction crew lunch pails—remained in a huge pile at ground level. The crack at the bottom of the lagoon that led into the dark unknowable earth below was only eight inches wide. The only things that fit through there were water and fish.

Chapter

28

The fact that Tim and Poppy were enjoying a delightful yacht vacation days after their lagoon wolfed down an acre of Denise's peninsula spoke volumes. Why not enjoy themselves? Why not take their mind off things? Why not take a deep breath?

"You can't Jet Ski across the ocean, sir," Stew tried again.

Tim cupped his hands and yelled back. "Tell that to Magellan! He was sailing around the world in a log cabin compared to this thing. It's got ten times the horsepower." He straddled the machine in a matching monogrammed orange bathing suit and life jacket.

The whole point of this cruise was to formally register the boat in Poppy's name in the Bahamas, and they'd been out for an entire day without a single signed document to show for it. God forbid they rush to accomplish something.

The boat bobbed offshore from Pearl Cay, a cupped hand of sand holding turquoise water where stingrays waved their fins into the air. The weather was typically spectacular, with an easy breeze pushing the right number of clouds across the sky so that the moment anyone got too hot, a patch of shade was on its way.

Denise felt as though she'd been running a marathon, and then at the final mile, someone had laid her down in a wheelbarrow and rolled her across the finish line. She'd been prepared to keep running, keep feeling exhausted and terrible, and now it was all just over in a flash, without any of the satisfaction of having spent herself completely. It was the outcome she had wanted, sure, but it was also a disorienting and unearned way to get there. She was left feeling dazed and disappointed, with a creeping loneliness of missing the effort. What to do now? What to do with all the energy her muscles had left to expend?

Even if she hadn't earned it, she needed this victory to mean something. The sick feeling that she didn't want to acknowledge was that it might not. The Falcons could easily climb out from under that rubble and live to lagoon another day. They weren't going to jail; they weren't paying any fines. They'd keep digging, filling, and building places like that—on other people's land. She wanted a lesson to be learned, any lesson, by any one of them.

"Hey!"

Denise flinched. Helen climbed up to the third deck and squeezed her sister's shoulders. She was supposed to be doing laundry.

"Announce yourself," Denise said.

"Every time? Fine—ahoy!"

"No, God. I mean, don't sneak around like that, make some foot noise or something. Are you barefoot?"

Helen tapped her toe ring onto the floor. "Tide times looking good." She fingered the map on the console. "Mom was always obsessed with checking the tide, remember? Like you couldn't just smell it. She'd make me go run over and check the shoreline and count how far I could walk out before I hit the water."

"Dad was obsessed with that, too," Denise said. "They were too cheap to get a pier put in. If the tide was up, we could get the boat out."

"High time for tide time," they both sang, then smiled.

"Did Dad make that up or Mom?" Helen asked.

"Dad. Of course."

Helen nodded slowly and looked down at her knees. "Right. Of course."

Denise scooted closer to her, and their shoulders touched, the sides of their sweaty thighs sticking and unsticking like double-sided tape as they adjusted themselves.

When Helen looked up, her lips were doing their best to lift at the edges. "Freaky week. I really am trying to be present, you know. I learned so much about meditation in Bali from this book of quotes a guest left in their room, but this is just . . . I'm out here actually trying to learn the job, which you won't believe, but it's true. I am. Chef taught me how to use the blender today—that thing is Jetsons. But I can't stop thinking about the building now, obviously. I am so completely freaked. Aren't you?"

Denise let out a long stream of air.

"You know what's really scary? All the other lagoons that are just sitting there, at the other condos. Lurking. They're like these big open mouths waiting to swallow up the buildings. It could happen, they could all go down, seriously, just like that one. People could die."

Denise's stomach turned. "Yeah, I know. There are four other lagoon properties," she confirmed. "All waterfront, all pulled off with some kind of bullshit legal weaseling. And they have plans for more. The permit applications are public."

Helen sat up straight in the chair, turned her body to face Denise, and curled her legs beneath her. She brought both hands out in front to prepare to emphasize what she was about to say. Denise felt a sudden urge to dive into the water.

"Listen," Helen started. "Don't say anything until I finish talking. I have an idea." She glanced around the deck to make sure they were alone. "Don't you feel like you want to prove that? That you knew people could've died? And you did something about it, your petitions and your calls and whatever, and this still happened? Just because the Falcons, like, donated a scholarship to a bird or something? They totally knew something like this could happen, obviously, and they just kept going, kept digging lagoons, putting even more in. When all along you knew that it was a super bad, super dangerous idea, and you were trying to stop them. Negligence!"

Denise crossed her arms. "You have no idea what that word means."

"Well, they do—and they're the ones being negligent about it. And listen, you're not hearing me right. You can prove it, *here*." She drew out the word and cocked her head toward the bow of the boat. "There is definitely, absolutely, probably some kind of unique, VIP business information on board here. Right? That is what the world needs to see, and that is something that literally only we could get our paws on—to blow this whole thing wide open."

Denise stood up and crossed her arms. "Helen, you're not going to understand this, but I have a job that I actually care about. I have spent the last twenty years working my ass off, getting every certification and license there is, putting up with torrential amounts of crap and abuse—stories I have spared you so you'd even be willing to get on a boat—plus getting told by basically every single owner they don't trust a woman to drive them. I'm finally, finally, the head captain here after two decades—when that asshole Captain Scott was given head captain after only six years, by the way—and I'm not going to chuck all that overboard because I'm pissed off one day."

Helen held up her hands in front of her, palms out. "I hear you."

"You don't."

Helen took a deep breath before continuing. "We—"

"No. Stop. There's no *we*."

"Yes. We are *we* now." Helen stood up and took a step closer to her sister. "And we, together, will make sure that no one is any the wiser, and you will not get fired. I'm going to cover for you. We can move fast, we can be cool, and we can do a lot more than you could do just by yourself, obviously. And we will be doing the right thing. We have to at least look. Trust me, it is not that hard to look around in guests' stuff; they don't pay any attention. And what if it's all right there under our feet, some kind of piece of proof that they knew the danger or cut corners or whatever. It could just be sitting there in one of those paper piles or whatever, and we're the only people who could ever help prove that they were doing negligence?"

Denise's fingers pulled so hard at her belt loops she could feel the fabric tearing. "You don't know what that word—"

Helen held up four fingers, and Denise closed her lips. "Four other properties. If we don't do everything we can, or at least, I don't know, if we don't just look around when it's this easy, when it's right there because why not, and that happens again? To one of the condos people actually live in? A bunch of people are all asleep and that happens? Come on, come on, come on. We have to. You know we do."

Denise hung her head. "Helen," she grumbled.

They did have to.

Chapter

29

Operational costs of running a yacht are around 20 percent of the purchase price. Easy math. Boat like that, I'd say fifty mil, so you're spending five, ten a year to keep it running. Funny thing is, the word running doesn't really matter. You're paying whether you set foot on the boat or not. Some of those boats sit in their slips year-round—honest to God, they don't go out once—and it costs the same.

That number includes everything, though. Not that I'm saying hey-what-a-deal, but you're getting a full crew, soup to nuts, whenever you want them, all that Ahoy concierge bullshit above and beyond. Plus full maintenance workups and safety checks, which is me.

But no, those boats don't require a whole lot of tune-ups. I'm down there four times a year, maybe, and one of those is just the annual required check-in. When I get a call, that means something is up or somebody wants to make a change. A lot of that stuff is preference, to put it mildly. We're not talking mechanical essentials here, more like how big are the bubbles coming out of the Jacuzzi, which is actually something that can be adjusted for, and I'm getting paid to adjust it.

Of course I remember getting that call. And the call I had to make right after.

Chapter

30

A lot of spas made the room completely dark inside with only something like a little yellow night light on and gentle music that always made her wonder what instrument was being played. Was that a harp? Piano? Maybe the whole point was to wonder, to get your mind off your troubles and think about flutes instead.

Poppy had been to so many spas since she met Tim, and this was one of the topics she most liked to talk about when she met new people now. *Do you know what those spa instruments are? I can never figure them out.* But it turned out other people didn't know, either. They never had an answer for her.

In this spa, the windows were open, and the breeze came in and fanned across the whole place. It smelled like a wet tree, but in a nice way. There was no music, just the rustling plants outside, those big palm leaves brushing up against the side of the building and the waves coming in from the beach, the nicest sound of all. It was pleasant knowing what all the sounds were, being able to pinpoint each one, more calming than the mystery music. She stored this thought away to bring up later.

She lay flat with her arms spread to the side, and her entire body was covered in a mint-scented seaweed wrap. The tall spa woman was using a soft brush to slowly layer fancy, cold slime over Poppy's cheeks, chin, and forehead.

She closed her eyes. "It's just funny, you know? Because I do meet a lot of people. Every week we go to a lot of parties, and I try to join all the clubs Linnie tells me to, but sometimes I stop and I think, 'Jeez, when was the last time I just hung out with someone one on one?' There's really no one-on-one time."

"One-on-one time," the facialist said.

"Exactly, like right now." Poppy smiled, then relaxed her cheeks as she'd been told to do. This was the absolute best part of spa time, the female friendship. It used to make her so sad when she went back to the same spa again hoping to chat with the same person, but a different one was there to do the treatment. But then she realized that every single facialist was so friendly. It was just their way.

"And so it felt really nice," Poppy said. "He asked me, just me, how I was doing. And I don't want to be mean, but Tim actually never even asked me, so it just felt extra sweet. I think he's only about five years older than me, but he seems really wise. I think it's his accent—it's like he really knows a lot. He's an Englishperson. And the whole thing must have scared him, too, which I understand—he works right at the marina."

"The marina."

"Totally, and that's the good thing because now I have this boat, or I'm about to have it, and I think I'll be spending a lot of time with it. So I think I'll see him a lot. And it's a little intimidating having this boat all by myself. It could be a lot of work. I don't even know about the whole boat world yet, so I'm just glad he'll be there, like a guide."

"He'll be there."

"He really will. I think if I needed something, he'd be there in a minute—he's very helpful. We talked on the phone once, did I tell you that? But in person he's got this light-brown, gray, dark, sandy kind of hair, it's a really interesting color. Kind of like yours. And he's pretty tall because I could see him still waving at us at the end of the pier even when the boat pulled all the way down the waterway. Like he was still looking for us."

"He was looking for you."

Poppy sighed. "I really think he was."

Chapter

31

"Here he comes! Gird your groins." Tim stood up from the table.

The spectacular sunset made it seem as though the boat was surrounded by fire. Orange-flamed waves licked the sides and spun in yellow and pink whorls every time the wind blew through. Helen was supposed to be watching Poppy and Tim eat and replenishing the scallop medley, but instead she was staring at the outrageous blaze.

A tiny yellow boat sped toward the yacht. It took Helen a moment to figure out where it came from; it seemed to whiz forth from the sun itself. She'd been staring into the light for way too long and had to blink a few times to see him.

At the helm was an enormous human being, whose giant hands on the little wheel made the boat look like a toy. The man wore black, tight-fitting shorts and a button-down shirt with a faint tropical pattern, like a Day of the Dead tiki drink. Behind a generous forehead, his remaining bleached blond hair was pulled back into a ponytail that reached his cantaloupe-sized shoulders. His lined, overly tanned face advertised that life had lived him.

The boat slowed and approached the stern, where Stew stood waiting to assist. Denise sped down the stairs to join him while trying to read the dossiers at the same time. Helen flashed on the memory of a pirate encounter she had had in Samoa once: It had turned into a nonevent when the pirates realized her group really was only carrying binoculars. They'd handed those over anyway, just to be safe. Helen also gave one of the pirates her number, but he never called.

Stew took the lines and tied the boat up. In one hand, the huge man carried a single, small duffel bag in a horrible shade of maroon; in the other was one of those tan folders with the little red string to tie it closed. A gust blew across the water, and his shirt flipped open to reveal a holstered gun on his belt loop.

Helen gasped.

"Tim? Honey? Who's that?" Poppy curled her fingers around the edge of the tablecloth.

"I'm on the list, cupcake," the man said to Denise. "I wrote the list."

"He sure is! You know it! Rocco taco, how's it hanging?" Tim hugged him with a loud back slap. "Best security team on the planet. One man, one plan. He got me airlifted from surf camp—I owe this man my life. You all just got a lot safer." He extended his arm and pointed up at everyone on the boat.

"Right on." Rocco fist-bumped Tim. "Got to hit the john."

Tim slapped his back again, releasing a plume of cologne.

Rocco elbowed past Stew and Kay. "Scram." He angled himself sideways in order to fit through the doorway, then disappeared down to the suites below.

Denise marched back up to the captain's deck without looking at anyone.

Helen lingered next to Poppy and whispered, "We're gonna need a bigger boat."

Poppy whispered back, "You mean like eighty feet?"

Tim put his back to Helen and placed both hands on Poppy's shoulders.

"We're made in the shade now, Popcorn."

"Oh. Great! But, I guess, how? Is he helping us with the paperwork?"

"In a sense, bingo. Bringing us some extra little papers for you to get your signage on, no biggie. And also, like, a little muscle around the paperwork we already have. Since we're going to be on the boat a lot more these days, working our butts off like this, it's just right as rain to get an extra set of eyeballs around to keep tabs on the old locks and keys, if you know what I mean."

Poppy nodded and then shook her head, making a circle.

"Think of him as a bouncer, babe. There's a lot of stuff on this water-puppy, you and me included. I mean, we are assets, technically, if you think about it. My mom's big on, you know, if people are hating on you, keep some bonus biceps around, get a little peace of mind, all that jazz. It's like how we have the team staked out at the house sometimes, checking on us, checking the home office for bugs, whatever and ever, forever, all gravy. Anywhere we go our information goes, and in this economy, you'd be crazy not to have a guy like Rocco around twenty-four seven."

"They're at our house?"

Tim kissed her on the cheek. "You want a marg? Let me make you a marg." He spun around to Helen. "Hey, ice up a few extra-spicy, extra-salty, extra-nonvirgin margaritas over here. Por favor. ASAP."

Helen's eyes were wide. She nodded once. "Of course."

She turned and stepped down into the living room suite below. The galley was to her right. "Pitcher of margaritas. Thanks," she said to the chef, who didn't even turn to face her before she reached into a woven bag of limes that hung at eye level and got to work.

Normally Helen would've gone over and explained how, in Tasmania, they have something called a limequat, which is exactly what it sounds like, only delicious. But instead she turned around and headed directly over to the office.

So there was information on board. She was so right.

The glossy wood office door had a half window that she peered through. Behind a giant desk and lumpy-looking chair were floor-to-ceiling bookshelves with row after row of binders and decorative mallards. The bottom shelves were lined with bankers boxes. She reached out to turn the knob.

"When I said 'scram,' I didn't mean scrambled eggs."

Helen froze.

Rocco hooked his wrinkled bratwurst fingers through his belt loops. "You like me? You want to go for it? Well, I don't have time for it, and you're not my type, not by a mile. If you ever come near this room again, you won't be hearing 'scram'—you'll be hearing water while it's filling your ears. I'm telling you this exactly one time, ditz."

The chef poked her head out from the galley holding the glass pitcher. "Salted rims?"

Chapter

32

What Denise needed was the geotechnical study. She had no idea that was what it was called, or how to read that kind of study, but something like that was what she was hoping existed, somewhere. She needed hard proof of what she already knew: that this construction was doomed from the start.

The technical terms were *compression test*, *density assessment*, *expansion capability*, and *bearing limit*. But she didn't know that. She didn't know that at every single waterfront site, a topographical survey was done, then subsurface testing, a water table appraisal, and laboratory testing of soil samples.

What she did know was that hot tubs too close to the shoreline slid into the water. And she knew her peninsula—how narrow it was and how the roots of all the old trees the Falcons had yanked out had been the fingers clutching the earth, keeping it safe from the relentless tide.

This gap between what she knew and what she could prove was making her feel insane. How, with all the lanes and lines, rules and roles that she'd scaffolded the world around her with, was there nothing tangible to cling to right now?

Ten years old. That's how old she was when she was on her own, when her dad was gone and her sister arrived and her mom became consumed with Helen. That was when Denise was out roaming this little patch of land alone, day and night. She was a child of that peninsula, in every sense, and she might not have been able to state, in so many words, that the soil had a granular organic structure or high particulate movement capabilities, but she knew it, alright. That ground was squishy as hell. She just had to prove it.

Chapter

33

Tim toweled off his shaggy hair and pulled a T-shirt over his torso, which was flecked with little red dots from acupuncture. He tossed the wet towel over a large metal bird statue, one of many around the boat, the largest flock being here inside the office. It was a humongous rhombus of a room that was half wood-paneled, half-sloped windows with a 270-degree view of the ocean. The shelves between the wood panels contained thick files, books, and Tim's late father's mini-globe collection.

Before he died, Mr. Falcon had loved working from the boat, and he'd made this space an exact replica of his land office. Assuming correctly that technology could not be relied on mid-ocean, he kept copies here of every single file he'd ever need, in row upon row of thick binders with tiny labels decipherable only to him. It was a floating Falcon archive.

The upper half of Rocco's body covered the window through the door.

"Tim? Do you think maybe Rocco needs to stand exactly right there?" Poppy squirmed on the sage-striped banquette. "What if someone needs to get in? I just don't want Helen to think she's not allowed. She's super nice—have you talked to her yet? Remember I was saying she's been to Australia, too. I thought you guys could talk about that. Maybe she knows how to do that big-wave paddleboard thing you did there."

Tim shook the remaining water from his hair like a golden retriever. "You need to stop worrying about them. They all get it. This is a primo example of what we've been talking about: This is it now, cake pop, you're staffed up. You're going to need to get comfortable managing all the people who work for you. That's what life is about."

They did talk about this a lot, and she knew she needed to improve. Tim said it was a habit she needed to shed from the many years she and her mother had spent taking care of each other, trading off after long days at work or school. It was always just the two of them, and they made each other feel special and supported no matter what. But now it was her turn to be taken care of, he kept telling her, and that meant she didn't have to think very hard about anyone else.

Still, she didn't like having Rocco around.

Tim sat down in the bendy leather chair behind the giant desk and put his bare feet up. He clapped his hands and rubbed them together. "So, here we go: What is the problem?"

Poppy sat up straight; she was prepared. This was their first brainstorming session together for the new brand expansion, and she was determined to bring some of her marketing department second assistant experience to the table. That was how they'd met in the first place, when she was asked to run and get the cream cheese for a morning meeting at Falcon headquarters.

"The building fell down," she said. She held a pen, and a notebook lay open in her lap.

"No, no, no." Tim held up a finger. "What is the need? What do people really need?"

She nodded again. This was brainstorming, ideas on the fly, the creative flow. "For the building to stay up."

"Okay!" Tim stood up. "Yes! Now we're talking. Strength. Confidence. Stability." He clapped after each word.

"Height."

He pointed at her and grinned. "God, I knew you'd be good at this."

She smiled. Tim strode toward her on the couch.

There was a knock at the door. Rocco stuck his head in, looked around the room to make sure it was safe, then opened the door just enough so Helen could slide in.

"Helen!" Poppy wiggled her fingers. She was relieved to be interrupted; she hadn't exactly wanted Tim to touch her just then.

"Thought you might want one of these." Helen held out a small tray with two cloudy white drinks and a bowl of fresh raspberries. "They're called sak-tails. It's sake, from Japan. Arigato." She bowed.

Poppy took a sip. "Oh my God, you are so multi-culti."

Helen grinned and clasped the tray at her hip with a shrug of her shoulders.

Tim plucked out the little tiki umbrella and nestled it in the breast pocket of his shirt. "Sayonara, señorita, s'il vous plaît. Hey, what's your name again?"

"That's Helen!" Poppy said.

Helen extended her hand, but Tim ignored it and took another sip. "Obviously, I'm not a native by any means," she said. "But I did get airlifted to Yakushima once when I got hypothermia on a cruise. One of the nurses there was gluten-free and told me about these."

"Time to go. These two are cooking." Rocco grabbed Helen's arm and pulled her, hard, back toward the entryway. "This room is authorized for family only." He turned to Tim. "Sir, you need to watch this one."

Helen stumbled against the door and rubbed her arm.

Poppy stood. "Rocco . . ." she said and scrunched her eyebrows together, but she didn't know what else to say. He looked straight ahead out the window. Tim fiddled with his notebook.

Helen held up her hands. "Totally get it—you guys enjoy. Ciao!" She scanned the room, then slipped back out onto the deck. Rocco hulked behind her, closed the door, and resumed blocking the window.

With the crisp click of the door, the room immediately went silent and stuffy. There was a thin layer of dust on the large safe in the corner behind Tim's chair, and all the binders looked so dated, their labels sun-faded to grayish-yellow and peeling at the edges. Were the Falcons against using computers? And did they really need so many bird statues?

"Tim," Poppy said, putting a hand on her hip. "What if he gave Helen a bruise?"

Tim sighed and sat back down behind his father's desk. He turned his palms up and shimmied his hands sideways. "Well, yeah, I think that's the problemo. There's just a lot of sore-subject stuff in here, babe, so Roc's just doing what we pay him to do. We've got to keep it senior level—just in this room, though. Okay? You get it." He reached out his hand, and Poppy slowly placed hers on top.

"I get it," she said, but she did not, and she did not return his squeeze.

"Alright," Tim pulled his hand away and clapped. "Now where were we?"

They brainstormed for a full half hour, then Tim went to the gym and took a plunge in the ice bath, followed by some sauna time and a long shower. Different temperatures helped unlock his ideas. Poppy had tried the routine before herself, but it just made her sleepy. He said they should keep the flow going after his workout, during dinner.

Poppy went up to the bow to sit by herself. After a while, Kaylee came and began cleaning the area around the hot tub, and they talked for a bit about astrology. She let Kaylee read her palm. It felt nice.

Poppy loved a lot of things about Tim. He had so much energy and so many ways to make the most out of every day, and she felt so much excitement and anticipation just being around him. His world was huge, and he was so generous with it. He wanted her to have what he had, and no one had wanted that for her before. He hadn't cared that she'd never even been to Canada or California. He was so entertaining, and it was so easy to be entertained by him. It was magically easy to be with someone like him.

And he pushed her out of her comfort zone—that was so important. She'd learned so much about little customs and rituals and the ways manners worked all around the world, like how not to bring up her family so much, or how foods and drinks could be different ages and you wanted baby meats but old alcohol. His family was so smart; they'd all been to college, but they were so nice about helping her learn the same things they knew. They wanted the best for Poppy, for her to be the best version of herself that they believed she could be someday, and that was very flattering to her.

Sometimes it felt like she and Tim were buddies. He was always saying "Come on!" and "Look at that!" and "I've been noodling on this idea," and waving her over, the way her friends had done in high school, when she'd been happy to run behind them. He was a non-stop show-and-tell, and Poppy had always liked the experience of sitting in an audience, the anticipation, the display. She wasn't shy at all, but she loved to absorb, liked to clap and tell people they were doing such a great job and see them happy and satisfied because of her reaction. It was one of the things she liked most about herself, her supportiveness of others, and Tim said he loved that about her most of all. Linnie had once called her "a terrific companion," with a soft hand squeezing her bare shoulder, and Poppy had never forgotten that.

Once, when they were in New York City and Tim took her to this beautiful restaurant with green velvet couches and they were the only two people there and it was raining outside and he ordered for both of them one of the most delicious potatoes Poppy had ever tasted in her life, she felt what she thought were butterflies. She thought, *This is romance—this is how it's supposed to be. This is how my whole life is going to be now, the best potatoes in the world.* And she hung on to that feeling; it really was there inside her, she knew. She really had felt it and knew that probably, someday, she would feel it toward him again. She just hadn't yet.

She had felt it with Geoff. It was less butterflies and more a feeling she could only describe as a warm spill. He placed a warmth inside her, there was no other word for it—an undeniable heat that had startled her, actually. That kind of feeling had never really been there with Tim, though she tried her best to feel it. The moment she'd taken Geoff's hand, though—a moment she thought about more than she was comfortable with—it felt as though her blood began to simmer, bubbling and steaming, like the two of them might disappear in a cloud of smoke that rose from the ground beneath their feet, and no one would ever see them again.

Between them there was a palpable sense that something was lost and that only together could they find it. *When will I see you again? When will I see you again? When will I see you again?* It was the chorus of a song that looped in her mind no matter how many other, different notes floated past her ears. There was no space for another tune except in the smoke-clouded corners where she wondered whether the same song was playing for him.

If only there was someone she could talk to about this—someone other than a spa person with whom she always had to start over from scratch. Someone she liked and trusted, someone who was knowledgeable and who would be around more these days.

"Shaloha!"

Poppy turned. Helen stood with one arm behind her back, one

holding up a pitcher of mojitos. "I officiated an Israeli Hawaiian wedding once." She whipped her other hand out in front of her. "Listen, I have two glasses here, and Stew said Tim's asleep."

Poppy perked up. "Come sit next to me."

She told Helen everything.

Chapter

34

Now, it could be said that Linnie was a genius. It might not be the first thing that came to mind at a time like this, but one layer down, it was the truth. Maybe two layers down.

Linnie had laid excellent groundwork. The boat was in Poppy's name or would be any minute, and that was quite a brilliant safety net, if Linnie did say so herself.

On top of that, despite what it looked like over there, iguana Chernobyl, the fallout wasn't nearly as horrific as she'd thought it might be during those early days. Had the whole thing happened a few hours later with one of those Realtors walking around giving a potential buyer a hard hat tour, then Linnie would've had her hands full. But right now it was all about saying the right things with the right level of emotion, matching people tear for tear. Facially, muscularly speaking, it was difficult for her to cry, but damn if she didn't pull it off.

She'd just returned from a few hours emoting on site and had immediately taken a scorching shower, as she did every time she was forced to hug her employees. Whatever happened to just waving hello? Shaking hands? Society egregiously over-hugged, and no correction was in sight.

Now she was stepping out into her yard, across the patio, past the pool, and onto the stone path that wound through the grass down to the water. She forced herself to take a deep breath. The warm wind climbed from the water and raked its hands through the gardenia and jasmine woven along the trellis by the pool house. Any minute now, her next meeting would begin.

It was essential for the collapse to be deemed an act of God—which it was. Their construction choices bore no blame for what had happened. God had acted, and down went the building; case closed, insurance reimbursement, a tale as old as time. This designation would allow for compensation for the cleanup and rebuilding, for the other lagoons to stay as they were, and—most critically—for more of them to be built. It had to be found an act of God. Which it was.

Raul, the expert, the gold standard in this kind of thing, had given the building his blessing, and now it was vital that he reiterate and stand by this blessing. He wanted them to keep building these things as much as she did.

But he'd been so difficult to get on the phone and impossible to schedule a team-wide meeting with. He'd responded with anything close to specificity only when she sent him a message from her personal number asking him to drinks after hours.

In the rare moments when she felt the tide rising inside her chest, the thing that gave her a sense of calm was watching the throbbing blue dots corresponding to her sons' whereabouts. Alden at the office with very brief trips back to his nearby home. Tim out in the middle of the Caribbean Sea. Just where they should be, where she'd planted them.

Her own throbbing blue dot was now waiting for Raul at the end of her pier in a custom Adirondack chair. Those chairs had the right look, but they leaned too far back, and she didn't like how that made her feel. She had several built with straighter backs, and she always sat in those, while making sure that her guests sat in the typical ones, which were absolutely impossible to get out of. In almost every circumstance, she liked to be the one to stand up first and not look hassled doing so.

The skirt of her crisp, white-collared dress draped over the sides of the seat, and it was warm enough that she thought about pouring herself a glass from the pitcher of Tom Collinses on the side table but decided to wait. He would pour one for her.

There he was. He was sailing over here, if you could believe it, on one of those small wooden boats that she had to admit did look beautiful, all alone and delicate against a wall of golden white clouds at this hour. It was never straightforward with him. On top of taking nearly a week to even respond to her or her team, he was now taking the world's slowest form of transportation to get to her. He couldn't just drive over. He'd sooner ride a tandem bicycle or have them shout at each other in the cockpit of a plane—anything that would render their meeting unserious. This juvenile predilection for accumulating hobbies with playthings that ensured you never held still was something Raul had in common with her youngest son. Something she'd tried to shake Tim out of a hundred times to no avail. Not that his poor taste had been completely pointless—at least his fiancée was useful now.

Waving was as far as she'd go, and as he approached, she didn't move a muscle to help as the boat pulled up gently alongside the pier. By the time he sat down beside her with a satisfying slide back into an inflexible position, he was sweating, and she knew he'd call a car later to get home.

"How are you holding up?" He wiped his forehead on his sleeve, then poured them both drinks. As long as she'd known him, he'd worn a uniform of matching linen shorts and shirt sets, beige or navy blue, and he kept tortoiseshell sunglasses at the ready in his breast pocket. He slid those on now even though the sun was low in the sky behind the homes on the other side of the water. "You're sitting on the end of a pier drinking by yourself—so maybe very good or very bad."

"Cheers," she said. "To being up the creek together."

He took a long sip, draining half his glass and then pouring himself a refill. "Oh, I wouldn't say that."

She scoffed. So he was off to the races. She turned in her chair and suddenly lost all interest in keeping up the pantomime of a social call. Her husband would've dragged Raul into the company conference room by what was left of his hair.

"Alright," she began. "I'm up the creek, and you're holding a gun that could shoot a hole in the bottom of my boat and sink it. Is that better?"

He smiled. "Melinda. *Dios mío.* Look around. Taste this. I did not come here to fight. I came here to have a cold drink with my friend."

Linnie wondered how much he weighed. A hundred and sixty pounds? One seventy? How hard would it be to shove the old man off the dock? Would he clamber up with those sunspotted hands and try to grab her by the dress and pull her into the water with him, or would he just drop from the shock of the fall and she could stand there with her hands on her hips and watch him sink?

"It was an act of God." She locked her eyes on his.

"Oh, I know it was." He crossed himself. "There is no doubt in my mind. Well, I shouldn't say that. I am devout, as you know, but to be honest there is always some doubt. Sometimes more, sometimes less, and never a lot. Right now I'm feeling about 12 percent doubt."

Twelve percent was his contractual share of the profits for all the lagoon properties.

She placed her palms on the flat armrests and stood up, quickly, nimbly, and now she towered over him. "You will personally speak to the investigators, show them the full viability documents, and confirm it was an act of God."

He took a sip and gave a small nod.

She removed her sunglasses. "And we'll do 20 percent."

He made a loud slurping sound while finishing the dregs in his glass. "Inflation. The truth is so expensive these days." With both hands on his own armrests, he tried to push himself up and out of the chair and couldn't. With a grunt, he gave up and slid back down in his seat. "It's a shame."

Without another word, Linnie turned and marched back down the pier toward her home. Her hands were shaking, but she was smiling. She'd been prepared to offer 30 percent. That stupid old man.

Chapter

35

Ahoy would tell you they had the best of the best doing maintenance on all the boats, but I'll tell you what—I was told never to set foot in the main building under any circumstances. God forbid one of them had to actually lay eyes on me. Like if they get a whiff, they're going to pass out from the smell of store-brand soap.

And get this, they made me do my rounds at night. For the quarterly engine checks, I worked nine to five—p.m. to a.m. Things break, salt water is corrosive, engines get old, some rookie crew goes down there and thinks she's turning on the music and flips the pumps off. Ninety percent of that stuff is harmless, standard, no biggie. Routine tune-ups and scheduled part replacements. But some of it is so dangerous it'd make your blood run cold. Gas leak in the galley seeping into the guest suite down the hall through a busted vent. A piece of the propeller breaking off and slicing through the water when somebody's swimming.

It's like they want the boats to be super safe—sure they do—but they don't really want to think about what that means. They don't want to see with their own eyes that I—one single guy in torn shorts and with a headlamp—am the difference between heaven and hell.

Everything working the way it's supposed to means you don't even think about the fact that you're on a boat. You're just enjoying yourself to the max out there, and the water's nice but in a nice-to-look-at kind of way. Something not working means you're thinking about how far you could swim and if there's any way you could hold somebody else's head up above water for that whole time. Somebody you love.

Unthinkable, maybe. Unsinkable, no.

And I get it, I guess. Who wants to think about this stuff? Not for what they're paying. Vacation buzzkill. But whether they wanted to think about it or not, I was all over the thing. Down in the engine room, in those little nooks and crannies none of them have ever even laid eyes on—switches and glitches known only to me and the Vikings and God—my fingerprints are all over everything.

Fingerprints all washed away by now.

Chapter

36

Oh, Nassau, you beautiful beast! Never before had Geoff properly appreciated the riotous vision of this place. The chaos of the lawless port, the thrill of open-air street crime, the sweet stew of marine engine oil, cigarettes, fish markets. He had missed it all, and how. He was very far from Ahoy's offices, of course, having landed at the public airstrip rather than on one of Ahoy's seaplanes, but he was making his way through the melee toward Bahamas HQ as fast as he could.

A horn honked as he crossed the street, but no amount of lewd gesturing and high-pitched colonial resentment could stop him now. He was here—and so was she.

Ahoy's Bahamas marina was even more beautiful than its state-side sister. It spread along a large cove that cupped neon-crystal-blue waters with white-sand beachfront on both sides. There was a curved white dock with slips for twenty yachts, and all along the piers were gigantic white pots overflowing with every color of flower. In between the water and the glass office was a wide expanse of grass landscaped with squat palm trees, clusters of perfumed flowering shrubs, and hammocks that swung side to side in the brisk breeze. There were ample private places and pairs of chairs that overlooked the water, hidden from view. Peppered throughout the grass were discreet speakers in the form of plastic, perforated iguanas and rocks that emitted a calibrated smoothness of steel drum jazz.

He was home.

"What are you doing here?" It was Kiyana, an excessively pregnant front desk concierge, his Bahamian counterpart. She walked into the office from the water side, one hand on her lower back, her tongue protruding slightly from her mouth. Geoff stood up very straight.

The interior of this Ahoy office was identical to the other one: glass-encased and decorated in inoffensive blues and beiges; side tables stacked with little piles of glossy yacht magazines that had circulations in the dozens. Abstract watercolors, Rorschach tests for land inheritors, were spaced generously across the walls, and a long, thin shelf displayed Ahoy's ten years' worth of angular glass Caribbean Yacht Society Notable Crew Awards. Two years in the middle were missing and, like everything else one paid for here, were best left unmentioned.

"I've been asked to escort a client to a legal meeting, if you must know. And how are you?"

She lifted up her shirt and rubbed her naked belly. "Some days you're getting kicked in the ass from the outside, some days from the inside, you know?"

He took a full step backward to emphasize that he did not.

"I'll be quite out of your way," he said. "What time are the Falcons expected, then?" He knew precisely when they would be here but felt he should convey the notion that he was, naturally, juggling a variety of responsibilities.

Her eyes flicked over to the schedule up on the computer, the same one he had himself. "Six thirty, it says."

He nodded and saluted her with his folder. "Bravo, Kiyana. Carry on."

He walked outside without knowing exactly why or where he would go. There were still a few hours before the boat arrived. He looked around and settled on a lounge chair behind a bush.

Behind his desk back home, he'd installed Fern, whom he'd once seen, when a phone rang, pick up a conch shell and put it to her ear. She'd had the good grace not to ask why Geoff was making this trip, and all would be fine as long as an owner didn't drop by expecting a standard human exchange.

The lounge chair was incredibly comfortable, and he let himself sink down into it.

The documents in his folder all pertained to the Falcons' change of registration request. Poppy had signed everything on her end, in a tiny spiral-flourish Geoff found utterly charming, establishing herself as the primary owner. Now they simply needed to file all this with the Bahamian authorities, as the boat was registered here for its port of call. That was one of Ahoy's specialties, to provide convenient places of business in either locale for whatever an owner might possibly wish to obscure.

Geoff's role in this registration process was entirely nonessential, but that hadn't stopped him before. It would be a treat to show off his talents to Poppy.

The sun sank behind the tops of the tallest boats. Gargantuan shadows crept inch by inch across the water, dock, and grass. Where was Poppy's boat? Where was she on it at this exact moment? And where in the world would Geoff sleep tonight?

Chapter

37

"Okay, wow, tons to report back." Helen hoisted herself up onto the half wall next to Denise's captain chair and rubbed her hands together like they were at a starting line. Denise had forgotten how tired her sister could make her feel.

Ahead of them, knuckles of land rose on the horizon as they approached the Bahamas. The smells changed as they came closer to land, the briny air opening up and making room for wafts of sand and flowers and charred hints of food. The sun was behind them, warming their backs, and the waves rolled out ahead of them, beckoning the boat forward.

They were about forty minutes offshore, when the navigation was most demanding and Denise was most tense. The last hour of any cruise was the hardest. The tides had to be monitored, docking system fail-safes had to be triple-checked, and the marina had to be radioed and the slip confirmed, among about fifty other urgent technical tasks that needed to be carried out in an extremely precise order. Helen was here to hang out.

Denise's eyes were locked onto the blue, black, and green screens in front of her. "Don't talk. You're supposed to be helping prepare to disembark."

Helen twisted open a bottle of the guests' water. "Poppy's not that psyched about their dinner plans, so she said there was zero rush."

"I—you—she . . ." Denise closed her mouth.

"Hey, do you know if the lady who lived in Mom's house after us ever fixed the hole in the porch? Is that how she died? Maybe she fell in there."

It was like someone had started explaining the concept of conversation to Helen but had been interrupted, leaving her with at best a partial understanding. She lived to pursue as many segues as possible and her curiosity was astonishingly pointless. Every comment was a trampoline she bounced off, and anyone who resisted her concussive style of conversation or didn't want to feel the burning light of interrogation was either suspicious or heartless.

Helen kept going. "And get this. Seriously, buckle up. Poppy has a massive crush on Geoff. Geoff! She could not stop talking about the guy."

"Geoff?" Denise blurted. That was not the right reaction, and she did not have time for this, but the woman's romantic taste suggested mental illness.

"I know! I'll tell you the rest later. But guess what else?"

Denise turned on the pumps, set the timers, and radioed Stew about the fenders.

"Okay, fine, I'll just tell you now. That Rocco guy pushed me."

Denise spun around. "He what?"

"I'm fine, that's not the point. I went in there to give them these extremely delicious sak-tails I whipped up—they didn't even ask for them, but I really just wanted an excuse to go in there, and it totally worked—and Rocco completely lost his mind. He's a binder bouncer. That's when he pushed me. He kind of grabbed my arm and yanked me out of the room."

Denise's heart pressed up against her ribs and was screaming to get out. To get out and throttle someone. The idea that someone, on her watch, had hurt Helen made Denise want to throw up and take a knife in each hand and lie down with a pillow over her head all at the same time. "What? Why didn't you tell me this before now? Are you okay? Where was Stew?"

"Blowing up the inflatables. Dude has crazy lung capacity. Did you know he used to be a singer, and that's how he got started on cruises? Do people ever have performances on board here? This is the whole point though: Rocco does not want us to get in that office, aka we absolutely need to get in that office, ASAP. Tonight."

The console beeped, and Denise forced herself to look down and regain some kind of focus. She punched in the coordinates to send the update to shore with their estimated arrival time.

Helen went on, "They're all getting off tonight, so we'll have a few hours to poke around. And I know what you're thinking, way ahead of you. I already asked Poppy, and she said Rocco is getting off, too—he's driving them to dinner. He started as a driver apparently. You know I love an origin story."

Denise brought a hand to her forehead. "Helen. Why didn't you just ask Poppy to put on a mask and grab a crowbar and come join us? That's about the least subtle thing you could've asked her. 'Oh hey, do these doors lock? Is the coast clear?'"

"Not even kidding, if we gave Poppy a friendship bracelet as part of the deal, she probably would. Super lonely, it's kind of a bummer. She's really sweet, minus the whole marrying-the-mob sort of deal. And I guess also the cheating-on-Tim scenario."

"Please stop talking. About this, about anything. Go help Stew. Tell Kay to call Kiyana."

Helen groaned.

Denise looked over as her sister was moving toward the stairs to return to work as slowly as humanly possible. "Listen. Why don't we go see Mom tomorrow morning? Some quality Janet time?"

Helen perked up. "Really?"

Denise nodded.

Helen pressed the palms of her hands together. "Perfect. We can recap. And about tonight, I'll just pop in there myself, okay? Compromise? That way, if shit hits the fan, you can fire me. I'll take all the heat. I know you only hired me so you could fire me anyway."

Her sister knew her after all. "Maybe."

A screen buzzed with a reminder to warm up the bow thrusters for docking. Denise opened her mouth.

"Go away," Helen said.

Denise yelled, "I can't go away, I'm—"

"No, no, no, I'm finishing your sentences. You were about to tell me to go away. See? We're a good team. Synced up already. It's going to be rock-solid."

Denise blinked. She saw all at once that Helen was trying with her; this was her trying. And yes, Denise resented how easy and natural it was for her sister to come up with these little elbow-to-the-rib moments. And yes, Denise was angry at herself that she couldn't pull off those moments herself—ashamed, even, that it never occurred to her to try like that. But there was no way that she was going to let herself be called the lazy one. She realized this was probably how Helen felt as a kid, watching Denise do something over and over, finally trying it for herself, then waiting to see how her sister reacted.

"*Paalam*," Denise waved. *Goodbye* in Tagalog.

Helen's mouth gaped open in a huge, stunned smile. "No."

Denise allowed herself a minor smile and felt a flush of relief. "When you were over there, I taught myself a few things."

Helen faux-frowned and put both hands on her heart. "She loves me."

"Cool it. It was in case I had to fly over there and perform some kind of rescue. Those boats you were on were ridiculous." She'd looked those up, too.

Helen downright beamed. "If that's all it took to get you to come visit me, I would've sunk something years ago."

Chapter

38

Watching the boats maneuver into their slips was a joy, no matter how many times he'd witnessed it, no matter what mood he was in. Geoff rarely gave the captains much credit—they all gave themselves plenty—but the very concept of steering a sixty-foot-long, thirty-foot-wide, seventy-five-thousand-pound object into a narrow parking space next to other ships of the same proportions without so much as disturbing a seagull was nothing short of extraordinary. The utter lack of panic among the crew calmed him as well. They were seasoned and skilled in their roles, and to watch them dock was to witness Ahoy's work at its finest. He did try to keep this admiration in mind when speaking to them.

Docking was a fifteen-minute, slow-motion performance, and Geoff walked out onto the pier to wait with his hands clasped behind his back and enjoy every moment of it. A porter, whom Geoff had met before but whose name he could not for the life of him remember, appeared at his side in overly short shorts and a yellow polo shirt. The staff were conveniently color coded.

"Geoff," the man said, with a tip of the visor.

"Yes," Geoff said and, lacking both the man's name and a visor of his own, did one little tug at the collar of his shirt for some reason, causing the porter to look down at his own.

Helen and Kaylee came down to the pier first, rolling suitcases behind them. Keen to avoid another noogie, Geoff kept his distance from Denise's sister, who immediately abandoned her post anyway and jogged over to the next boat to "scope out the competition."

Tim clanked down the walkway next in a bathing suit and white button-down with his initials embroidered on the sleeve in baby blue. "Ahoy my boy! Can't pay for this kind of service. Look at my man here—dock to dock, Popeye!"

Geoff endured a high five and nearly reminded Tim that he did, in fact, pay quite a bit for this service but then heard the unmistakable sound of a tiny gasp.

There she stood, pressing her lips together and looking down directly at him with the slightest, most beguiling expression of you-shouldn't-have. His heart soared.

Before Tim could, Geoff extended his hand to assist Poppy onto the dock. "Ms. Wojcikski. How was your maiden voyage as owner?"

"Just call her Miss Falcon already, right, Pop Star? That name's alphabet borscht."

Neither Geoff nor Poppy responded. Their eyes locked and, by the grace of God, she gave his hand a little squeeze. Geoff felt his chest might burst open.

Stew and Kaylee wheeled the suitcases toward a black SUV in the lot that had appeared without Geoff noticing it. He looked back and forth a few times from it to them while also trying to give Poppy his full attention, twisting his neck like a rag.

Poppy bounced on the balls of her feet, flouncing a long cheetah-print pink caftan with yellow tassels, which he now understood to be her adorable sartorial signature. "What are you doing here?" she asked.

Geoff tightened his grip on his folder. "Registration help, of course. All this paperwork is a handful and—not that you need it—but in case I might be of any assistance."

"This is so huge," Tim said. "No offense, Beverly Hills Pop, but I really did not want to spend tomorrow in some office with, like, two windows. I need to practice my flips off the boat. You're still down to do the slo-mo videos for me, right? The practice ones you took were pretty bad, but I think you could get there. Actually, I might ask Stew, he gave me this killer shoulder massage today—dude has some strong hands. Like he'd be really steady holding the camera, you know?"

Poppy nodded. "Of course, sweetie."

"Shall we say eight o'clock?"

"In the morning?" Tim's eyes popped.

"Eight is great!" Poppy beamed.

"Magnificent," Geoff said. He wondered how to professionally make this exchange last an extremely long time. "So, Denise and the team will be going over the boat now. A full inspection, tip to tail, is standard while we're docked. Refueling, of course, is essential, and the crew will be freshening everything up so that when—"

Tim mimed falling asleep and gave a loud snore. Then he cocked his head. "No, thanks. Vamos, like the locals say. We're outtie. I am famished." He started walking to the car. "Rocco! Shake a leg!"

A hulking man wearing an open Hawaiian shirt over what appeared to be a varnished chest stomped past Geoff toward the car without so much as a word. The man's hair resembled a blond coonskin cap.

Poppy put a hand on Geoff's shoulder and leaned her face toward his. "Eight." Her breath smelled of banana. She turned to walk away, then swiveled to wave goodbye again.

The engine of the SUV started up, and the trunk door slammed shut. A jet of courage suddenly spouted across Geoff's ribs. He shouted, "I'll be here all evening, in case you need me. I'll be right here, at the office, all night, not going anywhere, at your service. And if I'm not inside the office, it's the crew quarters then, where I'll be staying. Just right over there, right behind those hedges. So," he swallowed, "if there's anything you need—at all."

Poppy looked at him without a word, her expression unreadable.

"Mom and Pop Shop! Chow time!"

The passenger door shut.

The yellow-shirted porter returned and stood beside Geoff, joining him in watching the SUV slip beyond the iron gateway. "You want my advice?" the porter said.

"Absolutely not," Geoff answered.

Chapter

39

The nose of the boat faced the ocean, and through the wide mouth of the cove, a silver bracelet of the last sunlight slipped across the lower sky where the blue dipped to black. Low on the evening horizon, the faint first stars mingled, and the still waters in the cove were a deep, dark ribbon of purple. The beaches were empty save for a turtle scooching back into the sea over the wave-rippled sand. Palm trees arched over the shore and bobbed their green heads, agreeing at every turn with the wind.

Denise rarely came up to the bow deck and even now didn't feel all that comfortable sitting here. She wasn't one of those captains who thought it was the crew's job to clean up after her, too; she never left any trace on the boat, nary a butt print that had to be smoothed out. On her own rise up, she'd smoothed out plenty, and she'd always resented the captains who acted like guests.

More often than not, she went an entire cruise, an entire month of cruises even, without doing anything like this, taking a minute when the boat was empty just to look around. Of course she'd been to this cove a thousand times, but it was one of those things that didn't get old. The satisfaction came from the feeling that just behind her the colossal ship was safe, silent, and secure, its power conjured by her alone.

As soon as Helen had brought up the idea of looking through the Falcons' papers, a part of Denise knew she would do it. The pull was just too strong; she wanted it too badly, in a primal way she couldn't suppress. And it wasn't as though she'd never thought of doing this before. Helen, flung into Denise's world from a universe away, hadn't told her anything she didn't already know. But Helen did give her sister something she'd never had before. No one had ever offered to help her, not like this. Randy listened to her vent and signed the petitions and got nice and angry about it all right alongside her. But he never got proactive about it or said, "This is my thing too now, and I'm going to put this part of my life on the line for it." For you.

And maybe that's what she was doing here now, looking around— because even if she'd seen this view a thousand times before, there was always a last time.

She stood to go find her sister.

Chapter

40

The running lights were on, small yellow circles along the deck in the dark.

Stew and Kaylee were off the boat on a provision run and getting dinner in town. Ahoy was empty except for Geoff, whom they'd seen ducking into a crew bungalow usually reserved for storage. Neither of them knew why he was here or wanted to ask.

"Okay, we're going," Helen whispered. She and Denise stood shoulder to shoulder staring down the set of stairs that led to the lower suites. Neither of them moved.

"You don't have to whisper," Denise said.

"And you really don't have to come with me. You could stand out here and yell if someone comes."

"Do you have any idea what you're looking for? And it would be great if you could not destroy the place while you try. We shared a room—I know what you're capable of."

"I was seven when we shared a room."

"And now you're better?"

Helen huffed and went down the steps.

The living room at the bottom of the stairs had high ceilings and a glittering chandelier in the center from which thousands of tiny silver seashells dangled. The furniture was crisp white with gold flourishes and fixtures, including two large sectional couches and cushy armchairs that could seat dozens. Pale blue pillows were everywhere, each embroidered with a tiny *F* in white thread. The room smelled like peonies, fresh pink-and-white bundles of which filled a huge shell-shaped vase on each side table. A television the size of a small movie theater screen was embedded in one of the walls above a fireplace that glowed at all hours of the day and night, in the middle of the Caribbean, with a fake flame.

Their feet fell softly on the plush carpet as they made their way to the office in the back corner. "Also, the crew isn't permitted to know the door codes," Denise added.

"What if there was an emergency? What if you were trapped in there, and the boat was going down?"

"If I was trapped in there, the boat would be going down. And listen, this is an eyeballs-only operation, okay?"

Denise began tapping a lengthy string of numbers into the keypad on the wood door.

"So you're able to open drawers with your eyes now. I'll tell Mom. Kaylee said Swamp Fabio wouldn't even let her in to even clean the room earlier."

"Then they'll notice if someone went inside, so don't touch anything. It needs to stay clean. Completely pristine."

The keypad glowed green, and the door mewed a pleasant beep. Denise pushed the handle.

The office was strewn with half-finished snacks, empty glasses, papers all over the desk, and damp clothes. A small whiteboard in the corner had the word *brainstorm* written on it, but with *storm* crossed out and *hurricane*, underlined twice, written in its place; the board was otherwise blank.

"Disgusting." Helen smiled.

They stepped inside.

Helen dropped to her knees, tossed a pair of board shorts onto the couch behind her, and got up to her elbows in the nearest bankers box.

Denise circled the desk like a shark. It was covered in what looked like marketing briefs with mock-ups of graphics and logos and renderings of future buildings. She grazed her fingers across a few just to do it, to break the seal on this whole bad idea. They were in it now.

Denise scanned the shelves until she saw a set of binders from recent years. She knelt down and pulled one out, crouching behind the desk next to the safe. Her heart was pounding, and she knew she'd only let them stay in here for another few minutes; who knew when Tim and Poppy would be back from dinner, anything could happen. Her breath was coming quickly, and she could feel her pulse in her fingertips. She lowered her face to the pages and flipped through as fast as possible. Everything was in triplicate, which it took her a minute to realize.

"Do you think we should tell them about computers?" Helen asked, not looking up.

Denise's eyes slid sideways down the rows of binders and file cabinets. To get through this much stuff in a nanosecond without knowing what half of it looked like or meant made her feel suddenly overwhelmed. She felt stupid and small, a set of feelings she'd never had on a boat before, then felt angry at the Falcons for making her feel this way, resented Helen for putting her in a position to feel this way, and hated herself for letting it happen.

"I think these are take-out menus," Helen said. "Or maybe they're opening a restaurant. Either way, it should be illegal to sell edamame at Tongue Thai'd."

"Well, ex-squeeze me."

Both of their heads flipped up.

Stew stood in the doorway with his arms crossed, and Kaylee was right behind him.

"Harvest moon," Kaylee shook her head with a grin. "I had a

dream about this, only we were in the Sahara. We were wearing indigo camouflage."

Helen stood and put her hands up. "This is exactly what it looks like."

Denise shot up behind her. "Helen!"

"It's going to be so awkward when they find out about the internet." Stew walked in and ruffled some papers on the desk.

"Wires can become sentient and strangle their owners—they're the boa constrictors of the digital age." Kaylee began folding all the clothes in the room.

"No, no, no. Not this. Get out, everyone out," Denise said.

Stew snatched the binder from Denise's hand. "You think this is my first snoop job? Please. I was inside a Goofy costume during the Arthur Andersen cruise. Lots of pockets in those things. Go. Come on, this is the only way to have any kind of job security in this biz. Tell me what we're looking for. I'm a speed reader. Let's go."

Denise looked at Helen. Helen shrugged. "Soil samples?"

Denise let out a long sigh. "Anything about groundwater, soil, anything about condo construction, dirt, just give it to me. And . . . thank you."

Helen sank back down to the floor and pushed a box over to Kaylee, who started reading, then stood up.

"Is it alright if I keep watch instead? Words on a page aren't any good for my lower intestine. And I'm due for an exchange with Ursa Minor—you can only see her from the Southern Hemisphere and, alas, she's here now. It's all in flux, as you know. I'll give you a signal if anyone's coming. Do you want me to use the horn? I'll admit, I've actually always wanted to use the horn."

"Do not use the horn." Denise's voice rose from behind the desk.

"Say something normal, we'll get it." Helen patted Kaylee's shoulder.

Stew crouched next to Denise. "Seriously. Now if anything ever happens to me with these people—and life is long—all I need to say is 'soil sample.' Don't know what it means, don't want to, don't care, don't tell me. That is just some magic potion I keep in my pocket, and I chug it if I ever need to."

They worked in silence, the only sound the rustling of paper and the curl of waves lapping the side of the boat. Denise's heart pressed up against her throat. It was bad enough she'd gotten her sister into this, sort of, but unforgivable that the rest of the crew were mixed up in it, too. But it would be even worse if after all this they came away with nothing.

Helen crawled over on all fours, then sat down next to Denise. They leaned their backs against the filing cabinet with folders on their knees. "What about this?"

Helen handed over a set of charts paper-clipped together. Denise scanned the pages.

Raul's company—his logo at the top.

And all the right words: *compression test, density assessment, water content, expansion capability, bearing limit.*

Denise's hands went cold. "Raul just told me he wasn't involved with the Falcons."

Helen scrunched her eyebrows. "Why?"

Denise had no idea. She scanned the page. Tiny numbers lined a huge grid pertaining to different properties, values, and decimals that she had no idea exactly how to interpret. But it was at least a finger pointed in the correct direction. It was a start. It was the closest she'd ever been.

Raul's company.

She slid the paper clips off, pulled out copies of each chart—five pages total—and folded them into a square, then shoved them in her back pocket.

"Juicy," Stew said. "You're a major-league sneak, Denise. Didn't know you had it in you."

"My big sister," Helen preened.

Kaylee whispered from just outside the door. "Khakis."

The three of them scrambled to their feet and quickly shoved things back to more or less where they'd been. They dropped papers back into boxes and slammed the binders and drawers closed. They checked their pockets to make sure they hadn't dropped anything.

Helen and Stew darted out of the office, and for one second Denise stood in the doorway and looked back inside. Geoff's voice rose from the dock, so it was him and not the guests. She exhaled. The room looked basically the same as when they'd found it, a mess.

She went back in.

She took the empty glasses and dishes, piled them up, and took them out to a tray, then into the galley. She rolled all the clothes into a pile and dropped them off at the laundry. She tidied everything in sight, from the boxes on the floor to the papers on the desk. Neat, arbitrary piles. It had been years since she'd cleaned a room, and it felt excellent. She wanted Rocco, or even Tim, to know that her team had been in here, that they could be and would be in here, and that she was in charge. It was her boat, it was her charter, and this was her course.

Chapter

41

It was the longest dinner of Poppy's life. Usually when Tim ordered one of everything on the menu (he'd done this six times since she met him—she'd counted), it made her giggle to watch the waiter ask two or three times if that was really what Tim meant. This time, though, when he put the menu facedown and the words left his mouth, she shook her head ever so slightly, hoping he would notice, but he was already caught up in the excitement.

The restaurant was perched at the very top of Mount Bahama, or whatever it was called, and their table was set on a stone patio off the garden. The trees were all draped in tiny lights that mirrored the golden beads of the boat lights spilled across the black water hundreds of feet below. It had taken them thirty minutes of zigzagging back and forth in the car to get all the way up here; the tiny place was suspended above the island like the diamond perched atop Poppy's ring. Birds cooed from the branches, and in the middle of the table was a single white candle that kept flickering out in the breeze. Every few minutes, someone scurried over to relight it.

A bottle of something was brought over right away; then came a visit from the chef, followed by a relay of servers bringing forth plate after plate after plate. It had been magical the first time she'd experienced it—a childhood dream animated, a fantasia of food, with him telling her it was fine to take just one bite of something, who cares—but now she felt queasy at the prospect of hours and hours and hours of eating like this.

When it finally ended, long after midnight, and they slid into the car, Tim fell asleep immediately. Poppy fell asleep, too, as they wove back and forth down the mountain. She woke up when Rocco opened the back door and Tim was roused for the short walk back to the dock, up the passerelle, and onto the boat, where he collapsed into their bed.

Poppy waited to hear that he was snoring before she left the suite, checked that Rocco's door was shut, and went back to land to go look for Geoff.

Chapter

42

On a night like this, who was she kidding, there was no way Helen would sleep. Denise had crashed, unbelievably, but she'd always been a stone-cold sleeper. Helen's pacing drove Stew nuts, so he kicked her off to land, and now Helen was cocooned in one of Ahoy's deep, soft hammocks, delighted to be outside the cramped crew quarters on board. Denise might be pissed in the morning when she had to send someone down here to get her but whatever.

Tomorrow, they would dig into what they'd found.

The fresh air was remarkable: Sea air was even better laced with tree air, and the stars were out of control. The Ahoy campus was a neutered paradise, soft grass underfoot, trimmed flowers in every color combination so as not to offend any passenger of any nation, and a manicured coastline that standardized the crashing sound of every wave that hit the rocks.

It was a crazy thrill to break into the office and crazier still that they'd found something. Maybe. Who knew? Denise would figure it out. That was the biggest thrill: Helen had ducked into about a thousand places she wasn't allowed to, but Denise? Seeing her self-righteous-ass sister snooping around like that was the wildest sight of all.

People were completely different at sea than they were on land. On land, Denise threatened Geoff with violence and called city council members screaming, but at sea she didn't untuck her shirt and ate her breakfast burrito with a fork. Watching her switch places like this was exciting, and Helen couldn't wait to see what came next.

In Helen's experience, people went their very craziest during their brief stints on land. Stopping for an overnight anywhere that guests could disembark was like releasing sailors on shore leave. After being at sea, people felt like they'd been freed, as if they'd just realized how much space had been available on land all along—the better to run around on. A place definitely felt more exotic when you'd arrived there by boat. Helen was hardly immune to this feeling herself and had made several horrible choices on shore nights, from hookups with members of the Cambodian royal family to bad investments in solar-powered aquaculture, all in the spirit of *mea culpa, terra firma*.

Her eyes closed; maybe she would sleep after all. Thinking about all that paperwork down there, boxes and boxes of it, was having a powerful soporific effect. But then she heard the noise.

It was the unmistakable *squelch* of a smooch. She barely had to prop herself up, not that she could have gracefully moved within the hammock anyway. With a little shift to the side, through the mesh, she saw Poppy and Geoff kissing behind a palm tree.

Chapter

43

It was safe to say it was the best night of Geoff's life.

The layers of subterfuge were beyond erotic. First and foremost, he should not have been in this country at all—that went without saying. Second, Poppy was engaged, but that he didn't like to dwell on. But third, they were owner and staff, upstairs and down, right and wrong, and he was just kicking himself for not doing this sooner. The heat! It was verboten, unheard-of, a fireable offense, frowned upon, and it felt as if the entirety of his career, every step of the way, had led him right here. This night, this woman, this disaster—*my God.*

Not long after the Falcons had left for dinner, he'd fallen asleep pretending to read a book on one of the lounge chairs. He awoke with a startle in the middle of the night when he felt a hand on his shoulder. "Geoff," Poppy whispered.

He stood and kept his arms by his side. Then she took a step toward him, and he placed his hands on her shoulders.

"I feel like I've met you before," she whispered. "But I've never been to England."

He kissed her.

In between breaths, they whispered to each other about shock. At each other, at themselves, at the sharpness of palm bark, at the world for keeping them apart all these years and for now standing in their way still. None of it made any sense, but it all added up. They were two people making one beautiful, incredibly stupid mistake. It was outstanding.

"Geoff," she breathed. "Who are you? I feel like you were talking directly to me when you said you'd still be awake tonight. Were you? I couldn't sleep, even though I'm so full. My stomach, I can't even explain—"

"I was," he interrupted. "Thank God you heard me. You are so beautiful, Poppy."

"So are you," she said.

Had anyone ever called him beautiful before?

It lasted for no more than half an hour. He couldn't have taken her anywhere no matter how much he'd wanted to; he barely fit inside the bonus crew cottage by himself. But the chasteness warmed him to her all the more. She was moving slowly. There was more to come.

When she finally pulled away, ducked back for one more kiss, then stepped away for good, he was left standing at the shore a changed man. He'd done it, and in doing so, he saw what needed to be done. He'd spent years lifting his knees in order to raise one leg up at a time, step after step, and where had that gotten him? Not here, not to a garden across an ocean, not into the arms of an excellent-smelling woman, that's for sure. Now that he was looking out from this new shore, he marveled at what move he might make next and believed he could truly surprise himself.

Chapter

44

Somehow, at eight the following morning, thanks to a bracing outdoor shower, Geoff managed to look presentable.

Hair wet and combed with his fingers, he stood at the entrance to Ahoy with his hands clasped at his waist and watched the docks for Poppy's approach. Right on time, she stepped onto the pier and headed his way with a blushed, knowing smile on her face. She wore wide-legged linen pants and a matching top, both polka-dotted, and a cumbersome-looking sun hat that snagged on branches she passed by.

Behind her walked that same overbaked man in what appeared to be the same Hawaiian shirt. He caught up to her and said something Geoff couldn't make out. Poppy nodded and her lips drooped.

"Morning!" she said when she drew near. Her cheeks were aglow and her three to four necklaces dabbled a sparkle beneath her chin.

"Well, hello," Geoff said and reached for her hand. She did not extend hers.

"This is Rocco," Poppy explained in a tight voice. "He works with Tim's family. He's like a . . . helper, for us."

Rocco barked out a laugh and a cloud of coffee breath. "I'm a helper like a sniper's tossing you a tennis ball." He shook Geoff's extended hand and crushed his fingers. "Look. I specifically asked your crew not to clean up inside Mr. Falcon's office, and what do I see when I wake up at four thirty this morning for my P90X? It's as clean as a whistle. Now what are we going to do about that?"

"Uh. They are not my crew, exactly, and the cleaning is not my purview, but perhaps I—"

"Then what do you do?"

Poppy put a hand on Geoff's back. "Geoff knows all about the registration paperwork. He's done it before, so many times."

Rocco stared at him. "We're not done here at all. But let's get this over with."

Geoff sat in the passenger seat. For the forty minutes it took to drive to Nassau's financial district, he withstood a detailed explanation on the interplay of kinesthetics and protein. He stole exactly one twist in his seat to look behind him at Poppy, who delivered a nervous smile, fiddling with her bracelets.

Finally they arrived at the boat registrar. The tiny office looked like someone's home. Alone behind a low white fence on a tight square of grass, it was a pastel-pink cottage with yellow trim and neat stone steps leading to its yellow door. There was a golden turtle door knocker. The building's only admission of seriousness was a small hanging sign out front displaying crisscrossed American and Bahamian flags.

Inside, every single window was open, the shutters flung out as far as they would go, as if they were desperate for the sun's approval. Fans whirled above, and hidden speakers piped in classical music. The three of them were relieved of any obligation to talk when the gray-bearded, linen-suited man at the desk greeted them and began a long monologue on the vitality of American–Bahamian relations.

When a woman stepping into the room with a coffee tray interrupted, Geoff nearly wept with relief.

As the registrar spoke, he took swift care of business, scanning the documents Geoff provided, stamping every other one with an open-mouthed smile throughout. Rocco handed the man an additional folder, and he seamlessly swept its contents into the flow, page after page, pen stroke to pen stroke. It irritated Geoff slightly that he hadn't been made aware of all the documents, but in this mood, on this morning, he let it go without a word. In between sentences, the registrar responded to himself with nods, hums, and whistles, a one-man band of conversation.

After a hit of caffeine, Geoff suddenly couldn't hold back his own smile. He and the registrar kept locking eyes over the desk, smiling and nodding at each other as if filing these people's paperwork was the single greatest joy of their lives.

Poppy giggled when she signed on the final line. She looked over at Geoff with wide delighted eyes. The elated official asked if she had any questions. Geoff looked over at her expectantly, realizing for the first time in his life that he had none whatsoever himself. For someone who'd spent his whole life obsessed with next steps, consumed by plans and paths, right now there was nowhere to be but here, simply sitting in the same room with her.

Poppy put her hand over her heart and looked at the man with a serious face. "If I'm a citizen now, do I say the pledge?" Her eyes flicked up to the beautiful teal, orange, and black flag draped behind his desk.

"Oh," the man said, finally at a loss for words.

Rocco stood up and his chair scraped the floor. "It's all yours, alright? We done here? We'll be back after she gets married. Let's go, I need a shake."

Chapter

45

Denise and Helen's mother, Babs, moved to the Bahamas ten years ago and loved to mention that she hadn't returned to the US since.

She had sold the marine plumbing business for enough to buy a rundown blue house on the western tip of Andros Island, next to the scrubby marsh edge of a national park. It was a small working farm, ten slanted acres high up on a hillside that got full sun for twelve hours a day. A tiny strip of beach below was accessible by a steep, winding trail among knee-high vegetation. She had fixed up the house as much as she could herself, which was a lot—something she also loved to mention. The house had, everyone had to admit, some of the best plumbing on the island. In the early years, when the fruits and vegetables hadn't come in well yet, word traveled fast, and she stayed afloat lying on her back underneath her neighbors' sinks and crawl spaces.

When she looked into acquiring a cow for the farm, she met Janet. Janet loved to mention how much trouble cows were, and now they'd been living together for seven years and had chickens. Janet was a retired bovine veterinarian who, like Babs, still had steady work doing house calls. She'd desperately wanted children but never had any and had never married. Instead, she had an open-door policy for her dozens of great-nieces and great-nephews, whom Babs found extremely useful when it came time for strawberry picking, so long as she didn't mind a third of her inventory being eaten.

They were so happy it made Denise uncomfortable. Every time

she visited, about once a month when a charter stayed for more than a night or two, she could last only a few hours at the house before she had to get out. What drove her insane was her mother and Janet's hyperawareness of their happiness. They talked about it all the time. They'd finally figured everything out—romance, money, home, work, family, friendship, avocados incorporated into every meal—and could not stop patting themselves on the back about it. Of course Babs deserved to be happy—the previous iteration of her life was no picnic—but she didn't seem to understand that constantly announcing her own joy at having reached the most golden of years just threw into stark relief the struggles of everyone else who was still very much on the pewter path.

The sisters were coming up on their mom's place now. The morning after their heist had dawned bright and clear, and the water was the very same color as the sky. Helen sat in the bow of the Zodiac; Denise's hand was on the throttle. A lone, very long pier jutted out from the tiny beach like either a beckoning finger or an offensive one, depending on the viewer's mood.

Denise tied the boat up. Then they stepped into the brush at the bottom of the hill and began the hike up the flowered path to the farm.

"When was the last time we were here together?" Helen panted.

"Have we ever been here together?" Denise lifted her shirt to wipe the sweat off her face and took a swig from her water bottle.

"Give me some of that. Please." Helen snatched it.

"I told you to bring one."

"It's way too heavy."

"That's why you drink it."

"Christmas!" Helen finished half the bottle. "I think it was three Christmases ago. Mom made that disgusting stew. It had feathers in it."

"Was that when Janet made us those scarves?"

"I still have mine. At least I think I do. Never mind, I used it for a tourniquet after the coral thing. Don't tell her that."

"Are you insane? Last time I mentioned the honey here, and they tried to send me home with a beehive on the boat. Never bring up anything, ever. Say nothing."

When they emerged from the brush, their limbs were covered in a layer of sweat that acted like glue for the petals of every flower they passed. They trudged up the remainder of the hill past neat rows of crops and reached the yard behind the cottage.

"They're here!" Janet rose from her rocking chair and waddled toward them, the silver tail of a stethoscope flopping from her shorts' back pocket. She wrapped them both in a hug and came away covered in flower petals, which she brushed off. "How hungry are you? Give me this water bottle, I'll refill it. Do you want to do some laundry? How about just fresh socks? You need a shower? But do you want to go for a swim first? We have brand-new towels. And would you like salad first or a smoothie? Or just some cheese? Cow or goat?"

Janet jammed a lifetime of mothering into every single interaction with them, and neither sister was built to absorb it. The two of them could acknowledge that it was heartwarming but still found it profoundly annoying.

"Hi, Janet! Thank you so much!"

"Janet. No."

"My babies!" Babs had the body of a forty-year-old and ran over at a dead sprint, then dropped to her knees at their feet. They both knelt down and hugged her, and Babs pulled them backward so all three of them were rolling on the grass. Two dogs joined in and slobbered all over them.

"Mom! Ow!"

"Get off me!"

"It's my Helly Belly Smelly Jelly Bean!" Babs released Denise but continued raining down kisses onto Helen. When they stood, Babs roughly wiped off all the grass and dirt from Helen's limbs. The two of them held hands walking back to the porch, her mother squeezing her baby girl's fingers in a vise grip that made something in Helen's throat catch.

Babs wore long cutoff denim shorts and had a loose green bandanna around her neck. She pulled Helen down to sit on her lap and wrapped her arms around her daughter's waist.

Janet brought over plates of breakfast: eggs, plantains, and three kinds of homemade hot sauce. A rooster stood on the corner of the table, and Janet stroked his feathers between bites. Babs released Helen to eat but kept her chair close enough that their elbows kept bumping into each other, and she placed extra little bites on her daughter's plate. Helen ate every last one.

Babs placed her silverware down, then leaned back, slipped her hand in between her boobs, and pulled out a pocketknife, which she flipped open and started using to file her nails. Then she raised both eyebrows and seemed to remember something; she reached back in there to pull out a mint, which she popped in her mouth. Babs's bosom was like Mary Poppins's bag. Denise had once seen her pull a kitten out of there.

Babs held up the knife. "Girls, listen to me for once. Guava is the new pomegranate."

"It's true," Janet pointed her fork at them.

"I cannot keep them stocked and I'm working like a dog out here. Every single hotel is calling me to get new boxes of them, and when we're on the phone, I can't even hear what they're saying because they've got the blenders revving in the background—"

"Your mother is the smoothie queen of the island. I need to make her a crown. I've been wanting to get out my sewing machine again. Denise, do you need any new pants?"

"I actually am," Babs said. "They say it blends well, and if you put other stuff in it, spinach or chard, whatever, guava is a real punch in the gut. Crazy fiber load, which you know I love, because food comes full circle, life comes full circle, from one end of my business empire to the other. And also guavas are neon yellow, which I guess looks good in the pictures. All the hotels are asking me for them, I'm not kidding. But they only grow so fast."

"What your mother is saying is, you have the guava to thank for all the big bucks she's going to leave to her grandchildren."

Helen and Denise both groaned. Through a mouthful of eggs and hot sauce, Helen said, "Denise is closer than I am right now, for once."

Babs and Janet traded a grin across the table.

Denise sat up straight and turned on her sister. "Why? And no, not again. Randy and I are not getting married right now. His name's not even on my lease yet."

"Ooo, 'right now,' 'yet,' she says—those are new." Janet wiggled her head side to side. "We will take it."

"We will take that," Babs agreed. "But that's not what's going on. We do actually have a little discussion to get into. Gals, I want to tell you something, and I don't want you to get upset or anything."

Helen looked at Denise. She shrugged.

Janet took Babs's hand. "We're the ones getting married."

"Oh." Denise leaned back and put a hand over her heart. "Don't scare me like that. You're too old."

"Wait, I kind of thought you were married. What was that big party like five years ago? I flew here from Auckland. You know the plane flew over the South Pole, that was actually faster than going around? Yeah, I thought for sure that it was like an anniversary party, or you had a ceremony or something."

"That was your mother's sixtieth birthday. We did go down to the court to get a joint license to sell eggs around then. Maybe that's what you're thinking about, sweet pea. Oh, how fun is it going to be to have an *official* sweet pea?"

Denise patted her mother's hand. "This is great, Mom. When?"

"Next month, whenever, I don't care. We haven't really set a date. We'll just do it when everyone can come. The whole gang, Janet's whole family. Big old party. I'll make my signature stew, wheelbarrows of it."

Helen hugged her from the side. "That's great, Mommy. Will you do a dress?"

"Hell, no." Babs high-fived Denise.

"I am going to wear a dress big enough for both of us," Janet said. "And I'm going to make white collars for the dogs and sew some very fun white hats for you two."

Babs placed her hands down on the table. "Okay. Enough of all that. You know we love to hear about this stuff—your stuff. We always make Denise tell us everything about her clients—and I mean everything. And hey, by the way, give me some credit, I've been telling you to hire your sister for years now, so you're welcome, both of you. So, who's on the boat? What's their deal? How bad are they?"

"Wait, wait, wait." Janet held up a hand. "Babsy, we skipped the whole thing, oh my goodness. I've been so worried, and now we got all caught up with the food. Your place, the building that fell down up there, did you girls see it? Are you all okay? What happened to that place?"

Chapter

46

A wedding. Of course.

Geoff felt so silly. Naturally Poppy was getting married at the end of this—of course there was that. As if he hadn't felt the ring on her finger in his own hand last night. But the wedding as a certain event that would happen after a certain amount of time was something else entirely, and he felt so foolish, so simpleminded, for not seeing it for what it was.

This was his window.

Poppy was the owner of the boat—that was official now, signed, sealed, and delivered. Delivered indeed. Poppy was a vessel, he understood perfectly now, a temporary owner until she married into the Falcon family, which he knew would happen precisely when they wanted it to happen.

No one can control time, people said. But they were utterly wrong. He'd spent his whole career around people like this; he knew they could absolutely control time. And they were doing so right now. They would wait things out, thread a needle that looked like the hand of a clock, until the crisis had blown over and all assets were safe from scrutiny. Then they would bring Poppy and the boat back into the fold.

There was an opening right now. He had no idea how big or small it was. It could last a week or a year, and he needed to act quickly. It was a wormhole that could lead him to another universe, and it had just opened up right beside him, black as night and with an other-worldly gravitational pull. If he could make Poppy his, really his, then he could have all of it.

He'd been thinking about himself all wrong, limiting his path forward to the professional realm, believing it was his career that would take him higher and higher. But that was too small a scope. It was his personal life, his heart really, that was the fastest path to what he truly wanted. A promotion seemed ridiculous now, measly. He could skip over all of that, past every single rung, and land at the very top. He could marry into the Falcon yacht, Poppy's yacht. A love like this could make a man an owner.

Chapter

47

The stolen Falcon papers were laid out on the table.

"Fun brunch. When I asked what was up, I wanted to know, kind of like, who's sleeping with who on which deck?" Babs poured more coffee for everyone.

"Says the woman who sold the place to begin with," Denise said.

"Are you seriously blaming Mom for this?" Helen bumped her hip into Denise's.

"If I hadn't, I never would've met Janet," Babs said.

A streak of runny egg yolk plopped onto the bottom left corner of one of the papers. Denise, Helen, and Babs were hunched over reading the charts. None of them understood much of anything. None of Denise's late-night amateur research had prepared her for primary documents. And even though her years of working for owners had prepared her for the probability that Raul would lie to her, she still wished she knew why.

"I give up," Babs said. She slumped back in her chair. "I used to mess up the invoices for single jobs. That thing is just—" She waved at the pages and blew air from her cheeks. Then she turned to Janet. "You look. You read charts like this all the time."

"I certainly do. About cow urine," Janet accepted the pages that Denise slid over. She put on her glasses.

Helen finished the plate of eggs. "I got a UTI in Okinawa once, and there was a total lost-in-translation thing going on. It was like, *pee, man, pee, woman,* so for five minutes I could have sworn she was going to try something kinky in that exam room. It was intense. You really can't get cranberry juice in Japan."

Babs aimed a finger at her. "Hey. I bet guavas are good for that, too."

"Well, first of all, two of these pages are the same," Janet frowned, staring down. "There are five documents but only four reports."

Denise stood up and crouched behind Janet to look over her shoulder.

"See here?" Janet said. "The date is different and so is the property ID at the top, but otherwise it's the same data. Look." Janet's finger traced column after column, comparing one page to the other, and she was right. "No offense to you beautiful, gorgeous girls, but that's pretty easy to see. Babs, didn't you teach these girls basic data analysis? Every Sunday that's what I'm doing with my nieces and nephews, you know. It's a life skill these days."

"So is fixing a toilet. We're outdoor cats." Babs smiled and shrugged. "Reason number nine hundred why I'm marrying a vet genius." She put her hands on both sides of Janet's head and planted a kiss on her cheek.

Denise looked like she'd seen a ghost. She turned to Helen. "They fudged it."

Helen clapped. She did not need to be told something juicy twice. "They fudged it alright. We should totally go back in there and get more stuff. Then we'll have a big fat stack of evidence to send in. Where do you even send something like this? Who are we going to call? Or wait, do we go to them directly and do a whole 'Ha! Gotcha!' and *then* we send it in? Probably the whole big gotcha first, right?"

"We need more time," Denise said.

"You need time when they're not on the boat," Babs said.

"Like when the plumbing's down." Helen winked.

"Like bad weather," Babs corrected.

Janet lowered her glasses. "Sweet peas. You need the actual dirt itself. This could be a clerical error. I have given a lot of cows a lot of shots they didn't need because of clerical errors. The moos haunt me. You would need to get your hands on the dirt, or else, even with all of this, you're just hoping these people are telling the truth."

Denise scoffed. "I can't get the dirt. When we left, it was cordoned off like a crime scene. They'd never let me in."

"Plus it's all bogus now, all messed up," Helen added. "Full of concrete and asbestos and chlorine."

"Well, there would have to be the original dirt. Original samples are always best to work from. Whatever they used for this, when they first collected it." Janet tapped the papers.

Denise shook her head. "They probably tossed it."

Janet raised an eyebrow. "Would you?"

Chapter

48

The tenor of the conversation was bending their way—Linnie could feel it.

She was barefoot in the backyard walking the length of the grass between the pool and the pier. Probably about a hundred feet, and flatter than she'd thought; the grade wasn't very steep at all. It could certainly accommodate long tables, a dance floor, for Tim's wedding. It could be angled slightly so the sun would set just there behind the sweetheart table. Put the band on the opposite side nearest the pool. Line the pier with candles inside lanterns—or was that tacky now?

She'd never worked well with square footage and blueprints. Her husband had been the one who could look at a black-and-white floor plan, then see in his mind's eye exactly how the sun would come in through the windows and therefore what kind of art should go along those walls. But she had to walk it. It was important to think about a mass of bodies in the space, not just one but many, bumping and brushing up against one another and bottlenecking. She was a hostess at heart, and the entire point of any space, certainly any beautiful space, was to fill it to the brim with people.

The mood around the collapse had turned sympathetic. She knew it would eventually. This area was made up almost exclusively of waterfront homes with pools. So many had experienced flooding that the general feel was *There but for the grace of God swim I.*

There were some unfortunate murmurings from a few of her well-placed confidants at the statehouse level, however.

That was the only thing that worried her. Between their own ex-orbitant lawyering, airtight permits, and Raul's sign-off, they were as protected as they could possibly be—but was it enough? She had no control over the state-level mood, as much as she tried, and it was poor timing, no doubt about that.

There was a brewing sense of the need for sustainable building and socially responsible design and living in harmony with the nat-ural habitat and all that maudlin nonsense. Linnie rolled her eyes just thinking about it. Nonetheless, it seemed as though a larger clampdown might be in the works. Certain bigwigs might look at this collapse as some kind of showcase of wrongdoing, of putting de-velopment over environment, and try to make an example of them.

But it was only murmuring, so far. And she was doing everything in her power, which was quite a lot, to place fingers on lips and whis-per the soothing phrase *act of God*.

Once the cleanup was well underway, once the chattering crowds piped down, once they were working on the next lagoon site, then she would relax. Then she would set a date for this wedding.

Rose petals in the pool? Too much? Honestly, it would be a party she threw for herself to toast having clawed her way back out of these woods. Twenty lagoon properties, that was the goal she'd set for herself at the beginning of all this, and as soon as they cleared things up, she'd be off to the races again.

Maybe she would invite a few of the people at the statehouse to the wedding. Get out ahead of the whole thing, bring them in close. Why not?

The before and after of the event were the very best parts; she enjoyed those the most. The machinations of planning and strate-gizing, and then, of course, the autopsy afterward. In these phases, she could be alone, as she preferred. It would surprise people to hear that, since she was done up to the nines at every event, function, and fundraiser, the most inexhaustible one among their whole social set. But she was also always alone. The conversations didn't last long, volleys of fluff and flutter cut short by refills, and she was truly happiest on the drive home, going over it all in her mind and tallying it all up. There were so few people with whom she genuinely loved having a conversation. Her husband had been one, and Alden was another, both with minds like hers that floated above and looked down, in every sense, on the scene at hand. A wedding would be such a major operation, but worth it, a celebration. Should it be here at her home? A frame tent at sunset? Or at Tim's house? Where was the farthest hotel she could put Poppy's family? Or should they do the whole thing at the Breakers, where she could simply arrive and let them do it all, include it all, and she'd just sign the egregious invoice.

She didn't want to jinx anything. Things were going their way, slowly but surely, as they should, and the last thing she wanted to do was send up a flare, celebrating at a time like this when they were, of course, so sad, concerned, and contrite. Lanterns would look lovely by the pilings, she decided—wide white candles inside tall glass walls, one by one lighting the way out toward the ocean.

Chapter

49

There will always be clerical errors. Religiously speaking, human history could be chalked up to clerical errors. But this was no clerical error, Denise knew. This was an intentional duplication. Otherwise why would they have changed the date and the property ID and kept everything else the same?

And what would she do about it? After years of ranting and raving to every local environmental official in the zip code, Denise had zero faith that anything brought to their attention would command it. For all their talk of protecting forests and supporting the waterway, she didn't trust them to catch a Filet-O-Fish at a drive-through. With a flick of their finger, the Falcons could make a little complaint like this—the identification of a mere clerical error—disappear.

Heavy rain pounded the boat the whole way back, and the sea rolled enough to keep all the guests cooped up in their rooms. The crew wore neon-yellow jackets, in case they went overboard, and ducked in and out of the suites with bowls of sweet snacks and blankets warmed in the dryer. Denise didn't want to talk to anyone anyway; she needed to think. Her foul-weather gear was zipped up to her chin, and she shivered inside it.

Raul was lying. And what annoyed her most about it right then was that she felt disappointed. She didn't have a lot of friends—okay, fine, if she was being honest, she didn't have any—and it bothered her that the one person in her life to whom the word probably applied (what else were you supposed to call the person who let you borrow their snake-handling gloves?) had lied to her, about this. That he'd done it in her cockpit, sitting in her captain's chair, felt even more cruel.

The duplicate meant that either he never did a soil test at the peninsula site or, more likely, he did one and buried it. What did it say? And was it down there in the office? Or was it somewhere on land where she had no place to stand, zero jurisdiction, and it was out of her reach?

Never question the owners. Ideally, never speak to them at all. Ignore the owners, take matters into your own hands, because no matter how many pairs of gloves you borrow, no matter how high up they reach over your elbows, you can still get bitten.

She needed that dirt.

Chapter

50

They had found the motherlode alright. Helen was so vindicated, Denise would owe her for this for years. She had been home for a week and had basically already saved the family legacy.

This was quickly starting to feel a little bigger and scarier than she'd been anticipating, though. Super fun and exciting to sneak around an owner's office—who didn't love a good old-fashioned sneaking around—but now what? Tango with millionaires or lawyers or more people like that goon Rocco? None of that was her speed. It was important to stay in her lane and contribute to this ongoing investigation by doing what she did best.

She knocked on the door to Poppy's suite.

"Helen!" Poppy sat up in bed with a magazine in her lap and stretched her arms over her head, wiggling her thin fingers. Outside the rain pelted the sides of the boat. The large window that took up the whole wall across from the bed showed a jarring scene of choppy gray waves and towering white storm clouds that spit rain onto the glass.

The thick sky-blue duvet was dotted with half a dozen matching, monogrammed pillows that spilled onto the floor on all sides, as if the bed were a bubbling glass. The low lights gave the walls a warm yellow glow, and the velvet love seats and ottomans were draped in discarded dresses.

Poppy patted the bed next to her. This exact siren song had gotten Helen into considerable trouble in jobs past. Wait. Was Poppy into her? Was she into Poppy? Was that where this was headed? Had she learned a single lesson of any kind at any point in her entire life? Was it hot in here? Thrillingly, surprisingly, her mind actually darted to Jules, that pink hair. When Helen was back, she would go hop the fence again.

Tentatively, she sat down.

"How was dinner last night?" Helen asked. So much had happened last night and this morning—raid, betrayal, cover-up, her mom's engagement—she'd almost forgotten about Poppy kissing Geoff. It occurred to Helen now that she could use this knowledge in some way, couldn't she? She could threaten to expose Poppy to Tim if she didn't reveal every single thing she knew about Lagoongate.

But did Poppy know anything? It sure didn't seem that way. And blowing up their little friendship right now would be shortsighted. Better to keep a source like her close for the long haul. Helen was getting smarter at crime by the minute.

"Dinner took forever," Poppy sighed. "I'm still so tired." She yawned. "You know how they say eating turkey makes you sleepy? I think that same thing's in papayas. I came right home to bed after dinner and slept all night, but it's just never enough sleep, you know?"

Right. So she was comfortable telling Helen she had a big old crush on Geoff but not that she'd acted on it. "Well, you're not missing anything out there," Helen said, tipping her head toward the window. "Roid Rage Steve Irwin came out to try and do pull-ups and he slipped on the deck."

Poppy laughed and covered her mouth. She had a great laugh. "Too bad he didn't go overboard. Hey, I was thinking—and you don't have to say yes if you think it's weird," she started. Helen braced herself. "But would you want to come over sometime, for a drink? To my house? We could just hang out, like this. But no pressure, I understand if you don't think it's a good idea, or if you're not allowed to."

Helen relaxed her shoulders and smiled. Denise was so lucky to have her sister here; she had no idea. Helen raised her hand for a high five, and Poppy slapped it. "Game on."

Chapter

51

When Geoff returned from the Bahamas, the volume of nonsense that awaited him back at his desk was astonishing.

To no one's surprise, Fern had failed to keep visitors at bay, and there was a stack of what the woman claimed were applications—names penned on a yellow legal pad—of people who wished to store their boats here. Regular boats.

And, as usual, there were crew complaints galore, from the inadequacy of meals on board to the never-ending stream of personal vendettas between young staff members of opposite sexes. The problem with Fern was that she listened to these people and probably even went so far as to nod.

Fortunately the only owner issues that surfaced were simple enough—he'd been gone for only twenty-four hours, after all—and just required him to make a few polite calls to confirm a bar mitzvah performer's tolerance for wind.

On top of all this, Geoff was utterly bone-tired after staying up all night, flying commercial, and coming to terms with a potential new world order for himself. After he'd squirted water onto all these little fires, he placed his head down sideways on the desk and looked out to the docks for a bleary moment before closing his eyes.

When a police officer walked into the room, Geoff wasn't sure whether he was dreaming.

"Sir?" The bell chimed at the door. The officer took off her hat and uncapped a pen.

Geoff greeted her by wiping drool from his mouth. "Hello, yes, oh my, hello, miss, ma'am, madam."

She sidled up to the desk and put down her small notebook, in which Geoff could see the single word *Ahoy*, underlined.

He swallowed hard and stood up straight. "How can I help you?"

"Officer Liu." She extended her hand, and he shook it. "I'm here about what happened next door."

"The Falcon building? Oh, yes, yes. Quite sad. Tragic, really. Have there been any updates?"

"Yeah, no. Heracanes, actually." The officer cocked her head left toward the retirement community. "We found one of the residents passed."

Geoff raised an eyebrow.

"I know. But the deceased was found out in the bushes, under some of the plants over on the far side, the Falcon property side, yesterday morning. You didn't know about this?"

"I've just returned," he rushed to say and put a hand over his heart. "I was in the Bahamas until just this morning, at our office there. We have cameras all across campus, and the logs keep track of everyone's whereabouts. A memorable woman named Fern was here at the desk, and she keeps outstanding records. Truly, there are lists of everyone who sets foot here, from staff to sire, and who is on board every single one of our vessels at all times, so I can assure you that—"

She raised both hands and lowered them slowly. "Whoa. Not necessary. This is more of a courtesy call. The body wasn't on your property or anything, but neighbors and all. We don't really think anything was going on, but—"

Geoff opened his mouth and leaned forward.

"Yes, I am aware. They are elderly. But the staff at Heracanes called us anyway," she continued. "Came as some big shock apparently, so we're just asking around in case anyone's seen anything out of the ordinary recently."

"It was found . . . outdoors?"

"She. Yes. Next to one of those . . ." The officer used both hands to make swooping chopping motions. "The hedge trimmer things."

"Good Lord." Geoff recoiled and brought both hands to his neck.

"No, no, no. Sorry, nothing like that. I just always wanted to try those things, but I don't really have much of a yard. No maiming, really. But the hedge trimmer things looked like they belonged to you all—they had *Ahoy* written on the handle."

"Oh, God." Geoff deflated.

The officer tapped her pen on the notebook. "Have you seen anyone, not one of your normal people, come in and out of here recently? You said you have lists?"

Geoff nodded vigorously. "We've actually considered putting a stronger fence in, see, because we do get the occasional trespasser. A paparazzo or two has been known to pop by, if you can believe it, if one of our clients is in the news that week. We have very newsworthy clients. Is that interesting?" He found it very interesting.

"Not really." And yet she jotted down a note. "Yeah. Alright, well, here's a photo, ask around if you want, but no need to get people riled up. Please don't—I really don't want a bunch of bad calls. And here's my card. Call me if you hear something. But honestly, there's very little reason to think it was anything other than an old timer's time, sorry to say, probably some dehydration. Even in the winter, it's hotter out there than people think. Like I said, I don't have much of a yard, but you know, it's hard work. Anyway, sorry to bother you."

"No bother at all. Thank you very much, officer."

She put her hat back on, tucked her notepad into her back pocket, and left.

Good Lord. What if one of the owners had waltzed in and seen a police officer standing here, taking notes from Geoff, or overheard some kind of easily misconstrued comment about trespassers?

He watched as Officer Liu walked the fence along the property line. At the end where the fence reached the water, she put both hands onto the railing and easily hoisted herself over and disappeared into the bushes there, onto the Heracanes property.

Geoff shivered to imagine it, a patch of flesh through the leaves, a hand in the dirt, seeing a body on the ground when one was simply trying to enjoy some shrubbery in bloom. Thank God it hadn't happened here.

He stared down at the photo. Who was this person?

Part
Three

Chapter

52

An explosion is the easiest thing. Bing, bam, boom, and I mean boom. Twenty thousand gallons of gas in one of those tanks. And if the boat's in the marina, what do you call twenty thousand times five or six boats all lined up in a row? Not great.

Easiest by a long shot. Two main ways it can happen, and in fact, most boats have experienced some kind of fire—it's very common. Seems like a huge deal, but once you think about it, how much gas is around and how many ignition opportunities there are down there, it adds up. In 99 percent of situations, it's nothing a little squirt of the old extinguisher can't fix, but it happens all the time.

What are you doing on the boat nonstop? Feeding those people. Cooking all hours of the day—stove, oven, bananas goddamned Foster—from what I understand they just don't stop eating. Propane is a very heavy gas, as maybe you know, so it sinks down to the lowest point in the boat. Loose copper fittings, distracted chef, you name it, and that means there's just a lot of propane down there in general.

And what else, you ask, is down there?

The engine room is full of about a zillion sources of sparks. You've got dozens of ignitions that control everything on the whole boat. You're switching on the pumps, lights, motors, generators, all of it. So now you've got a room full of gas, and like every safety video's ever said, all it takes is one. One spark. And that's assuming you don't have any smokers on board, and you always do, no matter what. All those health nuts are lying.

Now, for sure, you're supposed to be running a vent check. This falls into the very big category of things that slip your captain's mind. You're supposed to run it during the pre-ignition check and post-ignition check, coming and going in and out of the dock, but does the vent check happen every single time? You're the insurance guys, you tell me. Vent check would, in theory, make sure your boat's not filling up with gas. But here we are today. If people stuck to the protocols in life, you guys would be out of a job.

Second way you see explosions happen is in the garage. Just like your garage at home, there's a whole area below the main part of the boat filled to the brim with every toy you can imagine—inflatables, Zodiacs, Jet Skis. Yacht's a babushka doll. And those things, even a little ten-foot blow-up with an outboard, have gas in them. Tiny tanks, sure, but gas tanks get gas leaks, and again, all kinds of ways to ignite a little spark down there. Call that one the Yamaha Trojan Horse.

Sorry, I don't mean to be rude. I see you trying to get a word in and ask something. But I already know what you're going to ask—it's the big, fat, obvious question. Isn't there some alarm? Sensors? Some big flashing red light if there's gas around? Red alert on the captain's dashboard?

I don't even know if I can explain to you how sophisticated the fail-safe systems on these boats are. I mean, I know I can't. Six years studying electrical engineering and another twenty doing it, and all I can say is, you have to be goddamned determined to screw something up on one of these things. These are machines that do not like to break, and when they even think about breaking, they whine like little babies. You clog a toilet and the captain gets alerted, I am not kidding.

So there's a bunch of gas down in the engine room? Uh, yeah, you're getting the alert of a lifetime. But where are you getting it? Five, ten years ago, big red lights flashing, a few annoying alarms going off that everybody can hear. But today? Your phone buzzes. There are lights on the console, don't get me wrong, especially for something like that, but you can see everything, check everything, hear about everything right on your *little phone. Captain likes it, he can go walk around or, better yet, press a button on his phone instead of walking all the way down there to check something out. Owner likes it, it's not freaking out the guests.*

I'll save you the tuition money and sum it up for you like this: Anything you can turn on, you can turn off. I bet you didn't think my little old NSA resume bullet point would come up in this interview, did you? But just think about it. You put something like that on somebody's phone, the ability to control every single mechanical system on an eighty-foot boat on something that fits in your pocket. All the fail-safes, alarms, alerts, engine controls, fire suppression, water-level notifications, you control the whole thing from right there. You can even steer the thing from your phone—the autopilot control is on there, no joke.

If it works, it can also not work. If you can check the engine lights and then go check the sports scores, you can get in there. Someone can get in there. You can stop getting those alerts. You can stop those alerts from even existing.

This is my point. Then I'll wrap it up for you. In a catastrophic situation like you're describing, there are two things that need to happen. First, someone needs to get in and shut down the alarms, so that when, second, someone breaks something, no one knows about it. There's a hacker and there's a hammer, and those are two very different people.

You're talking to the hacker.

Chapter

53

"So you found the jumbo load," Randy said.

He gave a thumbs-up to the two people in pastels who were sitting on the bench at the end of the wide pier. The taxi drifted toward them and gently nudged the edge of the dock. The couple stood up and held on to the silver railing at the front of the taxi, then ducked beneath the purple scalloped awning and stepped onto the boat. The older gentleman walked over and handed Randy a fifty from a wallet clipped to his belt.

"And no idea how to unload it." Denise ripped off a bite of her sandwich and loudly cracked a beer she'd taken from Randy's personal cooler at his feet.

The documents were safely in her condo. She'd slid them under one of her tanks, which were incredibly heavy and housed tarantulas.

Was she supposed to break into Raul's office now? Was there a lab somewhere? She really needed to stop breaking into places. She was not someone who did that; that was a one-time thing, under dire circumstances, and would never happen again. And what if she took all this to the authorities? Any leverage she had would be gone, forked over to some bureaucratic bonehead in the pocket of Big Falcon. And then the Falcons would probably get her fired from Ahoy, Geoff's dream come true, and blacklist her from every marina on the Eastern Seaboard.

Randy backed the taxi out into the waterway. He headed to the next restaurant for an exchange of passengers. All night long, he'd thread in and out of the neighborhood fabric, from hotels to happy hours to dinners and desserts, stitching W's along the water. It wasn't like he could tag along with Denise to her job—so, more often than not, these evenings on his taxi were the only date nights they got. Randy's captains came and went, turnover was high, and he ended up driving the boats himself most days to fill in the gaps. He pretended to be annoyed about it but loved the chitchat.

"Why don't you just get on the horn, call up Raul, and play dumb," Randy said. "Do some turtle talk or whatever you guys get into and just ask, 'Oh hey, I was just wondering, any reason why one place might have the exact same soil as another place?' Listen, not to advocate for the guy, but you like him alright, so maybe there's an A-OK reason. It's possible. I'm telling you, those big companies got so many gears grinding you wouldn't believe it." He shivered. Before he escaped to the water taxi business, he'd worked in mind-numbing middle management for a faceless insurance behemoth and spoke about the corporate realm in the traumatized tone of a released captive.

"Call him?" Denise shook her head. "He'd know something was up. We never talk about work, ever. And you know I don't call."

"Why would he want to work with those guys anyway? He's got piles of dough already. And man, I bet he's sorry now, damn. Big old investment right down the drain, boom, and take the worms with you. Does he really believe no one's going to find out about this? What is wrong with those people? I'm telling you, baby, you can trust absolutely no one in this world; that's all I'm hearing. Except you." He had an arm around her waist and pulled her close to kiss her on the cheek.

"Except I stole something," she muttered.

"Now, that was the right thing to do."

Randy turned away to burp. He wore his leather vest over his yellow Conch Cab T-shirt, and it warmed her heart. The vest was a security blanket, she knew, when he wanted to feel a little extra tough, and she understood he'd been badly spooked by the collapse. Every hour they'd had together since, he'd held on to her as much as he could, as though if he let go, she might sink down into the ground or something might fall and crush her. She liked it, and it surprised her how much and how quickly she'd adjusted to more overt moments of affection like this one than they'd ever had before. It was like they'd needed the excuse all along, a fear to huddle against.

Randy would have been handsome in any decade, any century, in any culture on earth. Tan enough to be ethnically ambiguous— people were always coming up to him and speaking their own language, and he loved it. He would tell you he could say hello in a dozen ways. Denise could picture him on a horse, in a railroad car, or in a curly white wig and white tights; see his face perfectly framed through the orange-tinted glass of an astronaut's helmet. An even mustache, a perpetual five-o'clock shadow, and a nose slightly bent so you might think he'd been in a fight or two, though Denise knew he was just clumsy. He was trendless and perfect and, somehow, hers, for going on two years now. It was so much longer than she'd ever allowed any other relationship to go on, but in the handful of times that she thought it was too much, that she needed to stay focused on her job, or that she just preferred her own company, the thought of never again standing here like this—side by side on the water, listening to his voice, her bare arm up against that soft leather—made her feel, in fact, like being swallowed into a dark hole.

He gave the side of her thigh a little squeeze. "Hey, if you do call him," Randy said, "do one of those three-way calls so the cops can listen in, or record it on your computer, just in case he says something, because you never know. I'm serious. That's how I nailed the lady who sold me the busted hot tub."

At the end of another hotel pier, an old couple stood too close to the edge and waved Randy down, hailing their chariot to Chris's Crab Club and beyond.

"It just pisses me off," Denise said. "It was completely buried in there. If we hadn't been on the boat, gotten in there—"

"And listened to Helen." Randy gave a huge smile to the couple and his twentieth thumbs-up of the night. "Where is she, by the way? Did you tell her she could come along? I was kind of hoping she'd come, too; she hasn't been out on a shift yet. She'd probably be putting on a show and getting this tip jar filled up." He clicked his tongue at the empty cheese ball tip tub. "You're distracting me from making big bucks, you know."

"She's at Poppy's house," Denise grumbled.

Randy raised his wooly eyebrows. "Slick thinking. She's a smart cookie, your sister. You think we should cruise over there and check on her? I'll get onto that pier and go piss in their pool if you say the word."

"What word would that be?"

"Justice." He kissed her on the top of the head.

Once all the passengers were off, the boat tootled around a bend, and the waterway opened up before them. The sun was setting, spilling ripples of orange across the water. The peninsula came into view as they headed home, the thick green leaves waving them to shore, but as they got closer, they could see that it looked all wrong.

The lagoon lot was an enormous gray blotch, spiky mounds of charcoal debris that took up the whole square. On either side, the flowers, pink and purple borders of bougainvillea, were now drooping and dying—long, thick vines coated in white dust, like a row of octopus ghosts.

The boat pulled closer and approached Randy's pier. It was

unusually quiet along the shoreline, and all they could hear was the hum of the motor and the flap of the scalloped cloth awning in the wind. There was no music, no clinking of glasses, no arguments, no doors closing, no one jumping in the pool, no smack of bocce balls, no voices at all.

Because at Heracanes, the entire yard was a crisscross hatch of yellow police tape.

Denise took Randy's hand.

Chapter

54

The gate wasn't picking up her bicycle. Helen rammed the front wheel into the metal a few times, and nothing happened. On either side of her were towering boxwood hedges topiaried into the shape of judgmental birds. It took her a few minutes to see the small metal box nestled among the leaves, and finally she backed up and pressed the button. The bike pedal scraped the front of her shin, and for the tenth time that morning she cursed Denise for not letting her borrow either her truck or Ahoy's golf cart.

"Yes?" It was not Poppy's voice that came through the speaker.

"It's Helen? Here to see Poppy?"

A long moment passed during which Helen plucked some little green branches and wove them into her bike wheels.

Finally the gate opened. The white stones making up the front wall of the enormous house were perfect rectangular boulders the size of refrigerators and for some reason made her think of half-naked Egyptians hauling them over here on wooden rafts across the river. Several cars were parked out front in the circular driveway around a mermaid fountain. Helen weaved her bike around them, barely scratching them. The windows were ten feet high and arced, and inside Helen could see a crowd of people.

The heavy wooden front door opened with a hard push. Inside, the foyer ceiling had to be thirty feet high. To her left was a light-filled pale green room with a grand piano and a long buffet table topped with a symphony of sandwiches. The condiment station alone took up the entire end of the table, with colors and textures of sauces Helen had never seen before. A dozen people in pleated slacks milled around and made themselves plates. She helped herself.

"Hey. Hi. What's up?" she greeted each of them, and they smiled tightly back and tried not to stare. She stuffed candies from a bowl into the pockets of her jean cutoffs. The setup was perfectly in line with her idea of what a mansion would be like inside: a massive buffet open to anyone who got in.

"Helen!" Poppy put a hand on her elbow. "Oh, do you want this?" She looked down at the sandwiches like they confused her.

Poppy sped through the house like she was trying to escape it, leaving Helen no time to look around the way she wanted to. They pushed through a set of French doors that opened to the outrageous backyard. The epic lawn looked freshly argyled by a mower in alternating shades of green. It sloped down toward the water, and along the way was a bean-shaped turquoise pool with smaller bean-shaped hot tubs on either side. There were three stone patios, each with slightly different water views and arrangements of lounge chairs. To the right, by the house, there was a full kitchen, grill, bar, and long dining table shaded by a pergola. A blue hummingbird actually hovered by the dining set, and Helen thought it might fly over and drape a napkin across her lap.

Poppy led them to one of the patios, where a bright green pitcher and glasses were waiting for them. A tiny bowl of pistachios confirmed that Helen had made the right choice with the sandwiches.

The waterway was widest here. There were so many boats passing by and so many houses to spy on from a nice, semi-hidden distance, Helen leaned back in her chair and never, ever wanted to leave. No wonder this woman put up with Tim.

Denise has got to see this view, Helen thought. But she just as quickly pushed the thought out of her mind. Denise had no interest in the people she worked for, she might as well have been a cargo ship captain, and last night she'd read Helen the riot act about coming here. The same old song and dance about how Poppy wasn't her friend, what was the point of getting close to those people, why couldn't Helen understand professional boundaries—the usual.

If all Helen ever got out of today was this fancy lunch, wasn't that worth something? Not everything in life required a mission, not every activity had to be "executed." If Denise had ever tried to get to know the people she worked for, Helen thought, her sister probably would've uncovered about a hundred scandals by now. She could be a total vigilante captain, pulling back the covers on all kinds of shady stuff these high rollers were up to. That's definitely what Helen would do if she kept working on the boats—this whole thing had given her a real taste of the spy life.

It tasted like margaritas.

Poppy released a high-pitched sigh in the seat beside her and lifted her feet onto a little decorative stool. Her bare toes were weirdly perfect, soft-looking, the nails painted with pink glitter polish. Helen tucked her worn brown flip-flops beneath her chair.

"I'm so glad you're here," Poppy said, turning toward Helen with a smile. "Sorry about the whole . . . crowd in there. It's just one of those days. This happens kind of a lot, with all the family stuff. But this is actually more people than usual. Sometimes they're at Linnie's house. Alyssa doesn't like them to be at Alden's house, though, with the kids and all? So they come here sometimes, when it's the weekend."

Helen twisted in her chair and reached for the margarita pitcher.

"Oh, no. No, no." Poppy tapped her hand, and Helen yanked it back onto her lap. Instantly a short woman in a white button-down rushed in front of the table, poured them both drinks, and disappeared in under ten seconds.

Poppy raised her glass. "Cheers! I hope you don't think this is weird, I know it probably looks like it's out of a movie or something. I mean, I used to think that! I just haven't really hung out with anyone in so long and, you know, Tim's mom introduces me to people but they're just kind of different than my friends from back home, you know? And old? And so it's been . . . well, and when I met you, I thought . . ."

"We could probably be best friends?" Helen downed her large glass and wondered whether she had to wait on that lady for every refill.

"Yes!" Poppy beamed as if Helen had just proposed to her. "And sorry I wasn't around yesterday on the boat—I was just so tired. Jet lag. Boat lag?"

Helen nodded and launched into her best story about how crossing the equator once on a cruise ship gave her vertigo. She desperately wanted to bring up the Geoff situation, but considering how well this was all going, having fallen backward into a dear friendship with a millionaire, she decided to wait a minute before she farted in the golden elevator.

"So who are they? They don't really look like the 1:00 p.m. spicy marg crowd."

"Lawyers," she whispered. "And some accountants, too, but I can never tell those apart."

"What do you think a group of lawyers is called?" Helen smiled and, screw it, helped herself to another pour. "A stiff? A frump?"

Poppy's eyes didn't budge. "I think it's called a firm."

Helen poured to the brim. "So, you windsurf? I saw one out there."

"It's Tim's life's work," Poppy said solemnly. "He's gifted. And I might be into painting, I think, as a hobby for myself. I really need one. I did some portraits of some people who work here. And Tim says I should sell them, but then I figured who else would want the portrait except the person I painted? So I asked Elena if she wanted the painting of her, but Tim's estimation was six thousand dollars for it, and so I don't know. I decided I'm going to give them to everyone as their Christmas bonus this year, because of the re-sale value. It's better than cash—it's an investment, that's what Al-den's wife, Alyssa, told me about the sculpture they got of their dog Hotchkiss."

"Hey, you want to hear something crazy?" She wasn't sure what she was doing, but a couple of drinks in seemed like the right time to level up their bonding in a grand-gesture kind of way.

Poppy leaned closer, eyes wide, and cupped her drink with both hands.

"So, the condo that just fell down, that location. You know I used to live there. That was my house."

Poppy's whole face fell. "What?" She drew herself back away from Helen.

"So weird, right? I grew up there. Before it was a condo and that whole thing, it was just a normal house. One story. Super small, just me and my mom. My sister, Denise, you know her—"

"Captain Denise is your sister?" Poppy opened her mouth wider than Helen felt that news really deserved. She was blowing this girl's mind with the basic boring facts of her life.

"Yup. Tough draw. Anyhoo, she's ten years older than me, so she was up and out of there pretty soon, and it was just me and my mom. I was basically a junior plumber in high school, so if you ever need anything . . . Then she moved, then the melanoma lady, and then I guess you guys bought the place. And now, here we are!" Helen looked over at the now-empty pitcher.

Poppy slowly closed her mouth, and for a split second Helen watched the turn of the woman's lips decide her fate. They curved up into a smile.

She reached out her hand to touch Helen's. "Okay, now can I tell you something crazy?"

"Please."

She put her hand on her heart. "I feel like somehow I already knew this. Because don't we totally have a connection? As soon as I met you, I told Tim, 'Helen is so cool, I feel like she understands me.' And now I know why! And guess what, it was always me and my mom, too. I always wished I had a sister. And how crazy is it that you guys lived at the same place as the condos? It's like destiny that we're hanging out right now—I kind of love it. I really needed this."

Helen relaxed her shoulders but felt a wave of guilt course through her. Poppy really was lonely, and Helen really was not her friend, at least not the way Poppy thought she was.

"I'm going to run to the bathroom," Helen said. "Be right back."

Poppy delivered a complicated set of directions that Helen paid no attention to. She started off over the lawn toward the doors.

Inside, she helped herself to a tour. She walked around the kitchen island, made a pit stop back at the buffet table, which had been cleared and cleaned, used the bathroom, then walked a figure eight around the living room. The number of decorative bowls filled with glossy seashells boggled her mind.

Voices rose from yet another room. Going down a long wide hall lit by rattan chandeliers, she glanced at all the family photographs along the maroon walls. These people were obsessed with horses and oars. Poppy did not appear in a single picture.

At the end of the hall, a set of double doors was open to a large library, filled with people. Helen stepped closer.

A large whiteboard took up one end of the room, and a bunch of papers were taped to it like on some kind of TV murder show, minus the red string. There was a small photograph at the bottom right of the board. White hair was all Helen could make out.

"Helen!" Poppy whisper-yelled from behind her. "What are you doing?" She had her hands on her hips, then reached out to grab Helen's arm and pull her away, hard. "Tim would be so mad at me," Poppy said as soon as she had pushed Helen out onto the lawn.

"It's your house, too."

Poppy shook her head and widened her eyes, looking down at the ground. "I hate it when they're here, it's so . . ." She flexed her fingers and shook them in the air.

They both sat down again, and Helen reached out to place a hand on Poppy's shoulder. "Hey, sorry. It's alright. This is your house, dude. You can do whatever you want here."

Poppy's shoulders drooped. "It's like I'm supposed to know how to act with all those kinds of people, and all the questions they ask me. But I have no idea! And we thought it was over. Linnie told me that it was all winding down—like no more reporters, no more lawyers. It was getting better. Back to normal, she said. But then just yesterday morning, a bunch of them showed up again. I don't know what's happening. Did we do something wrong? It's every week now. And I mean, I do like having people around—you know me."

"But not squares like that," Helen said.

Poppy smiled and nodded. "They are pretty nice. It just makes Tim all stressed-out, too—that's why he's not out here. We're supposed to be working on this whole rebrand for the business expansion, and obviously this isn't the most creative headspace for him. He's at the rock-climbing wall."

"Expansion?" Helen's eyebrows lifted. "Guess when you're down, nowhere to go but up."

"We have to be careful with the word *down* now. But, yeah, there are all these other locations they want to do the lagoons in, and people, like, really want them, they want to move in, and it's a lot of pressure on all of us. We're striking while the iron's hot, but it takes a lot of teamwork."

Helen was having a hard time parsing Poppy's own thoughts from fun corporate phrases she'd picked up. "What is the iron?" Helen asked.

Poppy plowed ahead. "We're going to tell Linnie and Alden about the whole new brand tonight at dinner. We're going to surprise them with our pitch. Do you want to hear it?"

"Absolutely."

Poppy sat up straight and tucked her legs beneath her. "At first, we thought it should be really focused on height and maybe also steel, you know, the big metals. It was all really gray and, like, beam themed. But then Tim had this thought, and he's so right, shouldn't it be about fun? That's why people move into a new apartment, because they're looking to have more fun."

". . . Right."

"Right! So we made it all about the beach. The big colors for the flowers, how you can walk down to the water, feel the sand on your feet, maybe see a dolphin, hop on your boat—powerboat or sailboat—order a drink."

"Community boats there? Love that. And a bar?"

"Well, no. But, maybe! I mean that's fun for people to imagine, way more fun. And that's what a Falcon building is all about, especially right now."

"Fun."

Poppy nodded so hard her hair bounced along her shoulders. "Right?"

Helen squirmed in her chair. She wasn't sure how much time she had left here. "Okay, feel free to tell me to go fly a kite, but I kind of wanted to tell you something. Sort of about what you told me the other day."

"Tim is big into kitesurfing, by the way." Poppy held the bowl of shelled pistachios and ate them one by one.

"Cool, so speaking of fun—I was sleeping outside in the hammock the other night, the Bahamas night, and I saw you and Geoff."

The temperature of the air around them dropped ten degrees. Poppy went rigid for a moment, holding a pistachio midair, before turning her head side to side, then back to Helen. Her eyes were drained of the excitement they had held a moment ago.

"It's awesome," Helen said, raising her hands in surrender. "It's me, you can tell me whatever. I know it's probably super complicated—I get it. I just wanted you to know that I know. Seemed like something I should tell you, since we're friends now. I mean, I know you told me you had a little crush and all that, so cute. But then I saw you guys, and I'm excited for you. Go for the gold, girlfriend. I haven't told anyone, obviously."

"You probably told your sister," Poppy crossed her arms.

Helen barked out a laugh. "Yeah, no, of all people, I would not be telling Denise. You shouldn't tell her either—she's not wild about Geoff. Though, now that I think about it, she would say he's better than Tim. Low bar. For her, I mean. Not you. He's great. Is he?"

Poppy took two handfuls of her caftan as though she was wringing it out. "Helen, this is really bad."

"Well, talk to me, what's up with you two? If you're really feeling something with Geoff and, I mean, not to be a complete creep but it looked like there was some genuine feeling there, then just go with that. You're not married. And I actually have no problem with him—I like Geoff, I think. He's got that whole British rom-com look going on with the hair, very vintage."

"I'm getting married."

Helen started to roll her eyes, then thought better of it and stopped halfway like she'd seen a bird. "When? And so what? At this point it's just a ring. Take it off, and you're free to go. Rip off that really nice cover-up, jump in the water butt naked, and swim to finer pastures, Pops."

Poppy leaned forward. "They would chase me. They gave me a boat. I own their boat."

"So give it back. They're not going to, like, sue you."

They both turned to look at the house filled with lawyers.

"I don't really want to talk about it anymore." Poppy stood abruptly and put her hands on her hips. "Now I have to get ready for my meeting, okay? I'm probably going to do a lot of the talking."

Helen fumbled up and out of her chair. Why hadn't she asked more questions about what the lawyers were doing? Why hadn't she talked to one of them? Why hadn't she taken a single sip of water?

"You can go out that way." Poppy pointed with a wag of her finger to a dark-green back door camouflaged within the nearest hedge.

"Okay. I guess, see you on the boat?"

Poppy nodded once and gave Helen a stiff little pat-pat on the arm. Then Poppy walked over to the house and stood in the doorway as if barring Helen from going inside again and creeping around—which was exactly what she'd planned to do on her way out.

Helen poured the remaining pistachios into her mouth straight from the bowl and walked toward the hedges, to the door for the help.

Chapter

55

Before she'd been to Tim's house, Poppy had never really considered how limited her thoughts about painting rooms had been. If she ever thought about painting interiors at all, it was all rollers, tarps, blue tape, picking out a color at the hardware store. But it made sense to hire a real artist, and murals didn't always have to be outside. This was a good example of how the family had expanded her horizons.

The Falcons' muraled dining room was beautiful, but she did find it hard to concentrate there. Every time she looked at one of the walls, there was something else to see, a full 360 degrees of art. It was a marsh scene, with blue-gray waters and swaying brown cattails, white lilies and green palms, birds and bugs overhead in every size, and all kinds of creatures along the water's edge: frogs, flamingos, half-submerged snakes, peeking jaguars. The mural wasn't menacing at all—if anything, it was strangely childlike wrapping for the room's chandeliered grandeur—but there was something eerie about it she could never shake. Maybe it did feel a bit like a nursery. She wished that tonight, her big moment to present the new brainstorming ideas to the family, they could have been sitting in a room where lizards' eyes didn't follow her around. But these were the new challenges she had to face in life.

Around the table, which had been relieved of a leaf for the tight-knit occasion, sat Tim, Poppy, Linnie, Alden, and Alden's wife, Alyssa, who'd greeted Poppy during cocktail hour with an oversize navy blue bow in her hair and complaints about mixing gin with acid reflux.

Tonight, the meal was buffet-style, and Poppy had just gone for seconds when Tim pushed his chair back and stood up. Poppy returned quickly to the table, sat down beside him, and put down her fork. She frowned at her crab cake.

Tim held up the stack of laminated and bound presentations, five pages long, that his assistant had finished that morning.

"It's Tim!" Alyssa shouted as if she'd just realized he was here. He winked at her.

"Oh, dear," Linnie said, and she looked at Alden, whose face was frozen with his mouth open. The ice in Linnie's drink dinged like tiny bells; summoned, a server slipped in to refill her glass and used small silver tongs to place a sliced lime on top. "You didn't think, I mean, not now that we're dealing with that woman—Aldie, didn't you speak to him?"

"It's a lot, don't I know it, so buckle up, fam." Tim clapped one of his verbal exclamation points. Everyone flinched. Poppy had told him before that he should maybe keep his clapping to the outdoors, but he told her he liked to live in his own soundscape.

"We start by picturing all of this, coming alive!" he swept his arms around the room's painted wildlife.

Poppy looked up at him and pushed her lips out into her biggest possible smile. Her waterlogged heart tried to soar; it really did. She usually loved watching him like this, but now, suddenly, her chest felt heavy and sealed off, unable to open itself up as usual to Tim's voice and energy. He was not having his usual effect. And as she looked around the table, she saw that she was not the only one who was unmoved.

"To feel like nature is all around, there are no walls, there are no roofs, no structures at all to even think about, only sand, sky, ocean, and you, under the stars, a child of the earth, hammocking in an Eden's paradise of Falcon properties." He slipped his hand into his pocket and pressed a button: Whale sounds emanated across the table.

Linnie rarely looked confused, but she did now. "Alden, you told me you spoke to him this afternoon."

Poppy kept her smile up just in case the talk turned to why she made the choice of a photo of a falcon in a flower lei for the cover page. She had an answer ready.

Alden swallowed a large bite of chicken he'd taken off Alyssa's plate and nodded. "Tim, about getting the legal team on the boat?" Then he turned to face Poppy. "Poppy, did you talk to Geoff? This is really your thing now. That was the whole point of this. I don't want to speak to the guy."

"Geoff?" All eyes turned to Poppy. She hadn't realized how loud her voice would sound over the whales.

"Yup, Pop Quiz is on the case," Tim said and spread his arms wide to clap again before he saw his fiancée's face.

"Tim?"

This wasn't at all what her part of the presentation was supposed to be about. And she had no idea what case she was on.

"It's cool, Popcorn. We're going to host some of the lawyers, the ones who were here today. You met them—they're chill, right? We'll all be on the boat tomorrow, whamming and jamming, so just let Geoff know. There's a list, I'll send it to you pronto."

"You haven't sent it yet?" Alden clanked his fork down.

Tim was still standing. "Hey, I'm working here! Little preoccu- pied with *your* rebrand, thank you very much. And this is just the dress rehearsal because we're going to give this same presentation to the legal eagles tomorrow. Only, check it out, for the whole 'Look around you, nature is three-sixty' part, it'll be the actual ocean."

Linnie put her napkin on her plate. "Timothy, dear, why don't you send over everything Poppy needs to make the boat arrangements. Let's get that settled tonight, since they're all arriving, from what I understand, very early in the morning. Thank you for this." She held up the laminated presentation.

Poppy shot up and stood next to Tim. She had been seriously looking forward to the moment that was promised to her, of standing up in front of the family to deliver a business insight. "This can really turn things around, toward the future. I think it's really good."

"I don't doubt you do," Linnie said. "But we're in a rather deep crisis right now, which I'm sure Tim has explained a bit to you. And we need to put this . . . initiative . . . on the back burner until things are sorted out. You are doing excellent work liaising with the boat people, and I'm sure you'll be as wonderful a host at sea as you are on land."

Linnie had attended one event hosted by Poppy, a fundraiser for mosquito bites, where Tim's band had performed and she had tripped over a cord for the smoke machine and fallen into the pool.

Tim hadn't told her anything about a crisis. The last thing he told her was that the cleanup at the peninsula site was going "tubular."

He sat down and leaned with both his forearms on the table toward Alden, who had yet to stop eating for a breath. Tim was saying something about Alden being shortsighted, how a crisis was the perfect time to rebrand and he was thinking too small, all of which Poppy probably agreed with. But she wasn't going to chime in; she wasn't even going to put her hand on his back and rub little circles.

She knotted her fingers together in her lap, and her belly roiled with a little flame of anger. No one was telling her whether this was a new crisis or the same one and whether they were connected, or if there would just kind of always be a little bit of crisis going on all the time here and she needed to grow up and get used to it, and whether

Alyssa knew about it while she didn't, or if Alden and Alyssa talked like that, if they talked about work and the family and didn't keep things from each other, and maybe she could talk to Alyssa about things sometime, pull her into that big bathroom after dinner and just mention—what, exactly?—something about Tim or something about Geoff; Alyssa had probably seen Geoff at some point, and maybe she was someone Poppy could talk to about whatever was happening, about this dizziness and this anger that really should be directed at herself, because if she hadn't been thinking about Geoff like crazy all week, replaying their time together in her head over and over again, then she probably would know why she was supposed to host a lawyer luau and what kind of a crisis it was, and she wouldn't have to try to talk about it with Alyssa, who Poppy thought didn't really like her all that much, but maybe they just hadn't had a chance to—

"Babe."

A palm covered her hands, which had balled themselves into fists.

"You good to ram it out with Geoff tonight? Just get him to come over if you need a powwow sesh. Just sent you the list—you two can make some last-minute magic happen. Not like we haven't pulled it off before, right, Ald-man?"

Poppy's lips parted, and it felt like she was nodding.

"Mmm. Squash it to me, baby," Tim said through a mouthful he'd scooped from her plate. "We cool?" He aimed his fork across the table, and Alden and Alyssa both nodded.

Tim had just told her to invite Geoff over to their house.

Her fingers puddled into her lap. He would be here, she thought; he would sit beside her, doing whatever it was they'd been told to do, together, and she would not have to look around a room and wonder what on earth anyone was talking about. He was like her, he understood her, he would know how to help her, and he would want to. He didn't want to be with anyone else; he didn't look over her shoulder when she talked. She wouldn't have to wonder about a thing. And if she did, she could simply ask, and she would not have to pretend. It wouldn't have to feel anymore as if her legs and arms were exhausted from treading water all the time, and that felt so, so good.

Chapter

56

Could he, at 10:00 p.m., assemble dossiers for half a dozen attorneys and accountants coming on board tomorrow at 8:00 a.m.? Of course he could. Time and again, he'd done more with less. Owners could bring anyone on board at any time—they certainly didn't require Geoff's permission—but the dossiers would provide the crew with primers on how best to host these people. They must be important if the Falcons were so keen to keep them happy.

Needless to say, there was no reason at all for him to do this work in person. He could be done with it in an hour on his computer. Yet he'd never burst from his cottage faster.

He called Denise on his drive over and had an extremely unpleasant conversation about her and her crew being back on the dock at dawn tomorrow. Just when he thought he'd mastered the American English language, Denise would call him something like "a flying fuckwad," making him wonder whether he really understood this country at all. But even her most anatomical vitriol couldn't dampen his spirits as he wheeled toward his destiny, which lay behind a ten-foot-high iron gate.

Because it was after hours, although he would be the first to tell his staff there was no such thing, he took the opportunity to wear a casual set of chinos rolled up at the ankles, an untucked chambray button-down, and a beautiful pair of blue loafers he'd found at a secondhand shop. Living among the wealthy elderly made for outstanding consignments.

Poppy met him in the driveway outside without a word and led him around to the hedges, through a charming side door, and out to a teak table by the pool. Lights had been arranged and snacks provided, along with a bankers box filled with miscellaneous office supplies, in case anything in the backyard needed three holes punched into it.

The two of them kept their sides to the house and angled themselves toward the water, with the soothing sounds of the pool-cleaning robot and the waves lapping against the breakwater muffling their chat. The moon's reflection wobbled its way across the dark water.

She passed him a pen, and he took her hand in his for the briefest of touches.

"You didn't have to come over," she said.

"But you knew I would," he said. "I haven't seen you since."

They locked eyes, and it took every ounce of his reserve not to pick her up from her chair and lay her down in the grass. Since his lips had pulled away from hers, he'd thought of exactly nothing else. Should anyone in his professional life find out about this, he would be exquisitely screwed. Should the Falcons discover it, he might very well be drawn and quartered. And yet being around her wrapped him head to toe in the fluffiest, fuzziest sense of calm he'd ever experienced.

The problem was established. The problem was love. Love was a natural disaster, and the greatest work of their lives would be cleaning up after it, rearranging the debris into some kind of shape that looked like a house where they could live forever. There was no preventing the storm or shoring up the shelter they had now; they didn't want to live in that. They wanted the wind to demolish everything, then the floods to wash it away, so they could start over completely and say, credibly, "I had no choice—this was not my fault, it was an act of God."

He loved her, he thought, and he was also very much in love with the idea of the kind of life they might lead together if everything went to plan.

If he couldn't touch her, he had to ask her. "I have to know what you've been thinking," he said.

Poppy shook her head, and the little curls at the end of her hair bounced like children on their toes, too excited about something to articulate themselves. "I've been thinking about us."

A two-letter magnificence. He put his hands on the table to steady himself. "And what should *us* do?" His voice dropped into what he considered his most seductive decibel.

Blissfully, he had lost it.

"Let's pretend we work together," she said with a smile. "And that's how we met. I got a job at Ahoy, and now I'm just helping you with your work. And look, wow, we're at this fancy house together. Now, let's get these dossiers ready."

He couldn't help himself. "The *r* is silent."

"—eady."

Collating with the woman he loved—it was perhaps the best evening of his life. This was exactly what they shared, the same little spot in this world, neither in it nor of it. A specific limbo he'd felt alone in for some time, and here was someone who understood it very well indeed.

Together, with a series of carefully laid steps he'd already prepared a draft spreadsheet about, they could make it their own. They could leave all this and, by God, own all of it, too.

She loved him, yes? That seemed obvious. Less obvious was whether she might be willing to go so far as to legally marry Geoff within the next several months while not telling her fiancé's family, in order to steal a boat from them. Time would tell.

Geoff assured Poppy that they could ignore most of what was in these dossiers. The guests were not owners, after all, or even family or friends; rather, they fell into the category of employees. Above crew, of course, and above staff such as nannies, tutors, masseuses, and security guards—but employees nonetheless.

It wasn't necessary to spend their precious time together tonight reading every detail about these people in order to cater to their every whim or to learn facts about them, such as that one of them kept kosher and would not partake in the planned pig roast or that another was allergic to the flowers in the leis Kaylee was currently preparing—or that each and every one of these attorneys, as noted in the thick file that had already been put away, was representing Poppy Wojcikski versus the state.

Chapter

57

It was seven o'clock in the morning, and Ahoy was buzzing. It was high season, midwinter—postholiday, pre–spring break—and guests were between ski trips and making the most of their boats. The grunts were in formation performing feats of calisthenics, the lunges and high kicks essential for yachting.

With a thermos of coffee in one hand and in the other a safety horn, which she blasted every time a grunt got too close, Denise paced around the marina. Her headphones were tuned to the Coast Guard's weekly meteorological report, as she was the only person alive who enjoyed listening to weather reruns to vindicate her experiences at sea. But she wasn't paying full attention. The next Falcon charter began in an hour, and she was psyching herself up to potentially go back down into the office to find more ammunition to use against them.

HR witch Fern wove among the crew commotion, a Wiccan swirl of purple and green scarves over her stretchy black dress. It always looked like she might burst into a puff of glittery smoke at any moment. She billowed toward Helen, who was trying to keep up with a school of jump ropers. Helen had never encountered a single group she didn't immediately want to join.

"Girls!" Fern grabbed Helen by the arm and dragged her over to Denise, assuming incorrectly that they'd be more likely to comply as a unit. Denise removed her headphones; Helen was panting like a dog.

"I'm trying to catch everybody, and God, will you stop moving for a minute? I'm going to sprinkle a little something in the coffee machine next time I need to get everybody to slow down," Fern said. "Just sign this already. I need to bring it over before the service, and I'm trying to get everybody. A show of respect."

Fern reached inside her fuzzy tentacled nest of neck accessories and pulled out a handmade card, on the front of which was a heart shape and the words *Ahoy forever*.

"I loved what she did with the gardenias over there," Fern said. "I used to pick them by the handful for my shampoo I make. I just boil them on my stove with some oils. Take a whiff." She tilted her head sideways and pushed her hair up into Helen's nostrils.

Denise took the card and looked at Helen. "Donna?"

Helen's hands went to her lips.

Fern sighed. "Oh, Donna's dead, sweetheart."

Chapter
58

Linnie understood she was easily annoyed. It was something she'd tried to work on for years, unsuccessfully. To try to just stand there and listen, to absorb incompetent conversations twittering around her and just say nothing, let things go. But it was impossible. Her involuntary rebuttals had earned her a reputation for abrasiveness, as her mother would've called it. Others simply called Linnie a condescending bitch.

Her husband had completely understood that when it came to enduring other people's stupidity, she had her limits. Whenever they rode home together from parties, he would sit back and let her get it all out, all her worst instincts and nastiest thoughts. She rained down torrents of complaints, insults, and judgments on everyone there, and he laughed and mostly agreed and didn't try to correct her or defend anyone. She always felt so much better afterward. In the last moments of the ride, she'd always end up saying things like "Well, I did like the slacks she chose," or "Their grandchildren really are beautiful." He understood that she just needed to extract it from herself in order to move on.

But what now? Linnie was all alone in this immaculate castle of a home, and when she'd tried complaining out loud to the housekeepers about all the terrible phone calls she kept receiving, they just started apologizing to her. None of it had anywhere to go, and inside she was boiling away.

"Be my guest!" Linnie screamed into the phone, then threw it onto the couch.

Ninety years old. This woman, Donna, was ninety years old. Seventy-eight, technically, fine, but still. It was hot out, she was dehydrated, she had bad hips, she'd survived breast cancer in the early aughts—this person was seventy-eight goddamned years old. What in the world did this utterly timely demise of a random retiree have to do with them?

Absolutely nothing! Which is exactly what Linnie had just told her attorneys. They had the gall to ring her up for the second time that same day to explain that they'd received yet another call from the police. They were proceeding with their investigation into the aftereffects of the collapse as a potential cause of death for this woman.

Were heart attacks delayed by weeks these days? Had this Donna person been retroactively crushed by a steel beam? Did staring over the fence at rubble give her an aneurysm? Why in the world was Linnie Falcon even aware of this woman's existence?

Things were spiraling.

Her nervous tic was fingering all her jewelry twice in a row in a specific order—rings, bracelets, necklace, earrings, rings, bracelet, necklace, earrings—and in the past twenty-four hours, the tips of her fingers had become practically gold-stained.

Her grip on this thing was slipping.

The most infuriating place in the world to be was on the receiving end of information. And she was finding herself at the bottom of that slide more and more often by the hour.

News of this local police inquest had somehow made its way to those waffling investigators at the statehouse. They decided that, yes, this was the push they needed to proceed with their own case against the Falcons, to make an example of them after all.

The state had filed the first proceedings and would now be officially looking into the cause of the building collapse.

Linnie's team was quick to tell her that it was all very slow-moving; the paperwork alone would be months in the making, and certainly nothing was criminal at this point. But Linnie had been raised to believe that ladies were in the wrong the moment they were in the same room as certain words. And *criminal* was one of them. How had this happened? How had it come this far? How did an old woman fainting from heat stroke by a fence near one of Linnie's properties crescendo to this?

There was time, she tried to remind herself, to pull together a plan.

When her husband died, she'd pictured herself sitting down at the boardroom table in his chair and slamming her fist on the table, or standing behind a podium delivering the company's speeches and then accepting those little angular glass awards at dinners. These lagoon homes had been her bullet train to the front of the industry. And yet what an industry it was proving to be. The world war–level logistics of hosting the company's holiday party all these years had not, in fact, prepared her for this.

"Just go on and relax," Rocco said. He walked in from the kitchen, buttoning up his shirt, and put his hands on the tops of her shoulders. He squeezed and began to massage, and she closed her eyes. Despite a shower, his skin still smelled of an old-fashioned cheap cologne that she was infuriated to admit absolutely unraveled her. They'd been having this little dalliance off and on for a few weeks now, and its power to reduce her stress was diminishing with each encounter.

"You're not touching nothing," he continued, pressing his thumbs beside her shoulder blades. "Even if something's going to stir up, it's not on you. We took care of that, all because you were the one thinking ahead. You're smart, Lin. It's all in her name, not yours."

Linnie smiled for what felt like the first time in days. It was true. She'd thought so far out ahead she'd scared herself, actually. What if she'd gone too far? What if she'd let the lawyers talk her into something that was just too much? They were so risk averse that sometimes she felt they prioritized peace of mind over profit. But they'd been right about the yacht. Putting it in Poppy's name had provided Linnie a lot of peace. *No matter what happens, at least we've got the boat to fall back on, a back-pocket, rainy-day safety net.*

And then when the building collapsed, she thought, why not go a step further? Certainly it was valuable to protect the good, but in the same stroke you could also put distance between yourself and the bad.

A poison chalice, diversified.

With the stroke of a pen, Poppy had become a magnate. It was quite a stack of papers to get through, but Poppy's lawyer, of course, was their lawyer, and finally, unknowingly, she'd signed on to become the owner not only of the yacht but of the whole LLC that owned the five lagoon properties, all bound tightly together now with an elegant legal bow.

If it all went underwater, and lately the tide was certainly pulling that way, Linnie wouldn't feel a thing. If things shored up, there would be a big, beautiful Falcon wedding.

The phone rang again. Linnie shook her head and waved her hand at the couch where the phone was still wedged between the cushions. Rocco went over and answered it for her.

"Raul." He put a hand over the speaker and turned to her. "When do you want to meet?"

Linnie's fingers went to her rings.

Chapter
59

Helen was crying. The last time she was crying and it was Denise's problem, Helen was eight, and ice cream worked.

"You want to find some ice cream?"

"What? No! How can you even think about eating right now? This is so horrible."

Denise looked around the docks in case anyone else might possibly want to come over and console her sister. There was nothing in this world that Denise hated more than people crying, and that was saying a lot.

"Donna," Helen sobbed. She sat down on the nearest striped lounge chair, and Denise crouched in front of her sister, elbows on her knees. "She's gone," Helen said. "And the last time I talked to her, she was so nice to me. She said it was good for me to have a fresh start and she'd moved around a lot in her life, too, and she said that's how she learned about so many different flowers. And it's just all catching up with me right now, all of it. I haven't even taken a minute to accept the fact that I was fired from my old job. I'm probably never going to talk about animals again or eat good kimchi, and I had to move home and hang out with you, and go work for you, which I told myself I'd never do, and I think Stew hates me, and we only went to see Mom once, and I feel so guilty about that because Mom's getting married now, and I don't even know if I'm going to be in the wedding, and then this happens, and now I'm part of this murder investigation."

"Wait, what?"

"Oh, Donna." Helen's shoulders shook, and she wiped her face with her palms.

"Breathe or something. Just cool down. Bring air into your lungs and repeat." Technical specifics always put Denise at ease.

Helen tried a long, shuddering inhale. Denise could say that much about her sister—she took instruction well. Helen reached out her hand, palm up, and Denise placed hers on top of it and squeezed.

"Good," Denise said. "Okay. You're overwhelmed, yes. Honestly, you're fine. You're stressed, okay, sure. But no one's been murdered. Alright?"

Helen shook her head. "All the police tape over there. And Donna was so healthy, seriously. She dug out all the shrubs for the whole flower bed by herself like it was no big deal. Huge holes—she just bought new shovels. Like two feet down, that's hard work! Have you ever dug a hole for a bush before? She was putting in new azaleas, lily beds, and some vegetables—I think cucumbers, because she likes to make pickles in the fall and fill jars to give out for Christmas. She says too many people make cookies. They were going to put up a little plaque on the wooden railing that said 'Donna's Garden,' but she didn't want that, she said it was too flashy, and after this lady, Antonia, fixed the tool shed, they put up a plaque that said 'Toni's Tools,' and everyone got confused and thought they were only for her and so, definitely no plaque."

"Jesus, how much did you talk to this lady?"

Helen shrugged. "Heracanes has a really nice hot tub."

"You've been going in their—" Denise closed her eyes for a second. "You really want to be in Mom's wedding?"

"Duh," Helen sniffled.

"Tell her."

Helen nodded. "Yeah, I will. Do you?"

"Absolutely not."

"Will you bring Randy? Please? I really like Randy."

"No."

Helen's lip quivered. "But—"

"OK! Maybe."

Helen nodded again. "There's something else. I think I saw a picture of Donna at the Falcons' house."

Denise looked around her. The grunts were in their uniforms now, freshly showered and racing each other down the docks. Stew and Kaylee were already on *Lagoonatic* getting it ready; she could see them out of the corner of her eye arguing over the correct angle of the sun umbrella. She wanted to be on the boat, alone on the deck behind the console with her maps, and not talking about the Falcons in public.

The very idea of those five pieces of paper being inside her home had made it impossible for her to sleep. She was exhausted and desperate to get rid of them, to move them in some direction, any direction, but she hadn't been able to figure anything out yet. Right now there was no room in her brain for an additional crisis, and an eighty-year-old dying was honestly not a crisis at all.

She sighed. "I seriously doubt that. Why would they care?" Denise stood and pulled up on Helen's arms. "Come on, let's go. Go time, get up."

"It was far away, but now that I think about it, I think it was her. And it did happen right next to their property. They found her near the fence, right where her garden beds were. God, now they probably will put a plaque there."

"So?"

"Hello? So, maybe it's connected somehow. The negligence! I told you it was a good idea to go to Poppy's, see? Couldn't we use this for the case?"

"Get up." Denise took Helen's hands and yanked her to standing.

Someone dying was not something Denise wanted them to have anything to do with. "You still don't know what negligence means, and we don't have a case—we're not case people. You need to calm down; you're projecting all your own crap onto this situation; just keep your crap to yourself. Inside. Let's go, you'll feel better on the boat."

With a hand pressed to her sister's back, she pushed Helen toward the pier and allowed herself one single look sideways toward Heracanes, where a police officer paced along the fence line.

Chapter

60

Kaylee stood at the edge of the dock noosing the pantsuited passengers one by one with purple orchid leis. Each recipient accepted the lei in the forced festive mood in which it was given, with slumped shoulders and closed-lip smiles. They carried aboard their own luggage—in one hand a briefcase, in the other a weekend duffel bag with a change of clothes, bathing suit, sunscreen, and for the boldest among them, a novel.

Denise had witnessed a thousand corporate retreat death marches like this one before. No one embarking knew which would be worse: to finally be rewarded with a trip to the Bahamas on your client's yacht and never even take off your Spanx, or to join a pool filled with your colleagues.

They would be out and back, a day trip necessitated by the embarrassing confines of the ship: It slept only ten people. In this decade, sharing suites was not in the cards. Some of the lawyers had been on board before and didn't waste time like the others, gawking over size and shine, but merely trudged directly into the office without a single glance out to sea. Stew waited by the door at an approved distance with a tray of Arnold Palmers, which all of them wanted but none of them picked up because they had bags in both of their hands.

As Denise passed her to climb the stairs, Kaylee patted the side of her pocket and whispered, "I saged the office."

Denise leaned over the gunwale and watched the suits mill around from above. She was extremely confident in Tim Falcon's abilities to never notice missing documents, but half a dozen hula-ttorneys was a different threat altogether.

Helen climbed up, joining her sister in the cockpit, and looked down at the working group. She was supposed to be prepping for lunch. "Hmm, these ones are different," she said. "But it was these same kinds of people at Poppy's house, their clothes are all the same, and the haircuts. They had whiteboards, a big table with little jars of pens, pasta salad platters, like the pasta that's all different colors, all of it. And . . . an old lady picture." Helen raised and lowered her eyebrows twice.

Denise rolled her eyes. She hadn't rolled her eyes in years, and it gave her a headache; her sister was bringing it out in her. "I see you're feeling better."

Helen stood up straighter. "I feel like Donna would want me to investigate. Wouldn't you?"

"You are connecting two completely different events. The lady got heatstroke. They lose like five people a year over there."

"Maybe the Falcons want to buy Heracanes and put up another shoddy condo there."

"Donna didn't own it—she mulched it." Denise lowered her voice. "And why would they need to kill someone to buy it? They didn't kill the lady who owned Mom's place."

"Or did they? And so you are saying Donna was murdered in cold blood." Helen smiled.

"I'm saying we're getting thrown in jail the minute one of those human cufflinks sees a missing paper clip from the office. Has that occurred to you yet?"

They were still docked and waiting for Tim and Poppy to arrive. The crew began serving a full spread of coffee and pastries. An hour after the office windows had been cracked, the couple finally graced the party with their presence and walked down the dock to ascend onto the boat. Tim had not buttoned his shirt, and the two sides flapped beside him like monogrammed wings. He, too, marched straight for the office, but rather than entering, he gave the door a hearty slap and asked if anyone inside needed anything from him. When a chorus urgently responded, "Yes, we do," he gave them a thumbs-up and left for the Jacuzzi.

Denise began the departure protocols.

They were supposed to arrive by lunchtime at a family friend's private island and were now running late. Stew double-checked the electrical in the engine room along with all the ignition fail-safes; Kaylee lifted and stored the fenders, then stood at the stern with a walkie-talkie; and Helen, a human walkie-talkie herself, was at the bow blocking her arms like air traffic control toward no one in particular.

Denise did not like the amount of space that was presently between herself and the guests. It felt way too small. The cockpit used to be a shield, the captain's deck a half-walled moat, protecting her from everyone else onboard. No one could touch what she did, and she didn't touch anything else. If she could've been dropped from above into her seat without ever having to set foot on the other decks, that would have suited her. The space she maintained between herself and the owners and guests was called professionalism, and it was a serious point of pride for her. It didn't matter who was on the boat; she had a job—safe, efficient navigation. That was it, no more, no less.

But she didn't feel so professional anymore. Her impeccable distance had taken decades to achieve, and Helen had collapsed it in weeks. Denise had left her perch; she'd gone down below. She was no longer just the captain, and she hated the low, dirty feeling that gave her.

She'd thought that getting the documents would feel different, triumphant, as though she was getting something over on the Falcons, outsmarting them and bringing them to justice. But she saw now that was completely impossible. Her domain was the boat, and now that the documents needed to go somewhere besides the boat, she was helpless and floundering. She'd made the mistake of thinking her mastery extended onto land, when it absolutely did not.

What did she know about soil? About construction? What did she know about finding original dirt samples? What did she know about any of this? Not enough.

They headed out into the ocean.

Denise could hear Tim's voice as he addressed the crew. The man spoke as if he were always pacing back and forth across a stage wearing a tiny headset. "Okay, right here, right now, we're focus-grouping this thing. Because you guys get it, am I right? You're the prime customer—real people. So keep it totally honest, don't just tell me what I want to hear."

Barred from their entire job, the crew fell silent.

"First, what attracts you the most to a condominium property?" He humped the air.

Later, Helen climbed the stairs and handed Denise a sandwich. They stood in silence for a moment watching the water ahead, a blue line of horizon blurring to yellow and white. The wind was gently flapping the napkin in Denise's hand. She lifted the sandwich over to the side, and Helen tilted her head and took a bite.

Slowly the boat approached Kamalame Cay, a ninety-six-acre private island owned by a merino wool tycoon, with eerie white sheep statues peeping out from behind all the palm trees.

The boat stopped about a hundred feet offshore, where it was still plenty deep, and Stew handled the anchoring. The water was so clear Denise looked down and saw a single lobster scuttle across the bottom.

A white pier with what looked like a gazebo at the end reached out into the sea toward them. Denise pulled up her binoculars and saw someone walking down the pier toward the small, lone yellow boat that bobbed at the end. He stuck out like a bug in milk: black boots, shorts, and tank top, with a revolting blond ponytail flying behind him parallel to the pier like an eel trying to return to water. He hopped on board the little runabout and revved the engine; Denise prayed for an explosion.

How had Rocco gotten here? A seaplane must've disgorged him like a bird dropping. What was he doing here? There was absolutely no way he was hitching a ride back on her boat—he was not on the manifest. She would gladly offer to tie him to the stern and drag him home, though.

On the deck below, the table was set with pale-pink linens, fresh flowers, and glasses in every shape to accommodate every kind of thirst. The chef made brief appearances with tray after tray of tiny sandwiches, handmade chips, and homemade pickles, plus salad speckled with herbs he'd brought onto the boat in little ceramic pots of dirt. He laid it on thick with words all identically meaningless to Denise: *artisanal, handcrafted, small batch, curated.*

The chef was infamous for always forgetting exactly one thing on every trip, some key ingredient or piece of the tablescape, and almost always he was able to compensate and make it work. Sometimes Denise thought he forgot things just to challenge himself, like a one-man cooking show competition: *And now, make an oil-free olive oil cake.* Today he'd forgotten those miniature chalk stands that he usually placed next to each dish on a tiny easel to tell people what they were about to eat. Everything here was self-explanatory, but he did like to let groups of guests know about allergens. On a white cocktail napkin, using two different-colored pens after one ran out of ink, he scrawled, "Peanuts!" He placed the note beside the bowl of snack mix, like a ransom note addressed to a desperate legume family.

The lawyers lumbered over to the table. A few minutes earlier, Tim had announced that after this huge lunch, there would be a fun mandatory team swim.

Tim snatched up two key lime bars, then left Poppy alone among the litigious. He took the back set of stairs in one jump and stood alone on the stern platform.

Rocco whizzed his little boat out from the pier toward the yacht. Without ever stopping, he slowed just enough to hand Tim, over the water, a briefcase, which he exchanged for a key lime bar. Rocco fumbled the handoff, and the key lime bar tumbled down the side of the boat, leaving a slime-green streak.

Rocco turned back to shore.

A hand clapped Denise's shoulder, and she flinched, nearly dropping her binoculars. Helen was back, holding a small plate of dessert, a tart peace offering. She took the binoculars and kept eating.

"These taste like Mom's," Helen said. "But, like, expensive."

"They are." Denise took a bite. "Chef's met Mom a few times."

Helen was quiet for a moment. "That's pretty nice. She's in the mix, in your life; I didn't really know that. How often do you guys see each other?" She sounded like a jealous high schooler worried her friends were hanging out without her, not someone who'd chosen to live on the other side of the world and had many times chosen to "do Australia" for Thanksgiving.

Denise shrugged. "Once a month, depends on the charter schedule. Honestly, I don't really go unless I'm there for work. And you know, you could be in the mix, too."

Helen frowned and seemed to think about this. "I do have a Bahamama now."

"Correction—it's Bamama."

Helen handed the binoculars back to Denise. Rocco had pulled the boat back to the pier and was tying up. "Mangrove Rambo is such an epic creep," she said with a shudder.

"Ahoy, my best amigos!"

They both spun around to see Tim Falcon climbing the stairs.

"Mr. Falcon," Denise said.

"Captain. Cap. Polar ice cap, gas cap, white cap." Tim saluted her.

"What's up, Tim," Helen said. She popped the final bite of her dessert into her mouth then spoke with a mouthful. "Do you need something?"

"Yo, Hannah. I totally do, and it's totally awkward, and I totally don't want to do it." He winced. "This is just not like a fun feeling that I'm feeling." He moved his hands in circles in front of his stomach.

"What's your concern?" Denise crossed her arms. She was her best self in a crisis, ice-cold. "And this is Helen."

"Dammit, I knew it wasn't Hannah. I was going to say Holly, you so look like a Holly. And hey, I look like a Tucker, or a Tripp, so I get it."

Tim held up his phone. "Two thingies. So my mom called, and she got a call from someone, who got a call from somebody else. Kind of how it goes in my fam, lots of who's getting all the ring-a-lings today. And she said that they said that there's some papers missing here? We keep, like, tons of stuff on the boat. I know it looks like it's all wild and crazy vacation times but, old habit of my dad's and all his lawyer guys who are super old but still alive, there are paper backups of the business stuff. We can't trust computers, like, 110 percent of the time, right? Makes sense."

"How can we help you?" Denise widened her stance.

"So the office was cleaned? And I guess that's the problemo. Because we don't really super-duper want people in there. Look, I asked Rocco if he could talk to you about this, but my mom's really trying to get me to make it my thing, handling more stuff like this mano a mano. Even though, between you and me, I already have plenty of things. Do not need one more thing, right? But, so, yeah, maybe one of you guys, or one of those other two on your crew, Sam and Renee, maybe they accidentally, potentially swiped something? From the office?"

Tim clapped his hands once. "This blows, am I right? I love you guys, you love me, we're the boat fam. For the record, I don't think you had anything to do with this, but my mom, Rocco, those guys downstairs, they all want me to ask, like I said. 'Get to the bottom of that, Timothy!' Just in case, never know, life's a mystery, blah. So here I am, being a CMO."

Denise took a step closer to him. Helen saw the look on Denise's face and stepped back.

"We clean every single room, after every single charter, that's standard procedure, company policy, for the sake of your comfort and for the sanitation of the vessel. When it's not being used, the boat is docked at a marina with forty-two employees and over two dozen vendors and contractors, one of which you just hired to paint the new name. Within the past week, it was docked at a second marina in a different country, with twenty-two employees and an additional ten vendors and contractors, none of whom, on that side of the Caribbean Sea, are subject to our same laws and regulations. But you're suggesting that an item you cannot find is the purview of one of us—your fam."

"Whoa!" Tim landed a hand on Denise's shoulder. "Exactamundo. See? Now we're back on the gravy train. I knew you were on the up and up, and you'd drop some knowledge, that's exactly what I told everybody. 'Captain? She is the most down-home cat around, believe me—I can't get her to let me do fireworks, ever! She's just not that kind of gal.' So that all sounds great to me, I'll pass on the good word. Lot of moving parts, don't have to tell me twice. Amen sister. Sorry I interrupted your whole celestial navigation thing going on here. I'll smell you later, ladies. Thank you for your service."

Helen beamed. "You are so welcome, Tripp."

Denise held up a hand. "You said there were two things."

"Oh!" Tim raised up two peace signs. "I heard you guys are one of us! Back in the day, your house was on one of the lagoon landing properties. Dude, it's so crazy. Every hunk of land has these wild and crazy chutes-and-ladders connections. We're out here discovering these little lots, but there's always somebody who was living there before. Isn't that insane? So you know what I was thinking. And let me start with 'You're welcome.' If one of you ever wants to get in on one of our condos, and dude, as soon as you see the lagoon up close, you're going to want in, I could probably bump you up the wait list. Scooch you right up to the tippy, Timmy top. Full price, nothing I can do about that, but I could get you into one, no prob. What do you think? You wanna join the 'Goon Squad?"

Chapter

61

Denise did not spend much time at home. As much as it drove her insane to be subjected to the grunts' slumber parties at the cottages, she was always the last one off the boat and the first one on, not to mention she liked to oversee repairs and redesigns, which kept her at the marina at all hours.

Truth be told, she hadn't had much interest in buying a house in the first place, but after enduring a series of rentals where the owner fought her over the number of bats she kept for mosquito control, she relented. She maintained that the neighbors should've thanked her.

The house was in one of those fancy neighborhoods with two curved brick signs on either side of the road leading in. All the houses were nearly identical, with white trim along the windows, porches out front, and decks out back. A single palm tree rose from each corner of each lot like parentheses around each little life. Out in front of every home was a manicured squiggle of red and purple zinnias. It was all waterfront, and wide slices of sea were visible in between houses when you cruised down the street. Denise liked to swim to work sometimes, right across the waterway, at sunrise.

Denise's yard, front and back, had been completely rewilded, her childhood yard re-created. The house was barely visible through climbing wildflowers, weeds, native vines, unwieldy bushes, and a visibly DIY pond. The towering grasses ended abruptly at both sides of the property line.

There were bat boxes throughout.

The neighborhood association routinely tried to fine her for violation of its beautification bylaws, but on the one occasion she attended one of these meetings, she patted her gun in its holster and reminded the group that her bats were doing more for mosquito control here than any of their toxic repellent sprays could dream of, and for that, they were welcome.

From the front porch, Randy waved to her as she pulled in. He wore shorts, boots, and a low tank top, revealing chest hair that had several black beans camouflaged within it.

"Fed all the critters inside. Everyone's got a full belly, myself included. I got the good Cuban, and I couldn't wait for you, I'm sorry. Left you all the plantains, though." He kissed her on the cheek as she stepped out of her truck, and Denise brushed his chest clean.

She put a hand on his back and leaned her head on his shoulder.

"That kind of cruise, huh?"

She nodded. "I need to go inside."

"Wait one minute," he said. "I have two things to tell you, and one of them I think you're going to like."

He led her around to the back porch, which overlooked the water. They slid down onto the plastic Adirondacks.

"First off, I made some calls. Not like I'm winning any Oscar here, but I did a pretty good job of pretending I was going to open up a new location for Conch Cab. I called up Raul's company to ask if they could help me with the soil testing, talked to some guy there."

"You did what?" Denise squirmed in her seat but then waved her hand impatiently for him to go on. They'd gotten back from the Falcon lawyer cruise just an hour ago, and she was too exhausted to really argue with him.

"And we were shooting the breeze, he was asking me about how business was going, and I was telling him he should come down and take a ride sometime. And then I asked, just real casual, like I was just curious and wondering and all, 'Hey, so, what do you do with all the old samples you get, from other sites you're all done with?'"

"And?"

"And they ditch them." Randy shrugged. "The guy laughed at me. He said if they kept everything they worked on, they'd have mountains of dirt around. Ninety-nine times out of a hundred, they can just go back to the site to get more. They don't save anything—just test it and toss it."

Denise slid down in her chair and groaned.

"He said for a lot of the testing they don't even take samples out, they just test it right there on site. Didn't ask how they did that, guess they bring the little vials over there with them or something. The only dirt that's in the office, he said—he was joking around—was like some dirt they put in a little jar with a ribbon around it that somebody might want for a souvenir, like when they broke ground on some big new place and they give those out to the construction honchos or something."

"Shit," she said.

Randy tossed up his hands. "That's the part you're supposed to like. I'm out here doing the legwork for you, working the phones. I know you two were about to try to go on some wild goose chase to try and find that dirt, so I'm taking that off your plate. You don't need another thing to try and weasel out, forget that. Now you just focus on what you've already got. That's a good thing. And you're welcome, by the way."

"Thank you." She reached over and squeezed his waist. "What's the thing I'm not going to like?"

Randy turned toward her and took both her hands in his.

She shook her head. "I don't like this."

"Cool down, I'm not proposing to you. Not today. I just want you to know that I'm in this thing with you, too. I'm serious here. You've got Helen mixed up now, a big part of it."

"She wanted to—it was her place, too. This whole part was her idea!"

He held up his palm. "I know that. And I feel like it's kind of brought the two of you close. Closer than you have been at least. And I'm glad. It's just, you have this whole big battle going on, and then I'm over here, and I'm not a part of that with you. And I love you."

"I love you, too," she said quietly. Saying it was one thing, but volume was another.

He smiled. "I know. But I want you to also know that if you ever needed me to do anything, I would. Like those calls. Or anything else. I can be in this thing, too, alright? If you want me to be, just say the word. It's so important to you, I feel like that's where your head's always at, and so that's where I want to be. Am I making any sense?"

Denise pulled herself up then stepped over and sat down on his lap, draping her arms over his shoulders.

He turned his head to kiss her arm. "Right now all I do is flip the bird every single time I drive by their place. But if there ever was anything, I just want you to know that."

"I do know," she said. She looked at him. "Hey, do you want to come to my mom's wedding with me?"

"Are you serious? What do you think? What am I going to say when you ask me to party in the Bahamas and see you in a dress and there's a good chance I'm going to get you to dance with me?"

"Hell, yeah."

"Hell, yeah!"

"You probably have to wear sleeves." Denise took his hand and led him inside the house.

"We'll see about that."

Later that night when she couldn't sleep, she wandered around the house. After Tim all but threatened her, knew way too much, and put her on edge for the entire ride, she'd been desperate to get here. Not that it would help, but she wanted to hold the papers in her hands. She had had a nagging fear that she would come back and the documents would be gone, that someone might have broken in and taken them.

Maybe she would put them back; maybe she should. Maybe this whole thing was stupid, and she had a job and a sister and a person who loved her, and her mom was getting married, and come on, what did it even matter that someone was digging big blue holes in the earth?

Inside her guest room, she lifted up the edge of one of the terrariums, and there they were. The tank was made with fine glass, had sophisticated ventilation, and contained three kinds of exotic plants she'd ordered to re-create their perfect habitats in miniature. With two fingers, she pulled on the edge of the papers and slid them out. She rolled them into a tight tube and held it in her palm, tapping it against her other hand.

The moonlight came in through the windows, and the glass of the cages gleamed, showing off browns of every color in a perfect row. Each creature needed a very specific soil, and she'd enjoyed the process of mixing it correctly and making it just right, a chunky dust for the tarantula, a thick mud for the lizard, a gradient from light to dark for the turtles that sloped down into the water.

And suddenly she knew where the dirt was.

Chapter

62

"I am not comfortable at all right now."

"None of us are, Raul, I can assure you." Alden paced around the room, and Linnie wished he would stop. He was wearing one of those fleece vests, even though it was eighty degrees outside. "This is not something we have anything to do with, obviously. It's a clear case of overreach, which is exactly what I've laid out to them. They're kicking us while we're down. They've got nothing to go on, so they looked over the fence and saw an opportunity. Clearly, we're not letting it go any further."

"Sit down, Alden, you're making me nervous," Linnie said.

The three of them were in the sun rotunda, a hexagon of a living room with wall-to-wall white carpet, love seats in the round, and a seashell wallpaper border that desperately needed updating. So much had been put on hold these past few months. On the blue tufted ottoman in the center of the room was a large rectangular tray with a pitcher of iced tea and three glasses, untouched. Linnie refused to default to offering the men drinks, the thought would never occur to her son, and Raul was too well-bred to either serve himself or ask for a glass. One by one, beads of water dripped down the cold pitcher onto the linen lining of the tray, counting the seconds of this unpleasant little get-together.

The local police had proceeded to question both Linnie and Alden about the death of that old woman next door who collapsed from sunstroke. They were both dumbstruck. What were they supposed to feel? Devastated at the loss of an almost eighty-year-old they'd never heard of or met? If they started caring about the hiccups of every next-door neighbor at every condo site across the county, they'd be overrun. Property lines existed for a reason. Legally, she was not responsible for feeling a thing.

For unimaginable reasons, the police were proceeding with a toxicology report, and Linnie had taken to praying that the woman was an alcoholic or, better yet, overmedicated. Thank God Tim was at sea and unavailable for comment—at least something was working.

But word had, of course, made its way to Raul. She wouldn't have thought that something as trifling as a local police officer poking her head around would even appear on the radar of the giant Raul Williams, but she was beginning to think he was quite a bit softer than she'd originally estimated. Too bad.

It had been an otherwise immaculate collapse, death-free, and Linnie was determined to return it to the harmless accident that it was. The insurers were extremely close to having the whole thing deemed an act of God, a designation that was more essential than ever now. A few little pen strokes away. So even if someone had died, it was hardly the Falcons' fault, despite what the brilliant officers seemed to be suggesting. But, of course, zero death in general was always ideal.

"Now, what can we do, Raul?" Linnie began. "It is, as Alden is saying, entirely unrelated. For the life of me, I can't understand why we're even hearing about these Heracanes people. When we first started building, we did extend an overture: We said that any of those elders would be welcome to take as many photographs of the lagoon as they liked, and I believe they took advantage of that. Quite a few birds drink from that water, and when they do, it's very photogenic. And now, after that, they try to embroil us in something like this. You know, I had one of my people check, and on average three to four people die there every single year—which is right down the middle for a retirement community of that size, apparently, and so it all makes perfect sense. With those numbers, some of them are bound to die outdoors. But here we are. When there's a crisis people will pile on—I don't have to tell you that. So all that is to say, I completely understand where your feelings are coming from. When it rains, it pours and all. And it's unsavory, certainly."

Whenever death came up, she found that strategic touching could be useful. She put her hand on top of Raul's, but right away he slid his out.

He placed both hands on his cane and began twisting it. If not for the thick carpet, he'd be boring a hole in her floors.

"Melinda and Alden, I need to explain something to you."

Linnie straightened her back and leaned forward. She'd felt ridiculous wearing a white silk blouse and tweed jacket in her own home, but now she was glad to be armored in what she considered work apparel if she was going to have to negotiate. Alden had come over earlier, and they'd agreed to offer Raul as much as 35 percent, but she was hoping it wouldn't go there. Though insurance would pay out handsomely, it was the principle of the thing. How much was the groundwork worth compared to what they, the developers, did?

"The reports we had done—" Raul began.

"The soil study," Alden was still standing, and now he nodded vigorously with his hands on his hips. Linnie wondered how much coffee he'd had. His energy level was all wrong for the moment, and she wished she'd put out cocktails rather than tea, regardless of the hour. "Sure. What about them?"

"Don't interrupt him, Aldie," Linnie said.

Raul took a long moment to look at each of them before continuing. "They were not right. The ground was much too weak for the kind of building you were planning. Well, it was fine for a building,

I should be clear, but not for a building and the lagoon installation, not for both, not with the amount of land you were working with. I don't want to get technical now, which I have a habit of doing, I'm told, but it has to do with the expansion capability, bearing limit, that kind of thing. Like a jelly donut. You went ahead and, well, jammed even more jelly inside that donut, so when you tried to balance a churro on top . . ."

He made a flopping motion with his hand. "You understand."

Linnie and Alden looked at each other with pairs of scrunched eyebrows, then back at Raul. His face was placid and ready, chin lifted. He'd stopped turning the cane, as if what he'd just said had relaxed him. Maybe they weren't hearing him right; maybe his accent was getting in the way after all. Did they need a translator? Did they have one somewhere? Should they trust one that Raul provided? Would he be insulted if she suggested one now? Certainly something was being lost.

Alden nodded and furrowed his brow. "Okay. But the report you produced was fine—it was a green light."

"Yes, it looked very good, but it was not. The real numbers were not. I'm telling you all this now, and again, I am very sorry. As you know, it will affect my bottom line as well, and it puts me in a terrible, liable position. I'd hoped of course to not have to bring this up any time, that we could proceed with just the small change of a few numbers and nothing would come of it. It really was close but just not quite there. But now, with what has happened, it seems possible that this adjustment we made may come out at some point. After the collapse, obviously, I thought maybe then I should tell you, but it looked like things would keep going, that you would be able to recover. Melinda, I have to say, you did a tremendous job. But I feel now, with what is happening, with where the winds are blowing, this woman who has died and what they are saying, it could become dangerous. So I am bringing this to your attention and now that we all have the same information we can proceed. I understand that sometimes knowing more can, funnily enough, make things more difficult."

Linnie's lips hung open. She tried to close them, to form a vowel of some kind, but they would not move into any kind of verbal shape.

Alden's eyes bulged. He tried to close them, to return them back to the normal dimensions of human eyes, but he was unable to, as if he were trying with every muscle in his upper face to squint but his eyelids would not budge.

The three of them turned their heads to look from one to the other and back again.

Raul continued. "Within the next few days, I will decide what to do. Or, I should say, we need to decide together—now that we are working from the same set of facts." He clasped his hands, and the edges of his lips lifted into a kind of resigned smile, as if this was an inconvenience for them all to bear, a moment of annoyance. "Most important, I've kept the original samples on my boat. Very secure. So we can refer to them if needed. I've always been a bit sentimental about things, and when we first began working together, I thought it could be a nice gesture to save the dirt. Sometimes on big projects we save the dirt, a celebration of groundbreaking and all, and for this I did the same. Someday, I thought, maybe I would present it to you as a gift. But now, of course, I am just glad that I have retained it for my records. It is quite valuable considering now that the ground is not the same at all, to say the least, after what has happened. It is a shame. If something like the death of this woman has been caused by this collapse—"

Alden regained the use of his face. "How? What are you talking about? There is no way in hell this sunburned geezer—"

Raul raised a hand. "Then I think it will make the most sense to share these facts."

"Then this whole thing would be your fault! You would be dragged to hell for this," Alden said. "That's what you want? You want this whole thing to come down on you? Because what I'm hearing right now is that it sure as shit should."

Raul lifted one shoulder. "My understanding is that this is your building, your site, your development, your history of these projects—your trust in an independent contractor that you thoroughly vetted and have a preexisting business relationship with. I bring all this up not to upset you, as I clearly have. I bring this up so that we may become bedfellows, that if things do indeed proceed in an unfortunate manner—which, again, maybe they won't, time will tell—that you know what we have in store for us, both of us. Because . . . if I am on the hook for this, and as you say, I certainly will be, it is my mistake, my own greed that has gotten us into this pickle—I was given a part of the profits from these lagoon sites and I wanted to see them proceed. It was going so well for so long, and when the peninsula came up not so good—it was pretty close, to be honest, the numbers were not very far off—so I changed what I had to so that it would all proceed. But make no mistake, I will do my own fair share of dragging down with me. If it comes to that." He held up his hands, palms facing each other, and knitted his fingers together for them both to see.

Alden rocketed up from his love seat with such force that the decorative orange pillows he'd been sitting on flung up into the air behind him like a burst of sparks. He stomped over toward Raul with both pointer fingers raised in the air. "Okay, holy shit, you have got to be—"

Linnie stood and placed a hand on her son's chest. "Sweetie. It's alright. Come sit down, right here next to me. Yes, right there. Now, does anyone want an iced tea?" She poured a glass for each of them, even though she had no interest in being in this room for another second. Her chest felt so tight the blouse had to be strangling her. But she had no idea what else to do, and she had to move her limbs, blood had to flow again, she had to do something, she had to think.

"Mom, stop. Just stop."

"Raul, thank you for making us aware of this. I'm very sorry to hear that, of course. But you're right, we are absolutely, inextricably linked together at this point."

"Yes, precisely." He took a glass in both hands then drained half of it. "Thank you."

"Of course. So what I think this calls for is more of the same. Call me crazy but what about a dinner, right? All of us together, hashing it out. Why don't we do it on the boat?"

"Jesus, Mom, are you out of your—"

She held up her hand. The moment lingered, and the sound of the gentle tumble of ice was a cool relief slicing through the thick, warm air.

"Alden, please. One moment. We'll have all the time in the world to go through things. Raul, as you've said, this is not the outcome that any of us want to see. We are nothing if not a resourceful bunch, and now, let's think of this information sharing as a blessing, shall we? We can put our heads together and be right as rain. We've worked together successfully for years now, and something like this, something local," she said the word with the appropriate amount of scorn, "has no business whatsoever putting us sideways, let alone standing in the way of future progress and earning potential. The day is young, there are jelly donuts to be had, sunshine to enjoy, and there is still a lot of money to be made here, and I would just hate to see us all derailed by something as small as a communication error like this."

Raul was looking down at the rug and nodding.

"Yes? Alright, then it's settled—give ourselves some time to put our heads together and see this through. It is simply more important than ever now that we are on the same page and determined to proceed together. For the country."

She wasn't sure why she added that last part, but it seemed to do the trick. Raul tapped his cane once on the floor then climbed his way up to standing from the couch. Linnie rose to face him.

He took both of Linnie's hands in his. "You are a special woman," he said. As usual, she tried to imagine someone taking the hands of her husband and telling him he was a special man, but she let it go. "And we will see where we are at the end of this week. Could be nothing. As you said, sunstroke. If we can keep going, then we have nothing to worry about."

"We will keep going," she assured him. She had no idea what that meant, but mirroring other people's words always made them happy. So did thanking them for no reason. "Thank you." She gave his decrepit, sunspotted empanada of a hand a squeeze and released it.

The moment the door closed behind him, Alden stood up and began stomping around.

"Mom, we need to torch him. We need to lay him down and knife his guts out like a fish. We need to pour gasoline down his throat. Goddammit, I'm talking about weird stuff, stuff we haven't done to people in this country in way too long."

"Darling, darling. Certainly, all of that. But sit down first. Please. I'll tell you exactly where we're going to start."

Chapter

63

Poppy's feelings for Geoff were solidifying into a kind of comfort she'd never known before, the warmth around her settling into itself, like lying down in the soft grass on a warm day, wrapped in a thick towel after a good swim, layers of bliss. She was tired, and the comfortableness was right there waiting for her, molded to fit her body. There he was.

They messaged each other constantly and talked about everything, from work to food to friends to theories they found they shared about where whales came from. They knew all the same people, really, because Poppy was spending all her time in and around the boat these days. It was a little world she'd built up for herself, and Geoff was part of it, too, and it was just magical. It felt like summer camp, she thought, even though they'd never been able to afford summer camp, but it felt like a summer camp she'd seen on TV, a sunny, miniature neighborhood where everyone had a little job and was happy to see you every morning and each day involved a new activity. She never wanted to leave. To Geoff, with Geoff, she felt like the most important person in the world.

On her most recent charter with the lawyers, she'd done a cooking activity. She asked the chef to give her a little lesson in the kitchen, just something fun to pass the time that it took to get to the Bahamas—and also she didn't want to run into Helen. What if she mentioned something about Geoff? The way Helen had said she'd seen them together made Poppy think she might. It was too bad, she'd liked hanging out with Helen, but maybe Tim was right, and you never really could trust people who worked for you.

The cooking class was so fun. After they made mini tarts with goat cheese and spicy pepper, the yacht chef asked her to carry out the tray and place it on the table. The lawyers were already seated, and as she approached, they all looked up and gave her a big round of applause as she put the tray down.

What a feeling!

Here, on the boat, she was in charge and appreciated.

All day long she was signing things right and left, repeating her Social Security number; it never ended. Multiple times that morning, people had stuck their heads into the kitchen, and she'd had to quickly wash her hands, take a pen, and initial something. She was a multitasker, a wheeler-dealer, as her mother would say—a leader.

And even though so much of it had everything to do with the Falcons (it was their business, even if Poppy did play a big role in it), Geoff made her feel like Tim's family had nothing to do with his and Poppy's world. Geoff always brought her back to herself and reminded her that she was the decision maker. He never, ever mentioned them at all, and when Poppy would say one of their names, Geoff would pretend he hadn't heard it. He only had eyes for her and made her feel like that was exactly what she deserved.

The funny thing about the boat was that it had given her this amazing gift, Geoff, but it was the one thing that was still tying her to the Falcons. The whole boat experience had taught her so much about herself—that she could stand tall, be in charge, pursue her own dreams, and be the owner of her own life. It opened her eyes in every way. Now that she'd experienced a love like Geoff's, she understood with neither regret nor resentment that she'd just never had that with Tim.

When she first met Tim and got lifted up into this whole, big new world, she told herself how lucky she was that he'd given her a second chance in life to make something of herself. But now she saw a third chance, and she was going to give it to herself.

There was no way she was going to let anything stand in between her and Geoff. The boat had brought them together, but it wasn't what held them together. Paperwork could hardly hold back the dam of an epic romance like theirs. She was an owner now, she decided, whether she owned the boat or not. Without the boat, she could have Geoff free and clear, and that was no choice at all.

Chapter

64

As usual, Helen looked like she'd come straight from an airport tchotchke shop where the salesperson had been told to use the word *authentic*. Everything she wore invited a question she was dying to be asked.

Denise flicked her sister's chest, hard. "Is that a brooch?"

Helen looked down. "Ow! You hate everything."

"I don't hate everything. I just hate the things you like," Denise said.

"Yeah, but I like everything."

"Cut me a piece already." Randy was at the helm of the taxi. He reached out a hand toward Helen, who was slicing a mango with a knife. They were cruising around the waterway with their coffees as the sun peeked out from below the tree line. The thick layer of mist hovering over the water parted before the bow of the boat. The air was cool enough that Denise wore shorts and a hoodie and Helen wore a jean jacket covered in show–off pins. Styx the dog was asleep on a pile of towels in the bow.

They didn't have a charter scheduled until tomorrow and agreed that they all did their best thinking on the water, though they'd been out for an hour now and had come up with nothing. Denise needed to get onto Raul's boat when he wasn't there without anyone at Ahoy knowing about it. Raul knew exactly what he was doing, hiding the soil samples in plain sight inside his terrariums in the middle of his boat. The tanks were ridiculously heavy, built into the center structure of the main suite, and filled with poisonous, biting creatures. The latter she had some experience with, but all in all, she was more concerned about what to do with the dirt once it was in her possession. Were they supposed to contact a university science department? Did the local government have some kind of unbiased soil sample testing team? Or did they contract out to Raul Williams?

Helen cut off another piece of fruit and handed it to Denise. "Okay, so the plan is still to try and weasel our way into the secret room when the coast is clear, Scoob?"

"That is what all this sounds like." Randy wiped mango juice from his mustache with the back of his hand. "God, I wish I could be there."

"Or," Helen said to Denise, "we could maybe make friends with those people on Raul's team? All those people that are always hanging on to him. You could try being an actual kind person that other people like spending time with and want to give things to? Just this once? Always works for me."

"When has it ever, one time, worked for you?"

Randy tapped the wheel. "Maybe you can just ask him real nice, 'Hey Raul, let me get a scoop of this dirt for my own spiders, they're real particular.' He'd get that—give the man some credit." Randy always assumed the best about people, and it always drove Denise a little crazy.

"Fine, I'll do it. I'll get up in there right in the middle of the night when the boat's at Ahoy. Probably no one will see me. I'll wear dark pajamas. I'll do it for Donna." Helen puffed out her chest. "And yes, this is a brooch. It's a lionfish. I got it in Tahiti. And actually this is not me bragging about all my travels, because they live here, too— I've seen them."

"Everyone's seen them." Denise held out her hand, and Helen handed over her knife. Denise pulled a new mango from her bag and began slicing herself a piece.

"Yeah, they're invasive pieces of crap," Randy said as Denise handed him a slice. "Those things are from Asia, alright. I heard somebody brought some over in a cooler ten years ago, thought it might be fun to let them loose in some river, and now they're taking over all the reefs here. Destroying the reefs, more like. You know, pythons and boars are invasives, too, and good thing the county actually pays you to kill them and bring them in, fifty bucks a foot for the pythons. Remember we made three hundred dollars that weekend just doing our thing?" He lightly elbowed Denise. "We should be killing those lionfish, too."

"The ones I saw are dead now." Helen chewed through a mouthful of mango. "They were in the lagoon."

Part
Four

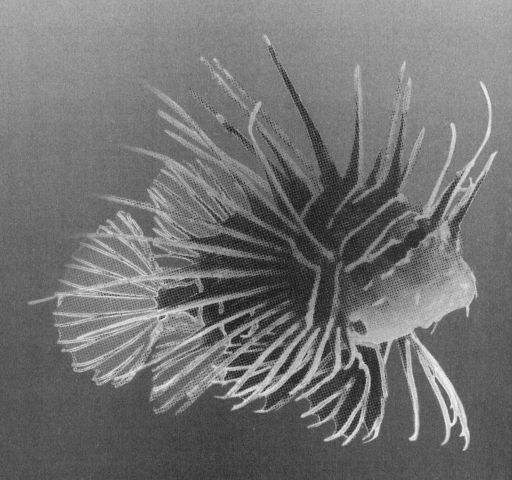

Chapter

65

So now you know half the story—you caught the hacker.

And, like I said, blowing it up? A breeze. Hey, a breeze would be great in that case—more oxygen, be my guest. That one's all about speed, one and done. Boom, boat gone.

The problem is—and you're smarter than me, you're just waiting for me to get to it—you're not going down there to light up a smoke or switch something on when you know there's a gas leak. No one's trying to blow themselves up. You might be trying to blow someone else up—aloha, human history—but not yourself, so an explosion is probably not what you guys are talking about. Because you're talking about setting something up for later.

You're talking about time management.

Sinking a boat is all about time management.

There's a fast way, and that's called blasting a hole in the side. About as common as you'd think considering the sheer volume of boneheads out there driving around. You do not need a license of any kind to get behind the wheel of a regular little boat, people. Ding-dongs crashing into your yacht right and left these days. And let's be honest, boat crashes are 50 percent alcohol, little accidents, and 50 percent on purpose, let's ram into these people and dent their fancy things. Either way, you've got water coming in.

Also, shipping containers. Holy collision. You'd be surprised how many of the big freighters manage to drop a container or two in the water. Happens way more than you'd think. And a thing like that doesn't just sink to the bottom, too much air inside, so it just sort of bobs right there under the surface, like a floating school bus. And those don't always show up on the radar. Crunch. I've seen plenty of those collisions—and then, of course, plenty of water coming in.

And those sensors I mentioned, here's where they'd come in. Your high-water alarm is going off if somebody spits, let alone when you've got a fish swimming in through your brand-new barn door.

It's about time management.

Let's just say you ram smack into the corner of one of those containers and rip yourself a big new one, you've actually still got a few hours before it's all underwater. You have to get towed in, it costs you about a million to fix, all in, but you live to spend another day.

But in your case, there was no evidence of any outside hits like that on this boat, not a single scratch on the hull.

So, the brawl was coming from inside the house.

Here's a very convenient thing about boats: They're easy to cool down. Surrounded by water, God's coolant. There's a big pump system that brings water in from the outside, circulates it all around the perimeter of the big engine to cool it down, then funnels it right back out into the ocean. All the time, going twenty-four hours a day. On one end of the pump there's a sea strainer that acts like a filter, so you're not getting sea-weed, fish, eels, or trash coming up into your system. It's a pretty sizable opening there since it takes a ton of water, nonstop, to cool an engine that large, and the pump controls that whole flow.

So, yeah, there is already a hole in the boat. If I were looking to do some damage, internally, I'd say that's a pretty good jumping-off point.

Finding me was no big whoop. Big surprise—niche line of work, some-one on the payroll with a background like mine, sure. Round of applause for you guys, really pounding the pavement.

Hammer for hire, though—pretty broad skill set.

And like I was saying about the Jet Skiers who like to ram into the sides of these things because they don't like to see how the other half lives, plenty of people out there share those feelings. Good luck finding them.

Chapter

66

A perfect storm required a perfect storm warning. A category one was a beautiful thing, a glorified thunderstorm. A two was confusing and could go either way. Three through five created absolute mayhem, and rightly so. Geoff himself had been trapped atop a minivan once for an entire harrowing night, having underestimated a three. But a one was absolutely fantastic. It was essentially benign but nonetheless triggered Ahoy's hurricane protocol, and protocol was where Geoff thrived.

All charters were canceled effective immediately, without exception. All crew were required to be present at Ahoy. All boats were to be moved out of the marina and into Potano Bay, a small harbor hemmed in by land and trees. All information flowed exclusively through Geoff.

A hurricane warning also required the presence of the engineer. That was protocol. Keith the engineer was a very unpleasant man to deal with, excessively talkative, and Geoff was always relieved that their interactions had a time limit built in, today's being meteorological. The man had just a few hours to pop into each engine room, one after the other, walk the decks of each boat, check the consoles and cockpits, systems and screens, and fully ensure that every single thing was shipshape before the weather struck. This was done for the same reason that valets take a lap around your car to clock any existing scratches when you hand them your keys. Should one's boat become damaged during the storm, it was vital that the storm be blamed.

In all Geoff's years with Ahoy, there had never been anything wrong, anything to note on these engineering checks beyond the usual. It was just another one of those services that a middle-management organization such as Ahoy offered to justify its existence. These services were the bulk of Geoff's purpose on earth.

The clouds were dragging a gray curtain across the sky. The wind was picking up and whipping the flags into a taut percussion. A thin white froth formed at the very top of each wave, and Geoff took a deep breath of the salted air, reaching out his hand to slap the edges of each flag as he walked up and down the docks, clipboard in arm.

As soon as Keith finished, they would move the boats out from the marina, one by one. Per Ahoy's guidelines for tropical storms, squalls, and hurricanes, the marina needed to be cleared. It would be madness to keep the boats all there side by side and risk them bumping into one another or coming loose from the pier, which was itself subject to strong currents and debris. Isolating the yachts from the imminent artillery of earthbound asteroids was their best protection.

All this was underway, and Geoff was blissfully in his element, delivering orders that employees were protocol-bound to follow. The frenetic energy of the swirling crews in their neon rain gear turned his little front desk into a command center. It was organized chaos, and he was very much in charge. Captain Denise, Captain Craig, Captain Chris, Captain Kevin, Captain Chris 2, and Captain Scott Dodge (an elderly seaman only conscripted in the most desperate times), along with their respective teams, were rolling, one after another, helming the boats out to the nearby bay to safety.

The word *courage* floated on the wind—directed at a grunt daring to finish a chicken wing left out overnight—and Geoff raised his chin at the sound. Yes, exactly. He was a hero, for all intents and purposes. He was a general conducting a land-and-sea operation to save the lives of billions of dollars. With all his heart, he wished Poppy could see him right now. The sight of him standing tall behind these swiveling monitors clutching the emergency instrvction binder would unravel her. He sent her a photo, which hardly did him justice but got the point across.

She'd been out of town the past two days, saying she had something to take care of for the family, and he hadn't pressed her. When it came to Falcon affairs—which, for the time being, she was still a part of—he did not like to give them any oxygen. When they saw each other later tonight, he would regale her with tales of this harrowing time behind the desk.

He found that keeping track of the crew members was the most difficult part of this operation. Admittedly, he'd never actually thought about them as distinct entities that he was obliged to keep safe. Now they were scattered across the boats, all on the water, away from home base here and manning their own stations, and he was the one responsible should anything happen to them. He was startled to feel fear, not for himself but for others, and the implication of their safety for his own liability.

Old Scott Dodge's team marched toward the farthest boat to begin its removal. A highlight of Geoff's day, if not his entire life, had been when Ahoy-admiralty Scott Dodge grumbled to him, "Keep it up, chief," as the captain clomped past the desk out toward the water, zipping up his fly. Geoff would hang on to that for the rest of his life.

Everything was going smoothly; the chaos played right into his plans.

Tonight, he and Poppy had an incredibly romantic rendezvous planned on her boat. Complete isolation, a whiff of danger, and a perfect setting for their very big discussion. She told him she had something special to tell him, a big announcement, and he could hardly contain himself. He was nearly bursting with anticipation. There was no doubt in his mind that she was leaving Tim. His response would be to merely suggest a timetable, one that she couldn't possibly be opposed to: that she delay her break with the Falcons, remain owner of the boat, and on paper at least (surely, they'd do a party at some point later), marry him. Then the two of them would be off to the races with a quite a start indeed to the rest of their lives together.

He hoped she was alright, even though he knew she would be perfectly safe down there, under the covers in the suite on *Lagoonatic*—like a stowaway waiting for him. The whole thing was outrageously erotic. As soon as the last boat left, he would jump into a Zodiac himself and join her, under the auspices of doing his utmost duty and ensuring that all the boats were secure in the bay.

He missed her. He loved the way she talked about the kind of life she was living because of how close it made him feel to living that same kind of life himself. It was extremely tempting to call her right now, just to hear her voice, but he would not, could not. People were relying on him. Nothing would slip through the cracks on his watch.

Chapter

67

Denise was losing her mind. The hurricane warning must have tripped whatever circuits had been running smoothly in her brain and scrambled her. Helen actually felt that her sister was thawing out. The two of them had been able to talk and stand next to each other around all this water, and neither of them had pushed the other one in—not once.

Helen was even feeling something akin to attachment, a small but satisfying warmth of possession, as she worked on a team alongside Denise—the sisters together and in their element—and as they wove themselves into a shady crusade to defend their former homeland. Helen experienced that warmth like a powerful drug. It made her like it here; it felt exciting. It felt like this didn't have to be the last time, like maybe she didn't have to leave again. There were plenty of slippery owners here. What was stopping them, the peninsula sisters, from taking them all down, one by one?

But now Denise was pacing around Ahoy in furious figure eights, and Helen hadn't been able to get anywhere near her without getting barked at.

The storm warning meant all crew members were required to sleep at the cottages until further notice. That the cottages were flimsy wood funhouses ten feet from the water did not factor into company policy. There were expendable assets, and then there were the boats.

The grunts had misinterpreted the situation entirely, treating the lead-up to the storm like an extended boot camp. At this very moment two were doing push-ups in front of her, and Helen was tempted to use them like ottomans. One was using a giant rubber band as a torture device around his ankles; one was jumping rope and whipping a divot into the grass.

"Helen!"

She turned toward the fence to see Jules hauling a sandbag across the Heracanes lawn.

Helen waved with big swoops of her arm. "Jules!"

"Happy hurricane day!" she shouted. The streaks of pink in her hair were the brightest sight for miles.

Helen jumped up and whooped; she could not help it. She saw Jules wink before she disappeared behind a group of women telling her not to hurt herself.

It was muggy, and the sky was silvery gray. The wind pushed relentlessly but couldn't sweep away the humidity; it just rolled waves of moisture through the air. Helen remembered this kind of weather in the days before the hurricanes of her childhood. Nothing on this earth was more ominous than the gentle flutter of a flower in the wind once a warning had been issued. Everything in sight became a petal about to be ripped off into a liquid firestorm.

Team by team, the Ahoy crews marched onto the boats, which pulled away from the docks one at a time. With the yachts gone, the view of the sky opened up above the piers, showing the clouds piled high over the water, mounds of bulbous gray about to burst. Helen stood at the edge of the grass in her life jacket, ponytail whipping the sides of her face, and watched the backs of the boats putter around the bend, their names disappearing behind the rising waves. One after another: *Tapped Out*, owned by a maple syrup scion; *Marlin Monroe*, a local news personality; *On the House*, another real estate person; *Issues*, a magazine distributor who'd gotten out at the right time; *Cirrhosis of the River*, a private practice hepatologist; and *Tax Seavasion*, Ahoy's CPA.

The main target of Denise's wrath was Geoff. Everything about Denise and Geoff's relationship could be summed up in the two of them waving their arms around about who was executing the protocols most correctly. Just now Geoff had handed Helen a wad of nets and asked her to cover the large pots of flowers along the docks. When Helen suggested just moving the pots indoors and maybe finding the extra life jackets instead, Geoff held the clipboard straight up in the air, clip side up, like a lightning rod wishing to be struck to make its point.

As a kid, Helen had loved hurricanes. She was told to stay put and play games by herself and not use up the flashlight battery while Denise and their mom sandbagged the perimeter of the house. When they returned inside, the three of them would sit around in the dark. Denise would be forced to hang out with her sister for days on end. For Helen at that age, a flooded crawl space had no repercussions whatsoever, and the whole thing felt like a camping trip—camaraderie, candlelight, and all. She looked around for Denise now to ask her whether she remembered the canned peaches their mom used to buy in bulk but saw her reaming out a grunt for wearing flip-flops at this barometric pressure.

"Hey," Helen approached her, hugging the extra life jackets, hoping to placate her sister with the sight of safety being taken seriously. "Remember the peaches? Every time I even see a peach now, total liquid scream, the vomnado, the chowder shower, the lunch launch. You, too, right?"

"Stop. I'm trying to get all these boats out of here. What are you doing? Do you remember what a hurricane warning is? Hand those out. You all need to be ready to go, right now." Her eyes were scanning the crews over Helen's shoulder.

"Yikes, fine. Calm down. Now you're in a rush, finally. All it took was a hurricane."

"What's that supposed to mean?"

"I mean you kind of haven't really done anything since we figured out they faked the reports. I know you're freaked out, and it's fine to be scared, but you were, like, paralyzed, I think. I'm just glad we're doing the next step, like actually pushing forward. I was worried you didn't want to power through to the hard part now that we're getting down into the whole Raul thing."

Denise narrowed her eyes. "Paralyzed? And are you kidding me? The hard part? I'm the one putting my ass on the line, and I'm the one who's been putting my ass on the line this entire time. If you get fired, who even cares? You'll just go back to whatever you were doing. This is my entire life, Helen! I still don't even fully understand why you care all of a sudden, out of nowhere. This is just some fun way to stir the pot for you before your next hilarious job. I actually care, it means something to me."

Helen reeled back. "Why wouldn't I care?"

Denise leaned in. "Because you don't remember. You don't even know what it was like. You just have this perfect memory of the place, so who cares if it looks different now. Nothing but good vibes and awesome memories for the ride. Hang ten!"

Helen's chin wobbled. "Screw you! What, like, I'm the luckiest, happiest girl in the world because I have nothing to go on, that's what you think? Because I have no memory of Dad, I should be super grateful?"

"It's better."

"Than what? You getting ten years with him? Did you ever think I might be jealous of you?"

Denise coughed out a brittle laugh. "Me? You're out there island-hopping. And I know what you're about to say, and no, not just like

I am. Not at all—because I'm actually working. I don't even look around me at all this, it's called work. And if you're so desperate to have some memories here, pretty funny way to go about it—you're never here with us!"

Helen's eyes filled, and she opened and closed her mouth a few times before she could speak. "You never tell me anything. Neither does Mom. How am I supposed to remember? And now, hello, I am here. Okay. Sorry if I'm late; sorry for living and ever leaving this place. I'm trying to help you with this, to do something about our house and get into it with you, and you're coming for me? Out of nowhere? You're still fifteen years old and telling me I'm doing it wrong, Denise. Which is it? Do I not care at all, or do I care too much, but wait, I'm not allowed to?"

"I never tell you? You never ask! You have never asked me, one time, a single thing about what it was like. You think I don't want to talk about it?"

"That's exactly what I think!"

"No. I don't have time for this." Denise put both her hands up, shook her head, and walked away toward the piers. "I'm not doing this."

Denise marched out onto the dock toward Raul's boat, and Stew fell into step behind her. But Helen's feet were rooted to the ground. The first rumble of thunder rolled through, and she felt it at the top of her chest and in the back of her throat—a deep baritone that echoed the water she felt roiling inside her. She heard the rain before she felt it, tiny wet slaps on the leaves.

Suddenly, a hand pressed her on the back. "Let's go, sweetheart," Kaylee said, sliding past Helen toward the water and putting up the hood on her jacket. "It's our turn."

Chapter

68

Denise made sure that Raul's was the last boat to leave, and she made sure it was hers to take.

Helen boarded the boat last. Denise did not look at her.

Since the minute she woke up that morning, Denise had not stopped moving. Now that her body was holding steady at the helm, her muscles were all still twitching, raring to go, screaming to be put in the game. It was perfect, absolutely perfect, and she was over-whelmed by the sense that after everything she'd been through, of course there was a storm to send her off into whatever next chapter this was. The wind had her back. She was destined to be here, to-night, burgling this boat.

Helen did not understand anything. And Denise could not spare an ounce of her focus for her dramatic sister right now.

People were not in their right minds. After being out all night dealing with his own boats, Randy had come home at dawn shirtless, streaked with grease, and shaking with excitement. She'd offered to help him with the taxis, but he'd told her no, to rest up for her own storm ahead. He'd hugged her for a long time until she pulled away and had to ask what was wrong with him.

She steered the boat away from the marina. *Waterproof* towed a large, orange Ahoy-branded Zodiac that they'd all pile into afterward for the ride back. The crew battened down everything, wrestling with the wind, moving things away from the windows, sealing them shut, and making final checks for anything on the decks that might take flight.

All she could think about was getting down there into the suite as soon as they moored. She'd brought her snake-handling gloves.

They cruised to Potano Bay, an elongated bubble a mile down the waterway; on a map, it looked like a blue python had swallowed an ostrich egg. As they approached the bay, the houses on the shoreline grew fewer and farther apart. The land there was preserved as a state park and circled the water in walls of green. Mangroves tangled beneath tall, sharp Fakahatchee grass. The low, thick branches of gumbo-limbo trees reached out twenty feet wide, as if to say, *Just try me*. The wind carried the sounds of screeches, trills, croaks, and calls that rose from the muddy banks.

This was where they kept the boats during storm surges, in this wide, perfect circle of a cove. It was a thirty-minute ride away from the ocean inlet and gave the boats a wide berth on all sides from each other and from the land. It was the only bay like this in the whole area, despite a million pushes for a million more park designations—a huge, tranquil loch that managed to shut out the storm surge coming from either side. On the outskirts, on the few inches that they were allowed, homeowners had built pools and hot tubs, to ruin the bay in order to look at it.

The moorings ready for them were gigantic, gentle cones floating in the water, yellow dots across the black surface forming a constellation. There were a dozen dotting the bay. The moorings were planted with a long chain of anchor line into the muddy bottom thirty feet down, and would give the boats a wide circumference. They would move in full circles throughout the storm, always pointing in the direction of the wind, and they would touch nothing else.

Moving inch by inch in silence, Denise brought the yacht toward the mooring they'd been assigned, and Stew bent out over the bow, extending his arm's reach with a long metal hook to attach the lines. They'd arrived.

Now the wind was fast enough to ripple the water into sharp-bladed reflections of the slate clouds overhead. The waves smacked the sides of the boat, and the rain drummed from above with fattening drops. The thunder purred beneath it all, and in the sky just above the swaying tree line, electricity lit the clouds to a yellow glow from within.

All twelve yachts turned ever so slowly to point in the same direction on the current, facing whatever was to come that no one else could see. Normally at this point, Denise would climb into the Zodiac and whiz around to double-check the mooring lines on every other boat, not trusting the other captains' work for a second. But they weren't her problem right now.

Helen stood at the bottom of the stairs waiting for her, not looking at her.

It was ransack time.

Chapter

69

Down in the main suite, Helen, Stew, and Kaylee were seated on the cream couch, shoulder to shoulder all in a row, like schoolchildren being lectured. Their hands were in their laps, and they stared up at the terrariums. A slice of lightning cracked open the sky just outside the nearest window and made them all flinch in unison.

"This turtle had a fascinating past life. He was a prime minister," Kaylee informed them. She stared intensely into its eyes and bowed.

"Do you smell that?" Stew scrunched up his nose. "These tanks are airtight and we've got a Bill Paxton and Helen Hunt wind out there and there is still a smell. I know I have a super nose, but why would you bring a smell like that into your yacht? That is bleach-proof—it's airborne. Imagine sleeping with that smell?"

"Some people like it," Denise said, pulling her gloves on. Her heart was pounding, not because she was about to reach inside the tanks but because this was it, the final mile. Robbing the Falcons had felt justifiable, but despite everything she knew, taking from Raul still felt wrong.

"Some people like that dusty little pretzel mix they put out on the bar that everyone's fingers have been in. People are wrong." Stew stood up and helped her pull the gloves up over her elbows. "This is so civilized, by the way," he added. "I'm making a note of this. Next time I do a snoop, I'm waiting on the weather."

The boat swayed ever so gently, and the rain blew sideways against the black windows. The sun had dipped below the horizon, and the storm had siphoned the last of the evening light. It was early evening but nearly pitch-black.

Helen carried in a chair and placed it next to Denise so she could reach up and inside the tanks. "What're you putting it in?" It was the first thing she'd said to Denise.

Denise held up a handful of plastic sandwich bags. A drum of thunder pounded through the air, and they all jumped again.

Helen shivered.

"If any of these things do that thing where animals go nuts in certain kinds of weather and start to attack, I am out of here." Stew pointed a stern finger at the tanks. "I know you know I'd take the Zodiac and leave you."

"I'm troubled about the snail. She seems lethargic." Kaylee frowned at a rock.

Denise kept one bag and handed the rest to Helen silently, then climbed up onto the chair. In the first tank was a tiny orange frog. Denise dunked her hand inside. One after another—she grabbed a small handful of dirt from each. The whole thing was about to be over in a quiet twenty minutes, and she'd make sure they labeled everything carefully. As Stew said, a civilized heist. The final tank held a snake, which reared back when Denise pulled up the lid. She lowered her arm inside, jammed her fingers in the dirt, and pulled some up and out just as the snake lunged forward with an open mouth.

"Ha!" Denise cackled. She was grinning from ear to ear, her heart thumping.

She peeled off her glove. Helen returned the chair to the table. Kaylee apologized to the animals, and Stew clutched the samples.

"We ride," Stew said.

They filed up the stairs onto the deck, and they all zipped their jackets up to the chin and pulled their hoods up. The deck lights were on and dotted the complete darkness with yellow orbs, hazed by water. Their Zodiac was floating behind the stern, straining at the line in the wind like a dog pulling on its leash to go home. The black bled from the water to the trees. Rather than being masked, the sounds coming from the mangroves seemed to grow louder the harder the wind blew—as if the animals on shore were yelling at Denise for what she'd just done.

The other yachts all faced into the howling wind. The only way to indicate their size were two small red lights, one each at the bow and stern, like the glowing red eyes of gigantic creatures peering out from the water, half submerged.

The four of them climbed and slipped their way into the Zodiac and huddled together in the back. Denise started the engine, but it was so loud with the rain beating on their hoods that they could tell it was running only when they felt its rumble on the backs of their legs. Denise kept her head down to get any kind of visibility as Kaylee reached forward to untie them.

Suddenly Helen's hand waved right in front of her sister's face. "Stop! Denise!" Denise looked up and followed Helen's arm, which pointed at the Falcon boat.

There was only one red light. Denise squinted and pulled the hood away from her eyes to make sure she was looking at the right thing. The gray silhouette of *Lagoonatic* was tilted, with its stern below the waterline.

Chapter

70

If the sound of rain was peaceful because the sound of water was peaceful, then it made perfect sense that the sound of rain falling onto the water would be the most peaceful sound of all. Poppy had never thought of it that way before, but Geoff had pointed it out, and of course, as always, he was right in the most charming way. The idea of being on the boat in the middle of a storm, a real hurricane no less, was pretty frightening to her at first. And she didn't love the idea of sneaking like a stowaway on her own boat, but then again, it was hardly hers anymore.

Now that she was here though, snuggled up in bed beneath the thick, fluffy periwinkle duvet inside the cozy master suite with the sound of the rain splashing around them on all sides, she understood that it was a perfect little escape. They could enjoy the thrill of sneaking around while they still had to. She'd kept all the lights off so none of the crew delivering the rest of the boats could see them and instead just lit a few scented candles on top of her dresser, giving the whole room a flickering golden glow.

It was so romantic she could just die—all the more so because it would probably be their last time on the yacht.

She bit her lip and rolled over to face Geoff, brushing a piece of hair from his forehead. He'd arrived, her brave man, on one of the Zodiacs, and it wouldn't be long before he had to get back. She could just picture him standing on the end of the pier, chest out, hair billowing back, facing the lightning head-on and wielding his clipboard like a shield against the enemy storm. Just when she loved him for his softness and gentility, he went and showed her a whole new side of himself: seersucker warrior.

"I wish I could stay." He kissed her.

"Are you ready for your surprise?" She propped herself up on one of the scallop-edged pillows. This was such a big gift, she wasn't sure how he would be able to leave tonight once she'd shown him. Her body felt so light and so strong at the same time.

He nodded, grinned, and pushed himself up to lean against the headboard.

At the bedside table, she pulled open the drawer, removing a glossy white folder and placing it on his lap. Her stomach did a little flip of anticipation.

"Ooo, darling, you do know my love language." With the folder on his knees, he pulled out the first sheet, and his neck extended forward. His lips parted, and she watched his chest rise and fall more rapidly. "What is this now?"

Poppy's quick trip to Nassau this week had been her first time on a plane by herself. Before she'd met Tim, she'd never been on a plane at all, and once they were together, he'd always gone with her, from Mexico to Tokyo even, and she realized now what a good teacher he'd been. She had no trouble whatsoever whizzing from security to the gate, especially in the tiny Nassau airport, and it felt so extremely glamorous to fly twice in one day, to use a plane to go to a meeting.

It also happened to be the first meeting she'd ever attended by herself.

The nice man at the Bahamas boat registration office was so happy to see her again so soon. He smiled so much she could imagine that he slept smiling, eyes closed and beaming in his dreams. He said he would be delighted to help her remove her name from the boat paperwork and revert the registration of everything back to the Falcons, to undo what she'd just done so recently, to erase it. Of course he asked why, and when she told him it was because she was in love and the boat was preventing them from being together, holding people back who truly belonged together, he smiled bigger than ever and clapped his hands. He said that was the best reason he had ever heard and was glad that something as simple as a signature could clear the way for two souls to join in this life. They hugged for a long time after she put the pen down.

"I did it for us." Poppy smiled. "I've been waiting to feel like this my whole life, and if we're going to be together, I can't be attached to all this anymore. This was my life with Tim, and it brought us together and I'm so grateful for that, but I want a life with you, so I'm going to leave all this behind."

Geoff stared at the papers.

"Maybe I can come work at Ahoy? I feel like I really understand boats now—that's what the silver lining is here. I've learned so much, because I've been an owner and a guest, so I could talk to anyone about their experience from any angle. And now I could help people who own but maybe don't want to own anymore. Do you have to wear a life jacket even when you're in the office? You don't usually wear one, but you're a much better swimmer than me."

A silence hung in the air for a moment. "Geoff?" she said. The wind whistled past the window, and even though it was impossible, Poppy swore she heard voices outside.

Geoff lifted his head up and lowered his shoulders. Suddenly his eyes grew wide. "Good Lord, do you hear that?"

They leaped out of bed, and their feet landed in a foot of water.

Chapter

71

"What the hell kind of moron is in there?"

"Hello! Ahoy! Hola!"

"If it's Rocco, we're turning around."

"We come in peace!"

In the total darkness of the bay, a small yellow rectangle glowed right at the surface of the water. The Zodiac sped over to the Falcons' boat in just a few seconds, only to find another Zodiac already tied up there. Someone had motored out here in the middle of a hurricane. A deranged person, which did not narrow it down.

The back platform of the boat was completely submerged, and the water lapped at the back staircase leading up to the first deck.

"Stay here." Denise barked at them.

"Oh, so don't get on board a literal sinking ship?" Stew took the line from Denise and handed it to Kaylee to tie off at the stern.

Denise stepped from the front of the Zodiac onto the stairway, and Helen jumped after her. The water was up to their knees. Denise spun, and Helen held up a hand.

"Don't even start. I'm coming."

They turned back to face the rest of the boat. At eye level there was a narrow window looking into the engine room. Inside they could see it was filled with water a third of the way up the wall. Shoulder to shoulder, they gaped for a long moment.

"Oh my God," Helen could barely breathe.

"Let's go," Denise grabbed her arm and pulled her up the stairs. "Do not let go of me."

There was a steep angle to the deck, and Denise marched past the heap of furniture that had been wrapped up and tied down. Helen stood at the top of the stairs that led down to the suites and shone a flashlight. The water was climbing the walls, an inky abyss. Helen had never been on a boat at night with all the power off, let alone during a storm. It really was just a giant hunk of fiberglass, teak, and aluminum, which was absolutely, unequivocally not meant to float in a giant body of punishing water without some serious technological intervention. She didn't understand why man had chosen ever to set sail when it was so clear that it was a horrible idea and that humans were born on land for a reason, and what was anyone thinking trying to battle water itself, because clearly—

"Helen! Right now!"

They waded down the stairs. By the time they got to the living room, they were up to their waists. Helen turned around; behind her in the foyer to the junior suites, she could see water coming through the bathroom door, a rippling black lip that made her gasp.

"Denise? Denise. Let's go, they're fine, they can swim, everybody can swim, they have a boat, let's go, we have to go. Right now. Please."

Denise turned to her and paused for a moment, opened her mouth as if she was about to say something. Then she leaned forward gently and put her forehead up against her sister's. "You're fine. I'm right here, and I've saved six people from drowning before."

"Out of how many?"

"Seven. When we're done here, let's get some canned peaches, alright? Does that sound good?"

"You remember?"

"Of course I do. They were disgusting."

"Here! Help!" Someone banged at the door.

Helen swung the beam of the flashlight toward the bow. They waded toward the master bedroom. The door opened just a few inches and there in the tight space was Poppy's face, eyes wide with terror. Even with just a slight opening, the water in the living room rushed toward them.

"Close it! Oh my God! Helen! We're going to die!" Poppy screamed.

"Back away, Penelope!" An unmistakable voice came from inside the room.

"Geoff!" Denise screamed. "What in the living actual flying fuck are you doing here?"

Poppy's face disappeared from the gap in the door, and suddenly Geoff's hands wrapped around the edge of the door and started pulling. The door wouldn't budge.

Poppy's face came back into the space. She was crying. "I am so sorry—I know I shouldn't have flushed that tampon down the toilet, but I swear I didn't know this would happen."

"Denise! Get us out of here right this instant. Right now!" Geoff shouted.

"Back up!"

Helen moved back and Denise stepped as far from the door as she could. She leaned back then ran and kicked the door open. The door slammed into the wall behind it, and there stood Poppy and Geoff in nothing but underwear. Water rushed into their room, swallowing their lower halves.

"Is there anyone else on board?" Denise grabbed their arms and pulled.

Poppy lunged toward Helen and wiped her eyes. "It's just us. What's happening? Can you get us off here? No offense, sweetie, but I'd rather go on the boat with Denise. Is that okay?"

Geoff grabbed Denise's shoulders. "Can you save the boat?"

Poppy looked back as Denise pulled her forward. "Wait! Can I get something from the room? Oh my God, can we turn the lights on? I don't know where I put my umbrella, did you see it hanging up out there?" She started crying again. "What if it blew away?"

Suddenly there was a loud metallic groan, and the boat lurched to one side. They all stumbled sideways. The water sloshed higher up the starboard wall.

Denise went down hard. Her leg caught on something and she fell, clawing at the wall on her way down. She splashed into the dark and disappeared under the water. A huge oil painting crashed down right on top of the water where she'd just been.

Drowned. Dead. Gone. Dead. Her sister was dead. Gone. Helen's heart left her body.

Helen righted herself, grabbed both sides of the heavy gold frame, and tried to pull it off, but the thin metal cord on the back was stuck on something. Each time she pulled, Denise's face appeared for a second, gasping, then the painting sprung back and slapped down onto the surface, pushing her back underwater.

Poppy started screaming.

"This could be priceless!" Geoff shouted.

Finally Helen reared back and punched the canvas, her fist blasting through and hitting both water and Denise's head. Her sister's face appeared, a red streak dripping from her left cheek.

Denise exploded upward through the frame, roaring out from the ripped painting. "You punched me!"

Geoff bolted up the stairs.

Poppy passed out.

"No, no, no!" Helen grabbed Poppy's body under the shoulders and started hauling her toward the stairs.

With the only air left in her lungs, Helen looked at her sister and huffed, "I'm sorry."

Denise's eyes were wide and unblinking and water dripped down her face. "I'm okay. I'm alright." She nodded as if to convince herself, then the muscles in her face came alert and hardened, snapped back into the moment. Denise reached out an arm and took half of Poppy's dead weight onto her shoulder. They pulled each other up the steep slant of the living room through waist-deep water.

Poppy's body bumped into everything that floated by: chairs, books, bowls, bird statues. She was making reassuring light groaning noises.

The sisters looked at each other across her slumped head.

"I'm here," Denise said. "I'm here."

Helen nodded and realized she was crying.

They hauled Poppy up the stairs onto the deck, which was now tilted at a sickening angle. The water was at the top of the back stairs, and the Zodiac was close enough that they could step right into it. Helen felt as if she might be sick. She could feel her blood pounding throughout every inch of her body.

"Mrs. Wojcikski!" Kaylee shouted. She scrambled up and over to them and dragged Poppy, who was able to stand woozily on her own now, into the boat. The rain was relentless.

Geoff was on the second Zodiac, frantically pulling the engine cord to get it started.

"Screw you, Geoff!" Stew yelled.

Geoff looked over and glared. With a face full of rage, he gave the engine cord one final pull, and he was off, steering like a drunk, zigzagging into the night.

Helen, Poppy, Kaylee, and Stew huddled in the back of their boat in silence. Denise slowly reversed the boat away from the yacht and made a wide turn to face the mouth of the bay.

They motored away, past the other yachts, one by one. Helen and Denise exchanged a look; without a word, Helen took over the throttle and steered them straight ahead. Denise pulled out her radio and called the Coast Guard.

As they listened to her describing the impossible, they shivered and all looked behind them past the boat's wake. The Falcons' yacht sank lower and lower until the yellow candlelit rectangle was snuffed out and the last red eye of the boat blinked down into the water.

Chapter

72

The ankle monitor was going to leave a scar. Linnie tried to stay vigilant about socks, but it was impossible in this part of the world unless one went around in athletic outfits all of the time—which many, dear God, chose to do voluntarily. But nearly all of Linnie's wardrobe required loafers or espadrilles of some kind, and even when it had gotten quite bad, when blood had dripped down her Achilles tendon and ruined the footwear, even then she refused. It was a different indignity altogether for them to tell her what she could and could not wear.

Next week was her day in court; after that, the monitor would be something she thought of fondly. A raw and bleeding ankle? What she wouldn't trade. Of course she hadn't the slightest idea of what horrors lay ahead. Sure, there had been husbands over the years among her set, one or two, who'd served several years, but she hadn't been close enough to the wives—or if she had been, she'd correctly distanced herself—to find out the gory details. The food, the drink, the beds, and the company, all the things she was keen to know about now.

In the month since the sinking, Raul, deservedly, was faring just as poorly. He was fighting for his life against the family of this woman Donna for his soil sins. By now they'd all learned more than they ever cared to know about the hellscape called *aquatic toxicology*.

Why hadn't anyone ever told her to stop? Why hadn't any of these people who were so angry at her right now stopped her at any point? She was furious at having not been stopped.

They were going to lose everything. The insurance investigators were a nightmare. They were ants crawling through the dark of every single crack and crevice in their lives. Apparently, they were interviewing everyone and their mother for hours to find out who'd set foot on whose yacht and what they were capable of. They would not pay a single dollar for that boat if they didn't have to. Forensic scuba diving, good Lord.

All of this for a little lagoon.

But what enraged Linnie so much she could spit was that horrible Poppy woman and her disgusting affair. After everything they'd done for her—a house, a boat, a marriage into a perfect family—she had snuck right behind all of their backs. She had the gall to return their gift! And in doing so, she had pointed the gun right back at them.

They'd seized everything now; it was all gone or going. That pointless girl had made a fool of Linnie and her best-laid plans to preserve something, anything, for her children.

The hardest thing in Linnie's entire life was knowing which members of her staff she could rely on. Even the ones she thought she could trust completely, the ones whom she'd leaned on for years, hired people below them, and Linnie could hardly trust another person's staffing abilities. To search for, vet, hire, and manage a staff was an extraordinary skill set that had taken her years to perfect. Or at least she'd thought she had perfected it.

See, they tricked you, these people. At first she'd been so impressed by Rocco. To say nothing of her tryst—which was pleasant enough but not worth muddying the waters over, in hindsight—she was heartened by his tenacity. He was a ridiculously hard worker, in more ways than one, and when Raul told Linnie and Alden that the ground samples were on his boat, the wheels began to turn for her.

And Rocco was right there, waiting for her up in her bedroom the whole time, awaiting her instructions. A perfect soldier.

How to get the samples off Raul's boat? What a simple question, actually too simple. The better question was why. Why would she want the samples? To have to worry about them for the rest of her life? Go to all the trouble of extracting them only then to be saddled with disposing of them? Accused of destroying them with plenty of evidence to go around? No, thank you. Much better to have them gone for good, and sweeter still if she could have them gone while twisting a knife into the stomach of Raul Williams.

As soon as Linnie had suggested that sinking the boat might be preferable, Rocco was in motion on a plan, no questions asked. He lined up the right people, those people lined up their people, and so on.

She was in the act-of-God business. In the past months, she'd spent every ounce of her influence convincing the powers that be that the building collapse was an accident caused by a storm. So it was perfect, divine even, that when an actual natural disaster was upon them, things fell right into place. The people Rocco had assembled now had a perfect cover. If anything could sink a boat, certainly a hurricane could. Finally, Linnie thought, the winds were in their favor. They deserved a break.

But of course, one never came. Her trust had been badly misplaced in Rocco, Poppy, Raul, everyone.

Everyone had failed her. Was it such an impossible thing to do? Build a nice, simple lagoon so that nice, simple apartment people could enjoy a view and pay a proper premium for it? Too visionary, apparently. To this day she believed, and always would, that none of this was her fault.

Chapter

73

"The thing about poisonous fish is that they poison people." Denise tapped the picnic table with her finger.

She and Helen were sitting across from Officer Liu. Randy sat on top of the table next to them, his feet on the bench, with Styx asleep on the ground below. The storm had left the sky white, a bright blank slate of clouds, and the wind was still making its way out, combing the trees clean of any last scraps it wanted to pull off. A million little waves carried all the tiny debris down toward the end of the peninsula, past the Ahoy lost and found, and out into the ocean.

Helen was having the time of her life. She leaned forward over the table, elbows bent, palms facing one another, with her worldwide bracelets pooling on the wooden top. "You know the saying 'The snake is more afraid of you than you are of it'? Totally the same thing. Lionfish aren't out there lunging at swimmers. But they do attack crabs and coral. And eels, if they're lucky. Yum, yum."

"Hold on. Wait a minute," Officer Liu took off her hat and wiped the sweat from her forehead. She looked down at her notes, then back up, first at Helen, then at Denise. "So you're saying Donna ate one of these fish?"

"Let me guess what was in the toxicology report," Denise said.

She leaned back and crossed her arms. To be fair to Helen, Denise was enjoying herself quite a bit, too. This always happened to her. She had these moments of clarity right after life-and-death situations, as if the adrenaline had dissolved all the clogs in her brain, and her thoughts could really let loose and fire away. At first she thought the breakthrough was about being nicer to Helen, but that wasn't it.

It was that she knew exactly how Donna died.

"Ciguatera!" Helen raised both arms into the air.

"Here they come. Watch out, baby." Randy clapped once. He was supposed to be giving them privacy, but Denise smiled over at him anyway.

The officer leaned forward. "How did you know that?"

Helen untied her ponytail, and her ridiculous hair erupted over her shoulders. She gave it a little shake, then sat up straighter, preparing for a performance. "Samoa. Okay, so the first time I ever even heard about lionfish was when I was doing a bike tour of the cenotes in the national park there. Did you know it's the only American national park below the equator? So we were riding our bikes—"

Denise put a hand on her shoulder. "We looked it up. That is what it's called, right?"

Officer Liu drew out the word: "Right."

Denise and Helen looked at each other, and both of them smiled. "You go, you can start," Helen said.

Denise took a deep breath. For over a year she'd been waiting to talk directly to an officer of the law about the development at her mom's place, and now it was finally her chance. She wanted to savor this moment. "The lagoon. It was full of these fish. And when the building collapsed, it punched a hole in the bottom. Those liners are bullshit, which I've left you guys a lot of voicemails about, by the way. So all the water and everything that was in that water went into the ground."

"Right next to Heracanes." Helen extended her arm in that direction.

"All those fish, in the soil, right below the property line, not that far down," Denise said.

She and Helen had been up all night at Ahoy. Denise spent the night on the phone for hours with the Coast Guard trying to explain what she'd seen. She still didn't know the whole story; all she could say was the boat was going down, and she had never, in twenty years on the job, seen a yacht go down. Helen spent the night playing referee between Geoff and Poppy, who swung between being catatonic, yelling at each other, crying, hugging, then returning to stunned silence, and ultimately breaking up very publicly. Helen also gave her account of what she'd seen to the police, EMTs, and two men from a nautical insurance company who showed up in three-piece-suits at three o'clock in the morning.

Denise was the one who explained that the engineer had been there just that day, before the storm, checking on everyone's boat.

Eventually, both sisters fell asleep inside Helen's cottage just before dawn.

When Denise woke up, that was her moment of clarity. The sun beamed its first rays of the day through the leaves across the water, and she knew. The rain had stopped. The debris of the night before had arranged itself perfectly into a clear picture.

She shoved Helen awake and, rubbing their eyes, they hopped the fence, walked across Heracanes, and checked Donna's garden bed. Then they hopped the next fence over to the lagoon site, soaked to a dark gray. Together they lifted up a few smaller pieces of the rubble and looked inside the lagoon. It was empty, a dark crater filled with detritus. A wide, jagged crack struck open a hole on the side nearest Heracanes.

Officer Liu leaned back. "Where the garden bed was."

Now Helen tapped the table. "Where Donna spent the entire week digging new holes, putting in a whole new irrigation system.

Up to her shoulders in it, all day, every day. Wiping her face, eating some of the tomatoes she'd grown right off the vine, all of that. Those azaleas were going to be gorgeous by the way, such an amazing green thumb on that woman. The crazy thing is, after the collapse happened she was even more determined to make the garden over there look tip-top so they wouldn't have to look at the construction all year."

Randy cracked a beer and placed it down in front of Officer Liu. "How good are these two, man?" The officer did not make eye contact with the beer and pushed it away with two fingers.

"The holes she was digging were two, three feet deep," Denise explained. "She was up to her eyeballs in that toxic stuff every day. Helen saw her—the woman was covered in it."

"It was pretty gross, if I'm being honest. And I'm saying that as someone who's lived in a shared tcpee before." Helen then placed a finger on her chin with a practiced flourish. "Now, Denise, do tell me. Would there really be that much poison in the ground from just one of those fish?"

Denise turned to her. "Helen, there were a hundred of them! And they were sitting there for weeks rotting and leaching all that shit out. Are you even paying attention? You're the one who saw them. You said she dropped her snacks in there and still ate them—that was you who said that."

"I know that! I was setting you up! To tell her!" Helen elbowed the police officer.

Officer Liu looked down at her notes. She finally looked up and shook her head. "Poison fish dirt. Jesus. We thought she ate some funky sushi. Only explanation for the ciguatera."

"Nope," Denise was full-on smiling now. She'd been drowning on a sinking ship less than twenty hours ago, and she hadn't been this happy in years.

"Is this murder?" Helen asked. "It's not not-murder. They basically murdered Donna."

Officer Lee held up a hand. "Whoa. Slow down there. I mean . . . I'm not a lawyer. But yeah, they probably wish they had just stuck with a pool."

Chapter

74

The hardest thing in my entire life is knowing that I can't rely on anyone who I'm working for.

Speaking of that, not that anyone here's paying me for my time, but you know I'm only saying all this because you're no kind of law enforcement. If I name names, nobody's getting handcuffed. Not because of me talking to you. This is between us, you and me, and you making sure you don't have to pay out insurance on a boat somebody sank on purpose. You want to keep half of this stuff sealed up as much as I do.

This was not an act of God—this was an act of Rocco.

Guessing he's on your list to have a little chat with, too. Well, Rocco sat down next to me at my bingo game, and he asked me if I knew anything about sinking a boat. Time-sensitive, he said. I told him the same thing I've been telling you today: Anyone who knows as much as I do about keeping a boat afloat knows that much or more about sinking it.

I did my thing—not all that hard. Honestly could've done it any night of the week, but the hurricane warning was just a bonus. I had to be out there in the rain doing the inspections anyway. Done and done while the crew's all running around two by two like the ark is coming.

So I get in and take Raul's warning systems off-line. But as you might've noticed, Raul's boat is right over there—floating, you know, like boats are supposed to.

Rocco asked me if I could recommend anyone for the other part of it, to punch a hole in the boat, and of course I had people in mind. Not my first rodeo. Denise's old deckhand Rod had done a couple odd things for me over the years without a ton of fuss, and on top of that, he was newly available. Not a shock Denise finally canned that guy. But he wasn't the only one. So many people have been in and out of Ahoy, it's like a revolving door. Ask Fern. I'm sure you have asked her—she's got every thought you've ever had in your head filed away somewhere. That bottle of soda she keeps on her desk is spiked, by the way.

Speaking of which, Rod's been on a bender since Denise fired him so that was a no-go. And I had somebody else in mind. Nonemployee, just a friend close by. Denise sent me over to Randy when he first bought the taxi business since he didn't know aft from his ass, and she asked if I'd do her a favor and check out all the taxis. Of course, I did. I've been working with Denise for years. We both know Geoff's full of shit.

And, boy, was Randy up for this when I asked him. Turns out he needed the money. Before he bought the taxi business, he was some kind of number cruncher, paper pusher, medical-claims back-office thing I tuned out for, so he knew the taxis were a good business. But he had no clue what kind of shape those boats were in. Lot of wear and tear when I checked them out, and that was a few years ago now. They could use some upgrades over there to keep things running. So he was all ears when I came down to his little palapa one afternoon and said I had an idea for him. You don't have to know a lot about boats to swing a hammer at a bilge pump system for cash.

But he swung at the wrong boat.

Or, I guess, if you're Randy and you're head over heels for a woman who hates the Falcons' guts and never stops talking about it, you hit the right boat.

Chapter

75

A wall made all the difference. It was never the desk itself that eroded Geoff's stature but rather its exposure, its nakedness in relation to the larger room, that blurred his abilities into those of a bag carrier. His desk now was ensconced behind a half wall that separated him from the rest of the open-air hotel lobby—the lowly front desk check-in team might as well be a world away. The head concierge had even been so kind as to place a medium-size potted tree between Geoff's desk and the main floor, agreeing completely that Geoff's value was in his scarcity.

Hotel life suited him. Just two weeks in, and he'd already been promoted from senior guest liaison to chief guest liaison, at his request.

Never underestimate the power of people wanting you to go away. Geoff himself had facilitated some of the great send-offs—second-marriage children to boarding schools, overly informed assistants to lucrative corporate middle management—but it was another experience entirely to be on the receiving end of one.

The hotel was not far away from the Ahoy Bahamas location, and he did wonder if he might see some of his former clients. It was quite a comfortable landing, all things considered. Of course it had been rather awkward at the end there, sitting across from a panel of his peers in Ahoy HQ, an equality of rank he'd been compelled to mention during the exit interview, since they, too, had the word *senior* in their titles. They were not able to provide severance, because technically he was being fired, but the in-house counsel kept referring to it as a transfer. The hotel had a long-standing history with Ahoy referrals, when owners needed a place to deposit guests they no longer wished to host on their boats. In the past, whenever Geoff stepped into the lobby to escort these people, he had admired the hotel's approach to making the guests feel that their stay was an upgrade.

Of course, he still thought about Poppy. Legally, he was discouraged from speaking to her, but through the grapevine he heard she was doing fine. In his new role, behind the potted tree, he had plenty of time to think about that night. A perfect storm, wasted. He'd wanted to catch what had been thrown their way and run forward, upward, skyward, while she wanted to retreat and slide back into what, exactly? Each other? Two people needed more than that if they were going to make it work, in his experience. After spending an entire life watching people with all the money in the world struggle to keep their relationships going, he knew that love required exceptionally firm footing.

Sometimes he thought back to the very first moment he saw her, framed in the doorway before he even had the faintest idea of what she would become to him. And he wondered, at first, if he could get that feeling back and want her as she was just then, the most beautiful woman he'd ever seen and someone who poured into him an overflowing sense of peace and energy at the same time, a soft hand on his heart, lifting it up. But he just couldn't untangle his feelings. Once he'd thought of her as an owner and then as someone who might pull him along into the ranks of ownership himself through their connection, he couldn't unravel those thoughts. He couldn't understand how she didn't see it, too, how her vision was so radically different from his, and so much smaller.

As a parting gift to Ahoy, Geoff's commitment to detail had been instrumental. On all the dossiers for the Falcon charters, he'd been obligated to note each time that the guest Ralph "Rocco" Flacco had brought a firearm on board. Geoff's dossiers had been extraordinarily helpful to both the officers on the case as well as to the yacht insurance team that descended onto Ahoy like vultures. Rocco was not legally allowed to carry a gun, and that was what tipped the whole thing over. Given the choice of facing those particular consequences, among others, evidently, Rocco freely explained what Linnie Falcon had asked of him and what he had, like any service member worth their salt, delivered.

At first, he was immensely flattered that an owner would try to kill him. It was a bit of a disappointment to learn that Linnie had wanted to sink a different boat entirely. Outsourcing delicate requests to lower-tier staff was a terrible mistake—as Geoff would've been the first to tell her.

Though he supposed he would never speak to a Falcon again.

Chapter
76

Timing is prime time. Even now, weeks after she'd last spoken to him, Poppy found herself repeating some of Tim's wisdom to herself. He really was right.

She kneeled down onto the thick rubber knee pad in front of her mother's cucumber garden and put a hand to her forehead as she looked up through the trees into the sky. It was going to rain soon, and she needed to get this done. The pickle process was going to take all day, jarring and pinching in all the spices, and then six days after that they'd be ready to sell.

Timing.

Like how when you're on a boat and it's sinking, you should get off before the water hits the thick red line painted halfway up the wall in the engine room. After that it really starts to go down fast, the way a beer can does when it gets to a certain point in the pool.

That night when she was on the boat, down in the suite, she'd heard the very loud beeping. The boat had just been parked in the bay, the crew left, and then she was all alone in the room. No one had any idea she was there. It was so dark, and the only sound was the whistle of the wind; then all of a sudden, just as she was lighting the candles, an alarm started going off. It took her a long time to figure out where the noise was even coming from, and in the crazy rain she made her way all the way up to where Captain Denise usually sat in the cockpit. There was a red light blinking on a humongous screen that was so complicated, and all Poppy did was push the button to say, *Okay, I get it*, and make it stop. She and Geoff were there in secret, that was the whole point—they did not need an alarm going off. And it went silent. The red light was still on, but at least it wasn't making any more noise. Bundled in her rain jacket, she went back downstairs.

Timing wise, that's when she should've called for help.

Sometimes at night, when Poppy closed her eyes, she could still feel the wet carpet squish between her toes and see the brown water of the bay slip over the top of the deck stairs. It made her heart pound so hard she could feel it in the mattress at her back, and she had to repeat to herself what her mom kept telling her: *Eighty miles inland, honey, you're safe now.*

And if only the two of them had been switched around—if only she'd met Geoff first. Of course, if she'd never met Tim at all, she never would've met Geoff, but still, she thought about it. Maybe they would still be together. It was hard to talk to her mom about Geoff because she hated him so much. It was because of him that her daughter had been on a sinking boat in the middle of a hurricane. But then Poppy reminded her mom that it was because of Tim that Poppy even had the boat. Her mom said she should focus on being a single woman for a good long while.

The only timing Poppy had prime-timed was her trip to Nassau. She'd taken her name off the boat at a very good moment, probably the best moment there ever was. The lawyers had asked her to repeat herself so many times because it just seemed too good to be true. But she told them, yes, exactly, Geoff had seemed too good to be true, and that's why she did it, for him. And even though that turned out to be a bad reason, it was a very good thing in the end. It really didn't go over the way she had pictured it at all, but lately she was finding it very hard to reconstruct what exactly she had been picturing. She couldn't imagine Geoff living with her here at her mom's house, and she didn't want to live in a hotel or even one of those little cottages at the marina, even though they were so cute and it did seem fun for a while to be with her friends there.

Tim broke up with her. The day after the boat sank, there were tons of police officers and even more lawyers than usual in the library room, so she and Tim were cooped up in the pool house to have their talk. It turned out Tim already knew everything that happened and knew a lot of things that even she didn't know, so she didn't even have to tell her side of the whole story—which was fine by her. She was so tired and sad, it would've come out all wrong anyway. He said a few cruel things to her that she didn't like to think about now, like how all the clothes he bought for her looked cheap as soon as she put them on. She'd tried to hand back the ring right then, but he told her it was ugly and he didn't want it. Just as well. Her mom had sold it and bought them a new car.

But his main point was that all this time, Poppy had been holding him back from living the life he was meant for, as the first semiprofessional dual wind and kite surfer. He even said it was also her fault that now he couldn't move to Lima, Peru, which was a very windy place, because she had messed things up for him and he had legal obligations here, where it was not nearly windy enough for his dreams.

When her mom drove over to pick her up at the Falcons' house, they had not been willing to open the gate for her. Poppy had to walk out through the little side door in the hedges for the employees.

But that was all behind her now. Even though it had happened just a month ago, the whole thing felt more like a blip in her regular life, rather than a whole life itself that she'd left. It wasn't just the boat timing she'd done right. The Falcons were in a lot of trouble right now, and it was probably for the best that she wasn't part of the family anymore. In a way, that beautiful lagoon had almost killed her.

Chapter

77

Janet had, conservatively, seventy-five to ninety relatives who all needed to give a toast at the wedding. Even the little white-flowered arch at the top of the hill seemed to sigh every time a new person stepped up beneath it and tapped a glass. A lot of Janet's veterinarian colleagues were there, and there were a lot of jokes about getting the milk for free. Randy was having the time of his life.

He held Denise's hand through the whole thing. He squeezed it during the ceremony when Babs looked out at her daughters with tears in her eyes. He and Denise sat in the back now, sweating, and watched as Helen helped herself to the microphone every three cousins or so. After he'd told Denise what he'd done, they agreed he should stay here in the Bahamas at Janet and Babs's house for a while, until the dust settled on the investigation.

Denise wore a non-chip clip in her hair and a green dress that Helen had exhumed from her closet and that showed off her sister's shoulder muscles nicely. Helen wore a very short kimono.

"Believe it or not, we have had the appropriation conversation." Jules drained her drink. Denise worried that she might like this woman.

Randy had trimmed his mustache and was in a short-sleeved button-down with the black leather vest, cargo shorts, and his boots. Denise loved clocking each and every time she caught another woman taking him in. He was facing fleeing or jail time, probably—

things that would've repelled her just weeks ago—and yet she had never loved him more.

Little yellow lights strung between the guava trees were swinging in the twilight breeze. Purple and pink flowers topped every table and every head, tucked behind ears and into updos. There had to be a hundred people here, spread in silk and sequins across the green-rowed hillside that sloped down toward the palm tree line and, beyond it, the water. The sun reached the horizon and tipped a spill of orange across the waves. Beer cans hissed open and wine corks popped, and finally, enough was enough.

"Okay, okay, okay." Janet ambled up to the white-flowered arch. She and Babs wore matching short-sleeved white linen outfits—a long dress for Janet, pantsuit for Babs—and were barefoot. They held hands, and Janet took the microphone. "Thank you to everyone. Please keep eating, that is the most important thing. And we have had so many people here tonight talking about our side of the island"—whistles and shouts rose from the crowd—"but no more speeches allowed now, please. I just want to say something to my new daughters, Helen and Denise, our beautiful girls. I want to tell you that now, whether you like it or not, we are tide-tied. That is an expression we have here: Tide goes in and out, but we are tied together either way. It's a bond for life, my girls. So the four of us now, tide-tied, alright? You hear me?" She laced her fingers together. Babs blew kisses at the sisters with both hands.

"Hey now, who's tying up to me?" Randy cupped his hands around his mouth and shouted.

Across the laughing, cheering crowd the sisters looked at each other for a long moment. *High time for tide time*, Denise mouthed.

There were times still, fewer now but sometimes, in the middle of the night, in her sleep, Denise would feel like she was still under the black water on the boat. She could feel the tilt of the hull pulling her backward, down toward the bottom. Everything was black, with blurs of objects and shadows floating across her vision, and she couldn't breathe. She would wheeze so hard Randy would wake up, and he had to remind her where she was. It was incredibly strange, in her dream, to come up for air and have Helen there; it didn't make any sense. Helen was a kid, eight years old. Helen wasn't strong enough to pull Denise out of the water. But she did. Denise gasped that first breath of air, and there her sister was, all grown up.

Sinking a boat is all about time management. The moment has to be right, and it's a delicate set of distances. Eight and eighteen are too far apart—there's no understanding there. Eighteen and twenty-eight, not enough common ground yet. Twenty-eight and thirty-eight would work; there's enough experience under both belts, and suddenly ten years doesn't feel like much time at all. And then you wait. One of you has to make it home; the other has to hold the door open. And both of you have to look into the water that's been very carefully controlled until this point, filtering in slowly, and decide *now*. Let it rush in.

Acknowledgments

Thank you, Claire Friedman. How cheesy can I get away with being here? You're my rock, North Star, #1, ride or die, all of the above. None of this is possible without you, especially this one and it's an absolute privilege to work with you every step of the way. Thank you to the whole team at InkWell for your support.

If you want to lose your mind while writing a book on deadline, I highly recommend having a baby right in the middle. It's been a wild ride, and it does indeed take a village: a huge thank-you to the HarperVia and HarperOne teams. To Gabi Page-Fort for carrying this over the finish line with excellent insight, kind guidance, and enthusiasm. To Gretchen Schmid for wonderful notes and steward-ship along the way. To Ghjulia Romiti for your amazing vision and sense of humor. To Daniella Wexler, the original champion who will hardly believe what it turned out to be. And a big thank-you to Ryan Amato for all your help.

Thank you to Judith Curr, Ashley Yepsen, Stephen Brayda, Sarah Kellogg, Tara Parsons, Juan Milà, Yvonne Chan, Crissie Molina, Sierra Delk, Amy Reeve, Anna Brower, and Cathy Cambron.

I have the greatest LA team in the game. Berni Barta and Will Watkins at CAA, thank you a million times over. You have made absolute magic happen, dreams coming true right and left, and I am the luckiest woman in the world to have you extraordinary people in my corner. A wild, shouting from the rooftops thank-you also goes to the team at Paper Kite: Kate, Jordan, and Amy.

Thanks to early readers Mimi Montgomery, Ashley Stephenson, and Sarah Rifield. Thank you, Zach Sergi, for countless conversations about this winding author life. Thank you, Virginia Evans, for the same, and welcome to the club, old friend.

Michelle Douglas, I could not have designed a more perfect friend in a lab. Thank you is insufficient for a thousand conversations about books, publishing, parenting, and small-city life. I love you, am profoundly thankful, and hope you're up for a hundred more book signings together. Thanks to our homes away from home, Curate and Leo.

Bailey Feldman, thank you for so many nights out and Fount days. I love you. Best hype woman, my true mom role model—my life is a lot better with you in it.

Thank you, Lauren Garcia, for sharing family life with me and for never making me feel crazy despite the many, many things I text you. We are in this together. Thank you to Hannah and Joe Carroll and Anastasia and Charlie Szold for making this community feel like one big, fun family.

Heather, "I could not have done this without you" doesn't even come close. You make our entire lives possible and better every single day with so much love, grace, joy, and bottomless patience. The world would be a better place if every mother had someone like you in their lives, childcare is the key to unlocking everything, and I am so deeply grateful to have you, the best of the best, in mine. We love you. Thank you.

To all the readers, thank you. I've loved meeting and hearing from so many of you. Every signing, book club, and bookstore event has been an absolute joy.

Huge thank-you to Matt Jones in Annapolis for sharing your expertise on the details of yacht mechanics. Much of what's in here is because of your incredibly helpful conversation.

In the middle of edits I took my daughters to the National Aquarium in Baltimore, and at the top of the escalator, above the stingrays, I saw Sally Andrew's quote up on the wall. Sally, thank you for letting me use your words, the Tannie Maria books are a delight, and I'll see you in South Africa someday.

Alex, Ray, and Joanna, I love you so much. Years in, I still can't believe how lucky I am to have joined your family. Paris Olympics forever.

Mom and Dad, thank you for absolutely everything. I love you. All the time together with Anna and Zoe, the luckiest granddaughters, is the greatest joy of my life.

Anna and Zoe, it's all for you. Zoe, you are part of every page here, bringing a pair of sisters into my world and infinitely expanding all the love in this house. You two are the most brilliant, beautiful people on the planet, and I love you a little bit more every time I breathe.

Paul, I put you through the ringer this year with a baby, a book, a weird haircut, and a marathon, and you had my back for all of it. I love you so much and thank you for believing in me, and this book, when I really did not. You are the very best, biggest supporter, and I can promise, at least, no more marathons.

A Note from the Cover Designer

When reading through the manuscript for *Salty*, I found ample vivid (and humorous) imagery to play around with. One of the first compositions I explored was the "fancy high-up bed" floating out in the middle of the ocean that we find in the first chapter. My initial instinct was to hone in on these little details, to hint at the wild ride found in *Salty*'s pages. However, the final cover we landed on was a more zoomed-out, big-picture image of all that the story encompasses. The sinking yacht and toasting sisters are clearly featured, but even more important are the natural elements we see such as the sand, sea, and sky. *Salty* is a book with weighty ecological themes, so it made sense to give the greatest amount of space to that which is, at the end of the day, in control of all the events that play out.

—Sarah Kellogg

About the Author

Kate Myers is the author of the national bestseller *Excavations*, which is being turned into a Peacock series starring Amy Poehler. Her writing has appeared in *Elle* and *Self* magazines, and on *BuzzFeed*. She studied archaeology at the University of Pennsylvania and has lived in New York, Los Angeles, and Washington, DC, where she's worked for CBS and CollegeHumor. She now resides in Annapolis, Maryland, with her husband, daughters, and dog.

Here ends Kate Myers's
Salty.

The first edition of this book was printed
and bound at LSC Communications
in Harrisonburg, Virginia, in May 2025.

A NOTE ON THE TYPE

The text of this novel was set in Freight Text Pro, originally designed in 2005 by Joshua Darden—the first African American type designer, according to *Fonts in Use*. The Freight font superfamily is known for its innovative approach to optical size and stylistic versatility, and Freight Text Pro provides its sturdy center. Aptly named, Freight is a workhorse font that can handle standard text sizes for small and large amounts of copy. Unique but easy on the eyes, Freight is a go-to typeface for everything from magazines to cookbooks to data-driven documents.

HARPERVIA

An imprint dedicated to publishing international voices, offering readers a chance to encounter other lives and other points of view via the language of the imagination.